The Breaking

Kathryn Heyman

THE BREAKING

PHOENIX HOUSE
London

First published in Great Britain in 1997 by
Phoenix House, Orion House
5 Upper St Martin's Lane
London WC2H 9EA

Copyright © Kathryn Heyman

Kathryn Heyman has asserted her right under the Copyright,
Designs and Patents Act 1988 to be identified as the author
of this work

A CIP catalogue record for this book is available
from the British Library

ISBN 1861590 35 0 (cased)
ISBN 1861590 54 7 (trade paperback)

Typeset at Selwood Systems, Midsomer Norton
Printed and bound in Great Britain by
Butler & Tanner Ltd, Frome and London

Acknowledgements

I am grateful for financial assistance from the Scottish Arts Council, in the form of a fellowship with Renfrew District Council, which eased the writing of this novel.

Some of the characters and ideas in this book first appeared in the short story 'Chasing Stallions', published in *The Flamingo Book of New Scottish Writing*.

Many, many thanks also to:
Lynne Alexander, for her supportive, perceptive and challenging coaching;
other staff of the MA in Writing at Sheffield Hallam University, particularly Archie Markham and Robert Miles, for their encouragement;
Sharon Heyman and John Selby;
Steph GM Leach, for years of love and belief;
All the godsisters of W.A., especially Megan Lawrence and Sarah Leach;
Giles Gordon for his energy and commitment;
Alison Walsh for her perceptive and enthusiastic editing.

The character of Kari was first developed in the play *The Princess Who Couldn't Fly and a Word or Two About the Crippled King*. My thanks to everyone involved in that first magical production, especially Kahren Hampton for her wonderful performances and friendship.

Mostly, thanks to Richard Griffiths, most kindred of spirits, for all of the above and everything left unmentioned.

Part One

One

The main road of Boolaroo begins and ends at the primary school – depending on which way you're walking. Or driving. Walk or drive it doesn't make any difference, you still have to hit the primary school at one end or the other. Now, this is assuming you're going to cover the whole road. You might stop half-way, you might be calling in to see someone, or to pick up some dog food from Fur Fin and Feather and then you might turn around and go back just the way you came. Let's assume you aren't going to do that though, because you want to know. About this place, this school, that little square police station you passed, the horses in the paddocks, the glass-fronted Catholic church with the red-brick convent, that yellow and white pub, The Penny's Head.

Sarah Sweet was one of the swarm of blue-checked small-bodied girls dribbling out of the Boolaroo school, with its cracked yellow paint. Sarah came out of Mrs Hallows' room. She was called Mrs Hallows because she was a Hallowe'en witch, she kept her broomstick in her Beetle car, everyone knew it was true. The school was two buildings, both verandahed and yellow-painted, with big high-ceilinged rooms. The bell-ringing, for school lunchtime, was taken in turns.

On the day it was rung by Sarah Sweet, her feet lifting off the wooden daïs, the rope reddened her hands to the point of bleeding, she gripped so hard. Sliding up and down the savage edges of the rope, her hands clenching, fists tight and tight and tight. It was the rawness, the tearing away, the sanding down of skin so hard it was like prayer. She rang, she rang, she swang from the bell, hands sliding, roughing, scratching. Feeling herself rubbed away. The bell was meant to be rung four times. On the

Wednesday Sarah rang, the sound called through the high wooden shed-like rooms, six, seven, eleven, twenty-four, thirty-two, forty-three times.

Her hands bled when she was stopped by Mr Cartwright, the fat, red-faced head teacher and her eyes stared over his shoulder at a place far away. He scalded her hands with Dettol and bandaged them carefully. 'Did you forget? About the bell ringing four times? Where were you Sarah, you must be careful mustn't you, you're not like your sister, don't pretend to be, you might get yourself into trouble. Okay? Go home and rest now, fresh for tomorrow.'

Sarah was still silent, slowly letting her eyes draw in on Mr Cartwright, kneeling at her feet with a red plastic bucket filled with warm frothy diluted Dettol. She rubbed the bandages against her legs, repeated the mantra carefully: *I'm not like my sister, I'm not like my sister.*

Kari Sweet, sister of Sarah, daughter of Mal, did not wear a blue-check uniform. She wore any clothes she liked, special clothes, her special favourite and best Chinese-girl suit, yellow hot pants – all sorts – with her big heavy calliper boots and big thick glasses. Special clothes. Special school. Kari (called The Spastic by Sarah Sweet) was a girl at the special school. One special amongst lots of other specials there. In the mornings before breakfast Sarah sat on Kari and farted joyfully calling 'I'm farting on the spastic's head. Farty farty spastic.' Kari squealed with laughter and then cried when Sarah bit her finger so hard she left marks in the skin, solid, good indents, like in chocolate. Later, Sarah bit the arm of Michael Maley who'd said, 'hey what's it like to have a spas for a sister?'

Spitting out his skin, Sarah said 'she's not a spastic you're a bloody spastic she just can't walk properly and her eyes are funny and she can think and talk just like you only not so stupid.' She yelled out that bit, the last word, *Stupid*, and her mouth dived for his arm again. Oh, but it felt good, to push teeth together over someone's skin, grinding almost to the bone sometimes, she would bite so hard she could be so tough so strong. She was Sarah Sweet, biter of flesh, defender of spastics.

Kari Sweet came home on the special bus, clinking and clumping in her callipers. Sarah Sweet walked the walk down the main street of Boolaroo, past the corner-store, past the red-brick doctor's room with its brown mesh-and-steel fly-wire door and the black pegboard at the front, with DOCTOR marked out in white plastic stick-on letters, past the brown square post office. Past the Catholic church, too, where Ruth Sweet, mother of Kari, mother of Sarah, wife of Mal, had once gone to find refuge. The priest (a pink skinny one with dandruff on his frock) told her to return to her husband and God would forgive her rebellion. Spitting powerlessness, Ruth Sweet pelted a rock at the dandruff-covered back. Ha. Still, it seemed easier to go back after that.

Just past the church, and on the other side of the road, was a brick house. Number Four, Main Road, Boolaroo. A flat squat square of a shape, with front and back verandah to climb up to and to jump from. There were patches of green and brown all around the square red house. Big, paddock-sized patches. On one patch, the patch next to the house, was the police station, not even separated by a gate or a fence. 'We own the police station, my dad is the boss of the police and nooligans' – this was Kari, at special school. On the patch behind the house was a white wooden prison. There were bars on the high windows (no glass, just air) and a solid metal door, with locks and locks and locks. Everything, you see. A real prison. A cell really. The wood was dark on the inside, there was no heating or cooling. Outside, there were six steps leading to the little veranda, leading to the door. Sarah stepped on to the steps, holding her bandages against herself.

A voice trickled out of the barred prison door: ' "Be thou my vision, o Lord of my heart." ' It slurred and dribbled, then eased off into a laugh. And again ' "save that thou art, dum da da ruler of all." '

Jasmine climbed around the walls of the lock-up; the scent played in the dreams of Sarah (*here comes the jasmine lady on a mat*

5

of pearls), and sometimes the sound of this singing, these slurred hymns squeezing out through the lock-up bars, was in her dreams as well. 'Amazing Grace'. 'There is a Green Hill'. These were the favourites, forced past a cheese sandwich in the throat of Jack Fir. Sometimes Sarah stepped right up to the door of the lock-up and held his small small finger through the barred window. 'I feel much better now, I feel myself now.' His finger shook inside her fist.

Jack Fir – born somewhere near Nundle, sometime around 1920, though there was no birth certificate or other record of his exist-ence. There was only his own word to go on as proof that he had ever been born at all. Arrested regularly for: vagrancy, trespass, disorderly behaviour, offensive language. Mal Sweet picked him up every Tuesday and Friday night – usually outside The Penny's Head, the green-carpeted Boolaroo pub, which smelt of vomit and Fosters. On Wednesday and Saturday mornings Jack would sit at the small brown table inside the dark lock-up, eating Heinz baked beans, sausages and four slices of toast with margarine (butter was kept in a dish inside the house, not for the prisoners). Monday nights he spent at the hospital. Wednesdays at the convent across the road, Saturday nights on the back porch of the school (two bottles of milk left out for him and a stale Lamington left by the canteen ladies). On Sundays he walked nine miles to the big Anglican church in Marmong. He ate his food too fast, trying to swallow and drink and sing at the same time. Three times Mal Sweet had opened the door of the lock-up to find Jack Fir hunched on the floor, his back in spasm, his face purpling up. Mal Sweet would slap him like a horse and call Ruth to clean up the neat little gob of toast which flew in a perfect ball from Jack's mouth and landed on the wooden floor of the lock-up.

Sarah Sweet's bandaged hand wrapped itself around Jack Fir's finger, while he sang ' "Holy, holy, holy, Lord God almighty" ' and pressed his monkey-sized face to the bars. He sang to her and she sang back at him 'Mr Cartwright is a fat red smelly penguin Lisa

Tredley ran to the toilet with her pants pulled down four times four is sixteen I hate my sister do you?' and they formed a harmony.

Sarah's wrapped-up hand was bleeding again, red began to seep through the white roughness of the bandage. Jack's song stopped – not in a trickle this time, but in a sudden shock of a stop. Sarah opened her hand and the monkey face through the bars stared with her at the clothed-up palm, striped red. 'I hurt myself, I was bleeding,' she looked back to his face. He nodded, waiting for more, but a wave of fury overtook Sarah Sweet and she snatched her hand away. 'Stupid old horrible leave me alone I'm dobbing and anyway you're too ugly to be married.' She saw his face become smaller, creased up, behind the bars while she reversed up the stairs to the back door. 'Stupid horrible ugly,' she called, while Jack Fir's face became more and more bunched up, his head retreating into his neck.

She used both fists to hit on the wooden door for her mother to open. Ruth looked small and crumpled when the door swung back. She had skin-coloured pantyhose on with blue shiny slippers. Black hairs flocked together inside the brown nylon of the pantyhose. Sarah told the black hairs, 'I got an early mark.' She held her bandaged hand behind her back and crabbed herself past Ruth, into the lounge. *I am not like my sister, I am not like my sister.* The words did not sing like before, but trudged through Sarah's brain, necessary visitors.

Bill and Ben, Flowerpot Men grew and mumbled on the television in the corner, their faces shades of grey and white and black and fuzziness. Sarah sat on her hand, feeling the rawness. Now and then, she pushed the nails of her unbled hand into the bandages, or her fist, punching the place where the skin had come away, punching until to not cry was something that only she, Sarah Sweet, could do. Kari would have cried. Ruth would have cried, that mother cried all the time. Only Sarah and Mal could be the not-hurting ones.

At four o'clock, Mal pulled the big heavy bunch of keys from his belt and pushed the lock-up door back. 'Orright then Jack, take care, keep off the streets.' Jack scuffled past and out the door, picked a stem of jasmine in his stumpy hand and banged the door of the Boolaroo house. When Ruth opened it, smiling above her nylon tights, he handed her the stem, said 'thank you very much lady,' and disappeared from Boolaroo for five weeks.

Two

Jack came back the same week that Fosters the cat had kittens and they found starlings in the roof. Jack was joyously arrested on Tuesday night, fed with an omelette, sausages, toast and two kinds of jam for breakfast. Kari carefully carved a basket from an orange, with a glacé cherry on top. Ruth put it on Jack's tray, with a white cloth and butter and family spoons. At playtime Sarah told Mrs White, the canteen lady with the wet marks under her arms, that Jack was back. On Friday night, the canteen ladies left half a box of Lamingtons and fairy cakes on the back porch. Jack saved three fairy cakes and left them on the back step of the Boolaroo house on Sunday morning, along with a half-dead Waratah flower from the front garden.

Kari heard the starlings first; the scratching in the roof happened loudest above her bed. She noticed them on Thursday morning. 'There's angels in the roof, Daddy.'

Mal pulled the high wooden ladder upstairs onto the dark landing, beneath the manhole. Sarah held the ladder fiercely while Mal slid the white trapdoor across and pulled himself up and through the hole, into the blackness of the ceiling. Sarah held her breath and said the whole times table three times in her head waiting for him. *Twelve times ten is one hundred and twenty, twelve elevens are one hundred and thirty-two.* Mal reappeared with blood on his hands and a flushed-up face. His eyes were sparky hard and his voice was loud loud loud. 'They're pests, they're no good to anyone, starlings.'

Sarah helped her father put the hessian bag of strangled starlings in the outside big metal bin. That was Thursday. On Sunday,

Fosters had kittens. Kari, who always fed and stroked the grey cat, had watched her grow big and nippled. Sarah Sweet had no time for sooky cats, like girls and spastics. Ruth, absorbed in tea-towels and hair-sets and casseroles, noticed the cat only if hairs were left in the kitchen. Mal noticed only horses.

Fosters was huddled in the wardrobe Kari shared with Sarah. Slime and blood dribbled on the clothes of Sarah and Kari, which had dropped down from their wire hangers. Fosters had found a solid pile of hotpants and tunics and dug herself in. When Kari opened the sliding door (chipboard, with a fake walnut-wood Laminex panel), Fosters looked up, startled and howling, biting on a pink worm coming from her own belly. Four small cases of shine and slime clustered around the pink worm and the warm belly. Small they were, smaller than Kari's hand, and slits where eyes should be, but too little to open. No hair, just shine. And more were coming, that was the thing. Fosters' claws dug into the clothes, her eyes and mouth widening as her catbody convulsed. Three more, before she breathed out like a sigh and licked and pawed the sad bundles. Kittens. 'Kittens on my clothes,' Kari rattled and clinked through the Boolaroo house, calling Sarah to come and see. Sarah pushed Kari out of the way; blood, blood on everything. 'She's bleeeeeeding,' Sarah was like a bell tolling through the quiet of the house. They were piled up, an exhausted bundle, seven silver-slimed kittens and Fosters' striped panting body. Occasionally, one of her claws tucked itself out and in.

'Shush, quiet, we'll put them in a box before your father gets home', Ruth moved through the crowd of two with a white Bartletts shoe-box, the one which had held Sarah's black school shoes with lion prints on the sole.

They were careful in the loading of the small parcels in to the box, lined with bits of old undies from the rag closet. Ruth tore the box open at one end, for Fosters to lie next to and let the pink blobs climb to her still swollen nipples. All were tucked up at the end of the wardrobe, the door left a teensy teensy fraction open, for air and light to just dribble in. It was a secret.

*

Kari, tucked up tight with the secret, kicked her legs at dinner. She drew patterns in the mashed potato on her plate, pictures of two circles on top of each other, with whiskers and tails. *Stupid stupid stupid* – the song in Sarah's head had changed, and she kicked at Kari's callipers beneath the Laminex table. Kari looked happy and bewildered, singing to herself beneath her breath. Mal knew nothing about the secret. He ate mostly in silence, sucking his teeth ferociously and telling Sarah, 'eat it up, eat it all up.' This was the dinnertime song. Sarah thought about little starving children and swallowed, thought how she would turn into a nigger girl if she wasn't civilised with her knife and fork, thought about the little slimy pillows bleeding on her best yellow skirt, nearly gagged on her lamb chop. Kari sang, 'Five little kittens have lost their mittens, they don't know where to find them.'

At bedtime, Mal dusted Kari in Johnson's Baby Powder and helped her into pink flannelette pyjamas, laid her callipers carefully by her bunk, said, 'Prayers now, Blossom.' He helped her to kneel, holding her beneath the arms and lowering her down. He sat on the bunk, helped her begin: ' "Little jesus meek and mild, look upon this little child, now I lay me down to sleep I pray thee Lord my soul to keep." '

Mal sat silent then, letting Kari do the Godblesses on her own. The Godblesses were a kind of way of saying 'I love'. 'I love Mummy, I love Daddy.' It was like saying 'Atishoo' for sneezes, you just said it or you had bad luck. If you missed anybody out in the Godblesses, they would have very bad luck and probably die. 'Godbless Mummy, Godbless Daddy, Godbless Sarah, Godbless Miss Pound, Godbless the horses, Godbless everybody in the whole world.' Kari stopped, breathing hard, trying to whisper the secret into her hands, to save the kittens from the bad luck of not getting a godbless. 'Godbless Fosters and her babies.'

She said it quickly, and though a soft thumping came from behind the sliding door, Mal was calm and soft, said 'go to sleep now, my Blossom,' and kissed her goodnight. Sarah, waiting outside the door for her turn to say prayers with Mal spat inside her head at Kari the stupid spastic big mouth can't keep a secret

11

spastic. Bloody bloody. Mal stepped out through the door and let his hand ruffle about in Sarah's hair. 'In bed now mate, garn.'

No mention of prayers. Sarah took three big jumps to her bed, playing the if-your-feet-only-touch-the-floor-three-times-it-will-be-all-right game. The light clicked off and Sarah hung her head over the edge of the bunk, staring at Kari's callipers lined upon the floor. Fear and knowing and mad all tumbling around inside her. 'Da-aad,' Sarah's voice called after him and the door swung open again. Mal's face popped in and out of the darkness; he was like a dream. Sarah let her eyes see the dream, a disappearing shadow. She told it: 'Kari saw Fosters have kittens she hid them in the wardrobe I didn't know.' The door closed and there was the dull thump of Mal's feet on the hall floor.

They were gone in the morning. The kittens, the box, the undies, nothing was left in the wardrobe except neatly hung hotpants and dresses. All the shoes were piled up at one end of the ward-robe – Sarah's gym-boots and school shoes all mixed up with Kari's special shoes. In the kitchen, Ruth was bright like a moon, 'toast or Froot-loops, toast or Froot-loops?' talking quickly and putting things on the table, concentrating hard. 'Get dressed for school quickly, blue clips or pink, Kari? Sarah, put long socks on please, quickly quickly.'

Sarah could walk to school on her own. Ruth walked with Kari to the bus stop on the main road, waited until the yellow bus full of yelling and laughing arrived. Sarah let herself out through the back door. She could see Mal in the far bit of the back yard, way down near the paddock. His back was bare, brown as brown in the sun, while he piled bits of tree and kindling wood onto a big bonfire pile, like for cracker night. Sarah sucked her breath in, held her tummy in tight and ran to the gate on tippy toes.

All day at school she felt bits of sick rising and falling in her mouth. She hid her face in bits of paper and stayed in to colour in her Cars and Trains project at playtime, playing with the burn of shame, her head feeling like a merry-go-round. People's voices seemed to come from far, far away. She could hear the sea in her ears.

There was the dry dead smell of fire in the afternoon when Sarah walked home. She smelt it before she even reached the gate of the Boolaroo house, left-over smoke clogging her nostrils. There was a big dead black place in the yard, near the paddock. Sarah sucked the smell in to herself, willing the sick to rise up, daring the dizziness to just try it. She watched her feet moving one after the other, closer and closer to the black charred circle. The grass around the black circle had turned brown, the way it did at the heat of Christmas when everything was born. Grey ashes had floated about, settling on the cement path, the paddock fence, the green grass as well as the brown. There was an unburnt bit of wood, only grey from the fire, not black and ashy, and seven black shapes, little corpse-parcels with crooked necks.

Sarah could see the tiny ears and the slits for eyes. They were black and hard and still shiny, but like melted plastic now. Sarah picked them up, one at a time, and placed them on the outer rim of the circle. She dragged her foot in a figure of eight, making a smooth track in the ashes, and knelt down, ramming the black bodies against each other. Ram, crash, crack. Dodgem Kittens. Sarah made the sounds of cars playing a knock-out comp. When one Dodgem Kitten got hit, she chucked it into the centre of the circle. 'Out!' She was driver, dodger and commentator. The kittens did nothing but leave black marks on her hand and they didn't skid well, having no wheels. Sarah kicked them into a pile, their twisted necks all poking over each other, and banged on the back door.

Ruth was in the laundry, pushing a line of Mal's police shirts through the wringer with one hand. Sarah watched above the loud rumble of the machine. Ruth pulled the blue shirts from the washer, fat and alive with water, and fed them one by one through the squeeze of the wringer. Like two rolling pins stuck together. *Squeeeeeze, squeeeeeeze*. Sarah fed the wringer words it did not want. The shirts flattened, grew lifeless, flopped onto the other side of the metal tub, where Ruth quickly pushed them into a wooden basket. Both her hands worked at the same time, one pulling a dead shirt off the wringer, one feeding a live shirt through. When Ruth looked down, Sarah could see a blue, black and purple mark on her cheek. When the wringer stopped, the laundry was shocking in its silence.

Mal was bright again that night, his face all gleaming and shining like before, with the starlings. Thwacking Sarah and calling her his little mate, ay? His mate. Kari sat still all through dinner and did not play with her food. No-one mentioned the kittens.

Three

'They're ya mates, horses, don't let em smell fear, give em a strong hand and they're mates.' Mal held the end of a lasso in one hand, holding it lightly, like air. A new mare was on the end of the lasso, stretching like a crossbow and kicking her hooves.

'Like women ey Mal?' Frank Johnson, 'Johnno', sat on the white-and-black wood fence. The fence that Mal built. Johnno was a roll-bellied man with tattoos on his back and arms and a can in his hand.

Sarah put a finger on the picture of a red dragon on Johnno's arm. 'Where'd ya get the pictures from. You've got em on ya back, didya know?'

Johnno rippled his fat, so that the undressed lady on his side thrust herself up and down, while Johnno went 'uh, uh, uh.' He looked at Mal, ready to laugh with him, but Mal Sweet was wooer and breaker of horses, with his hand gentle on the lasso and soft sounds coming from his mouth and his eyes all liquid at the gold-bay mare.

'Why?' Sarah tapped again at Johnno's back, letting Mal whisper to the mare in the sun of the paddock.

Johnno bulged his arm muscles up, looked down at Sarah, said 'some kids up the track needed a blackboard and I said they could have a borrer of me. Not bad scribblers, whaddaya reckon?'

Sarah rubbed her fingers on the undressed lady, watching her jump up and down. 'Uh, uh, uh.'

Johnno's eyes were on her and she felt tight inside. 'Children scribbled on Johnno, Dad,' she called across the paddock, in her loud voice, and the mare's eyes fired up, spit foamed at her mouth.

15

Mal's voice was flat as the paddock. 'If ya can't be friggin quiet like a bloke, don't flamin well come out.'

Sarah swallowed her words way back in her mouth and just let breathing be there instead.

At the Boolaroo school, playtimes were for games of Breaking. Sarah used the sash from her sports tunic as a lasso and took turns with Peter Clarke and Ian Mackintosh (Macka) being the horse. All mad and fierce one minute, then soft and quiet like a weak girl the next. They tried to catch each other out, begin by talking low and silky to the horse, then suddenly jump on its back going 'Heeya Heeya'. The washroom was home and if you touched home, you were safe. Sarah could let her voice out in a big loud yell, or a scream, or a neigh at those times, yes sir. She wanted to tell Johnno this, that she could yell as loud as she liked at the Boolaroo school and no-one even said shut up get out of my way. But Johnno was waving his dragons in the sun, staring hard at Mal in the paddock.

There was always a man there, on the paddock fence, watching Mal do the breaking. Mal was good. Talking down in his throat, making the horses trust him, but hard with them, like they would know. Who was the strong one, the not-afraid one, they would know that for sure. Men came from Teralba, Booragul, the Point, all around, for Mal to break their horses. Other times on the fence were: Crocka (Bill Crockle), Whitey (Allan White), Rollo (Ivan Rollinson), Smithy (Bob Smith), Wog (Sam Luciano, whose grandparents had once been Italian), Mad Mick Riley and Davo (Mick Smith), watching Mal break their horses. All the horses round – Booragul, Marmong, Cockle Creek, the Point – they were all broken by Mal. You could ask anybody, they'd tell you, Mal Sweet broke the best. All the sweat dripping on him and the flush on his face. He was boss with them and never frightened. *Dad wasn't even frightened in the war. Not even with the Japs making him walk all that way through the jungle. Nah. Hates Japs, but. Mad stinking bastards Japs.*

Sarah thought a Jap was a kind of animal, possibly with claws, lurking on jungle paths. Like Niggers. Nigger was a kind of water animal on account of catch a nigger by the toe. *You catch him going up a creek, like a platypus. Like you can never catch a platypus. And Dad says you can never catch a nigger.*

Mal still held the end of the lasso, with Johnno's new mare on the other end. 'Come on girl, easy, eeeeasy.' Mal's words were as warm as the sun on the bay mare. She tested him at the end of the rope, baring her broad teeth, cantering in and away from him. He stood steady, his hands facing up, with the rope slack. It had taken three days to get this far, she was difficult this one, randy. Johnno had backed her into the corral at the end of the paddock, reversing his red trailer right to the fence. That was the exciting bit, not all this slow talking and blowing kisses at the horse. When they let the trailer door open, it was like at the rodeo, with the horse rearing and spitting down the ramp and into the corral. *Gettaway! Come near me and I'll kill you with these hooves.* This one had backed right up to the corral fence, shaking and with her eyes all white and rolling, but her teeth bared. It was the way Ruth looked, backed up against the wall sometimes, with Mal yelling over her. *Come closer and I'll kill I swear I will.* She was only sixteen hands, Johnno's mare. Johnno wouldn't give her a name.

'We'll see what she's like after Mal gets his leg over her before we name her heh heh. If anyone can ride her that bastard can.'

Two years before, driving to Gundegai, they had stopped at a rodeo. There was a sign saying, CHALLENGE BUCKING BOBBY BROWN: DARE TO RIDE THE WILD BRONCO. The bucking bronco didn't have a name, it was too wild to have a name. Mal had lasted twelve minutes and fourteen seconds and won twenty dollars. They had driven the rest of the way to Gundegai singing 'The Quartermaster's Store' and 'The Dog Sat on Me Tucker Box' in loud, laughing voices. Kari's callipers had clinked like cymbals. 'Where the dog' (clink-clink), 'sat on me tuckerbox' (clink), 'five miles from Gundegai' (clinky-clink-clink). Mal had zigged and zagged across the road to make Kari and Sarah squeal and Ruth go 'oh, Mal luvvaduck,' and rub her hands on the back of his neck.

Johnno's mare wasn't even a bucking bronco and she was taking days to break. Sometimes Mal could do it, the whole thing,

17

in two days. This one would be slow. After Mal swung the lasso in a beautiful singing circle over her neck, he had let her run with the lasso trailing on the ground. Mal had stood in the paddock, let her run from him and slowly, slowly, slowly, lifted the end of the rope in his hands. Just stood there, like that, with the rope in his hands, a bridle at his feet, and the horse bolting about. He didn't pull it tight though, the rope, just let it hang easy on the mare's neck. Mal talked all the time, way down in his throat, his eyes looking right at the horse eyes, little words and sounds and cluckings coming from his mouth. Clucking and clucking. Being kind, so kind, and soft. Her ears started to stand up again, her lips closed in over her teeth, her breathing gentled up. She watched him.

Mal let one hand slide away from the rope, careful, careful. He moved like thick honey, slow, slow, slow. He kept his eyes on the mare's, he breathed in and out, in and out, so deep she could hear him. In and out, in and out. They were both still. Mal breathed. The mare breathed. In and out. Like quiet wind. Mal dropped his hand – slowly, slowly – away, further away. Whispered and clucked at the mare again, as he reached down to his feet, bending at his knees, his eyes still on her. 'Easy girl, eeeeasy.' She was easy, watching him bend, hearing him whisper and breathe. Safe. Mal's hand rested on the bridle, his knees bent, his eyes on the mare. Sarah, sitting still as wood on the fence, counted inside her head *one cat and dog two cat and dog three cat and dog* to forty-seven cat and dogs, before Mal's sun-spotted hand eased around the leather strap.

He came up straight and slow, the bridle hanging from his hands. 'Shh girl, ssh my love.' Mal saw nothing now, except the mare, her chest shining with sweat, her nostrils going small and big, small and big. 'That's it, thaaaat's the way,' he opened the fist holding the rope, let his palms face skywards. The rope dangled over his hand, unheld. The mare raised her head, dropped it again. Sarah breathed only through her nostrils, keeping her stomach muscles still. Johnno's hand gripped the rail next to her. 'That's it, thaaaat's it.' Mal was crooning to the horse. It was a song, coming softly from the belly of him. Sarah's mouth was open. Watching him, her father. Her father watching the horse. His hand half closed around the rope, so that three fingers touched it, but lightly. The mare's ears twitched. Mal stood. The horse stood. Sarah sat. Johnno burped.

The mare's mane flicked from her eyes as her head jerked up and around towards Johnno on the fence. Mal let a long slow breath out, through his nose. 'Carn girl, carn love, that's it. thaaaat's the way.' The mare's head turned back to him. 'Shh, s'okay.' The bridle strap rested in the dust. Mal waited. Breathed. Sarah could hear the sounds of trees, grass, dust in the air, people on the moon. *Ssshhh*. Mal lifted his hands a fraction, just enough to lift the bridle from the ground. He stood a moment, then rolled his weight forward, towards the horse. Her tail flicked, then was still.

Mal lifted his foot, held the rope, whispered, moved his foot forward. Waited. Whispered. Watched. He moved forward another step, not stopping this time, but making each movement roll into the next, like music. Mal was an ancient dancer when he did this, his body somehow never stopping the inch forward, but never moving. He was like cloud, changing and changing, still and moving. Sarah's insides trembled with this, with being invited into this dance, oh, so so gentle, so slow, so sweet. This was magic, make no mistake.

Mal was closer now, his arms, his legs, his arms, his back, all one song. His voice singing to her, his beauty, his one. The mare's neck lowered, her eyes drooped. He was so close now, his breath skimming her cheek, soft and dancing. His hand was smooth in its moving, both still and moving his honey hand, touching her mane, resting like breath on her mane, his song falling from him like tissue-whisper, his hand sliding liquid down her neck, oh, around and the strap slipping on, and the metal just slipping in, just slipping like a tongue, you wouldn't know, wouldn't dream, wouldn't dare. She felt the bridle, felt the oddness of straps about her head and face, the metal in her mouth, between her teeth. Spit. Spit it out. Her head pulled back and to the side, her eyes rolling back. Mal took three steps back, silent while the horse battled the bridle and bit. He left his palms open, facing her. 'Good girl, let it out, that's my girl, that's the girl.' He leant towards her, palms open, breath slow. Her head grew still, then flashed towards him, teeth bared, snapping them together. 'Bitch,' but he caught it in time and made that sound slow as well. They watched each other, eyes sparking. Then Mal stepped back, bent himself, and climbed through the paddock fence.

Outside the paddock he lifted a hessian sack full of chaff and bran onto his shoulders. Chaff dribbled out onto his wet blue singlet. He walked away from the horse to a cement trough at the far side of the fence and poured the food in. Sarah wanted to put her hands in the trough, for the bran to trickle through her fingers and the smell to clog her up. Mal left the empty sack near the trough, walked back to Johnno, said 'Make a friggin noise like that burp again and yer out on yer ear, I don't care if she's yours, she's my bloody breed. I'll be on her tomorrow, no thanks to you, ya miserable old bastard, give Davo a call ey? He'll wanna see, and Macka. How bout a bloody beer.'

Sarah held her breath until both the men had gone.

Four

'She might be spittin at me but she's still eaten me bloody food. Reckon yer right Johnno, just like bloody women ay?' The black and white fence rocked with the rumblings of Johnno, Macka, Davo. Heh, heh.

'Yair, but most women don't buck as hard,' Macka roared out.

'Speak fer yerself mate.' Johnno's thighs opened out, as he rocked himself back, held upright by the laugh, rumbles moving up and down the fence.

Sarah was small on the end of this line: Johnno, Davo, Macka, and red-haired Blue (Simon Park), recruited the night before at The Penny's Head. Sarah's feet hooked back and over the lower rail of the fence. She banged her foot against the wood: new boots. Riding boots, proper ones. Brown, and Mal had said he'd teach her to crack a stock whip if she wanted. Macka, Davo, Johnno, even Wog when he was around could crack whips easy as anything, but Mal cracked them loudest and quickest and no girls did it, not like Sarah Sweet would, no sir.

'Carn, ya gettin on her or chattin her up?' The fence chorus hissed and booed, while Mal breathed at the bay mare, her ears tensing back. She was still bridled up, chewing at the metal bit. Her front hoof slammed into the ground. Mal stepped forward, his teeth brighting up his face, his breath and hands steady. The mare's head pulled back and back, her ears flat on her head, back and back, so that her feet were pulled off the ground, her hooves – unshod – hammering at the air near Mal's face. He lowered his head and took two steps sideways, straightened and stepped forward again. One step. The horse stayed, four feet planted.

'Looks like she's winnin, Mal. Carn, I'd a stayed in the pub if I thought you were gunna do a dance.'

Mal stuck his thumb up behind his back, 'in yer dreams, Blue.'

Blue's face creased. 'Nah, in me bloody nightmares, I reckon.'

The fence chorus tilted back and forwards. Sarah was flushed up with their laughing, with their backslapping and knocking of each other. She felt wild, as strong as them, ready to call out, to jump on the horse, going heeya heeya.

Facing the mare, and making a soft voice to her, Mal walked backwards to the corral end of the paddock, and climbed onto the lower rail, swinging out like an awning. 'Give her a crack, Johnno.' The mare bolted at the thunder sound shooting from behind her. And again. And again. White foamed at the corners of her mouth, her nostrils went wide and small. And again, the crack, the thunder sound. She ran forward, forward, a shrieking coming from her mouth. Mal swung out further and further, the whip cracked, the mare's mouth opened and sound bleated out. Her hooves pelted up and down, bash, bash, bash at the dust. Mal's arm went taut as he stretched, pushed back with his leg and threw himself to the wind galloping past. His arms swung around the mare's neck, his legs flopping about on one side, his stomach folded over her backbone. *Get off off off I'll kill don't think I won't.* Mal's leg lifted, arced above the horse, and came down on the other side, so that he straddled the horse, and sat half upright, his hands moving along the bridle strap, grabbing fast and smooth for the reins.

Cheers and whistles cannoned along the fence. The mare's neck arched up, snaked from side to side, spit running across her lips at the shock of weight on her back. Her front legs reared off the ground, her head swinging. Mal pulled at the reins, so that the bit edged into the mare's mouth, forcing her head up. His thighs were tight against the roundness of her panting. Sweat gleamed beneath his legs, his hair glinted.

A young stallion, a wild one, had battled Mal Sweet once, bucking and pig-rooting for two hours, with Mal holding on all wild-eyed and fired up. After two hours, the stallion rolled. Mal went down with him, kept the reins medium tight, somehow flattened himself and rolled with the horse. The brumby, apparently, had kept all its reserves for that roll and gave up then. It spent the next day trotting around Mad Mick Riley's Teralba paddock, meekly nuzzling Mal. This had become legend not just in the pubs of Boolaroo, Teralba and Booragul, but had spread as far as Port Maquarie and even Gunnedah. He could hold for ever, Mal Sweet, his eyes glazed over, like he wasn't there. A kind of trance is what it was.

The spine of the mare dug between Mal's legs; he liked it bareback, liked to feel the breathing beneath him. He knew when they were ready to give up, and when there was breath left in them for one final fight, he could feel it beneath him, in the breathing. Johnno's mare was strong for a young one, but she wasn't big. He kept the reins back, just enough to have no slack, to keep her head up, but careful not to let the bit cut her mouth. The mare ran at the wooden fence, charging sidelong, rubbing her flank against the rails. Mal relaxed his muscles against the wood and pulled the reins back. Foam speckled at her mouth and wet slipped and dripped from them both. She ran again at the fence, hitting herself against it hard, hitting Mal's leg against it hard. The reins jerked back hard on her head, Mal's hands fisting up white, pulling back, back, back.

The metal of the bit pushed against the rim of her mouth, pushed further. Mal's legs squeezed around the horse, hard. He jerked the bit back, white traced her mouth, blood marked the bit, began to dribble out. Her lips were folded back, her eyes only white. Sarah looked at her new shoes, new riding shoes going, *one cat and dog only girls are chickens two cat and dog Dad was not afraid not even in the war three cat and dog.* Mal kept the bit there, back in the mare's mouth, with Johnno yelling, 'you're drawing blood, ya bastard, yer damaging the horse ya frigger.' Mal could hear nothing, only feel the heaving beneath him. He was holding on, he was the stronger one, the lasting one, no question, don't question it.

The mare stopped. Just still, there, like that. Ramming and

frothing, then stopping still, like a photo. Stopped. Mal jerked on her back and waited, loose, holding. She stood. The fence chorus did not ripple. Then, just sudden, just like that, she ran a mad circle and did a half buck. She was smart this one, worth breaking, worth having once she'd been done. Mal had bred her for Johnno, an Arab–Palomino cross, his special breed, beautiful rich gold bay. Glinting and wild like this, she was a beauty. Mal was away, lusty drunk on the wild of her. He moved with her, let himself be loose, not tense. Rag-dolled about when she jerked from side to side, when she bucked. Holding on, but so loose you'd think he was part of her, growing out from her skin.

She ran again, bucked. Stopped, panted. He'd loosened the reins, so that they were still tight – she couldn't pull her head down – but not gashing. But she knew it, the feel of the metal cutting in there with him on her back. Sarah's legs were numb, her hands blistering on the rails. She could feel the beat of the sun on her head, on her nose, could feel it beginning to peel already. Her mouth was dry, she daren't ask for water, daren't move. The horse began to run, then slowed, slowed and walked. Walked with him on her back. Circuited the paddock, Mal turning her this way and that, barely even touching the reins. They walked a figure of eight in the centre of the corral, he kicked her to a trot, and to a canter. She breathed hard. He slid off her, rubbed his hands down her neck, her rump. Her legs folded under her, she lay, panting. The fence chorus cheered.

Later, Sarah would help him comb her and rub her down. In the shed behind the paddock, sacks and sacks of bran, hay and chaff mingled, waiting to be mixed. Tomorrow, he would ease the mare and soothe her. Like the others, it was easier for her to give up, in the end.

Five

Kari was home from special school, peering down through white net and roll-up blinds to Boolaroo main road. Staring across at the Catholic church, at the zebra crossing, at the round rock garden in the front yard of the Boolaroo house. Sitting up high above it all. There were red spots on her back, on her cheeks, on her chin. The pox. The chicken pox. Sarah was over her dose (had lain pathetically in bed, begging lemonade and *Archie* comics) and had run from the room that morning calling, 'Spastics got the po-ox, spastics got the po-ox.' Sarah was back at school, miserably lining up for milk and playing kiss-chasies behind the wooden weather shed. Kari watched dust float on the edges of the air, felt the quiet of sick days fold around her. She saw specks of dust swirling in a strip of light coming from a high window and settling on her callipers, rested against the wardrobe door. This was the secret daytime world.

The air, the day, was thick with Ruth padding about doing this, doing that, important chores which mattered. Ironing sheets (sprinkling water from a Tupperware cup onto the white crinkle, smoothing it into straightness with the smell of the crisp heat), making mayonnaise (the trick is to use two eggs and a hint of sugar), planning table settings. Ruth was endlessly, numbly busy, her feet muted on thick green carpet, her hands moving over things, her eyes skimming past, thinking what next what's left to do. Keeping the best for last, the polishing of windows.

Ruth Sweet polished and cleaned windows, always wanting to see through, to get more. Her arms fierce, moving side to side and side to side, squeaking clean. On both sides she would go, blowing and spitting and rubbing on marks. She used two bottles of

Windex every week, had three special window chamois cloths. Ruth Sweet's windows were immaculate. Kari could hear her squeaking at the window of the lounge, soft TV voices filtering in and out, while the light, the dust, the specks, danced, while Kari's eyes watched and lay down. Watched and lay down. Watched and lay down. When she woke, it was to a new Ruth, a new sharp Ruth standing on the bed of Kari, on the top bunk and making noises in her nose as she pulled and tore at the gauze of the curtains, falling back with them in her arms, stumbling to the floor. Kari watched as Ruth scooped the curtains up and whooshed out of the room, tearing a corner of the gauze on the metal door hinge. Kari could hear her stampeding about, catching curtains on doors, tearing them from windows.

Ruth loved to see clearly, could not bear the scarring of a window by dirt or grime or marks. Her face shone with the satisfaction of the clean, of the seeing surface. She tore curtains down with the passion of rage, her arms and cheeks mad shining. Kitchen, lounge, three bedrooms, bathroom: all gauze and net, then the white calico in the outside toilet. She was panting in the laundry (uncurtained) with the mound of gauze and net and calico at her feet, the bottle of Dr White's Miracle Bleach in her hand, when Kari called for lemonade. Ruth brought one bottle of lemonade and one of Windex, stomping up the stairs. She scrubbed again at the square window, triumphant in its bareness. Kari touched the face of Ruth, saying, 'you're shining Mummy.' They pressed their faces together at the naked shining of the window. Ruth felt words bubble up inside her, then swallowed them back.

The house, every window in it, was clear now, clear and shining, with light banging in, banging in, welcome as Larry was happy. Ruth glowed with the welcome of it, her face pressed, she was light herself, opened her mouth, said, 'would you like the story of the ice-queen, Bloss?' Kari squirmed beneath the pink chenille bedspread, squirmed in the light coming from her mother. Ruth told the story of the glass caught in the little boy's eye, while she breathed in the window. Happy as Larry.

Ruth Sweet, before she was Sweet, before she was bitter, before, when she was Ruth Cregg, everything had been in dark rooms. Might as well have been a lean-to, the house in Tabulum where Larry Cregg had buried his wife with a rusted shovel and cooked fried eggs for his daughter, Ruth. There was a wooden cross outside, marking the spot where Ruth's mother rotted. She'd begun to rot before she died, that was true enough, cancer cells eating through her stomach and intestine. Ruth had learnt not to breathe in the pantry-sized rooms, keeping a silence for her mother to be ill in. That house, who'd have believed it? Two rooms, both dark and windowless, but for a small slit at the upper edge of each wall – no wider than an inch. The air was thin and tight while that woman, Ruth's mother, lay being eaten alive, her mouth a straight pale line.

After she died, it got thinner in there, harder to breathe. In the nights when Larry Cregg's shoulder heaved over the girl, his chest fur rubbing against her mouth while he pushed, Ruth took small gasps of big air through the gap between his shoulder and arm, swallowing air and staring hard at the slits at the top of the wall, thinking, *my mouth is at that slit and that slit is a window and my face can see the window and can see through the window into the fresh green and flower field fields beyond I can see the sunshine shining I can see the flowers through I can see the window I can I can see I cannot hear this grunting feel this pushing I can see the wind.* She also learnt to count the bricks in the wall. There were one hundred and twelve bricks in the wall above the only bed.

When she moved to Sydney, forgetting her father's name, Ruth Cregg rented a room in Bondi with a whole wall full of windows, the room was full of light. She'd asked for the flywires to be taken off the windows when she took the room, and what the heck, she seemed a nice enough girl. So Mrs D'Arcy (widow) had a man take the screens away and Ruth Cregg let air and light in, discovered Windex and the joy of polishing windows. She polished twice a day in those first months, it took the place of words or friends, even acquaintances. Oh, there was Maureen, from her job at the Pavilion. They'd had an ice-cream together once and sang 'We'll Meet Again' in fake vibrato. Maureen had co-ordinating lips and nails and a crowd. Maureen did things with the crowd, while Ruth waited on the edges to be invited in: drifted back to her light-filled room and polished windows.

Mal Sweet had been like a dream, of course, in his policeman's uniform. A protector, pacing up and down Bondi Beach, with lifeguard shoulders and golden hair and a long brown face. She noticed his hands the first time he came to the Pavilion. Ruth showed people in, took coats and bags and smiled, dressed in green stripes and a skirt above the knee. He had huge hands, long and broad, both, with fair fine hairs winking on his raised knuckles. Brown hands, with neat nails, clean nails. Clean. He smelt of Palmolive soap and Brylcreem, oh god, she could really really have swooned. Ruth Cregg's hands were tiny, like her waist (eighteen inches, only an inch above Jayne Mansfield, how about that). He could fit his hands around her like a piece of wire. She was tiny, too, only five foot one, like a child or a doll with a round face, she needed someone to protect her. The stripes, the policeman, the hand around the waist – Ruth Cregg felt like a cloud, a white one, fresh and ready.

Mrs D'Arcy sewed the dress for her, spreading white satin and tulle across the downstairs lounge while Ruth danced with pins in her mouth. Mal paid for the cake, Maureen and the whole crowd showed, Mrs Ruth Sweet nee Cregg, thought she would fly away to the moon on tulle and satin wings.

They had a honeymoon. Five days in Noosa. The windows there were enormous, ceiling to floor, and ran right across the hotel room. You could open them like doors and step through them, French they were, but a single pane glass, like normal windows. Ruth pulled the curtains down on the second day of the honeymoon, and used a bottle of methylated spirits to polish the windows. She rubbed inside and out, with newspaper, meths and elbow grease, while Mal lazed about on Noosa beach. When she finished, you wouldn't have known there was a window there.

The Boolaroo house windows gleamed and were invisible in their brightness. These were the happiest days, the days of curtain washing and drying, when nothing but light came in through the panes. Kari caught the edges of the glow from her mother, asked for Lolli Gobble Bliss Bombs and was not refused. She was tucked in light and gentleness, sleeping, waking, sleeping. She slept past *Adventure Island* on the ABC, past Sarah banging in through the back door, woke to the smell of savoury mince and something moving under her chin. A scratchy something.

'Hey, Blossom, who's come to visit you? She was lonely, I found her on the street.' Mal's whisper did not rustle her hair, soft as for the horses. She was a pink raffia doll, with long plaited legs, a cork-ball head, a sparkling pink-gold-blue dress. Mal's hand floated over Kari's hair, touched her cheek, kitten-soft. 'Up for a bath now, ay, Bloss?'

Kari held the raffia doll tight to herself. 'She needs a bath too, Daddy.'

You could ride a canoe down Mal Sweet's laugh. 'Yair, she does, I reckon she does, but she'll have to sit just on the edge, ay?' Then calling downstairs, over his shoulder, 'Garn runna bath for ya daughter.'

Ruth let the bath run, while she set the table with the grey cloth and the placemats from Nimbin. She was careful in the laying of the knives and forks and spoons, superstitious about knives pointing inwards and spoons touching forks. She finished setting and ran to the bathroom, reaching the tap as Mal carried Kari through the white door. He sat her on the edge of the bath, slipping her pyjamas over her arms and off her legs, while Kari held the raffia doll in one hand. His hands slid under her arms to lift her up and in, her feet hitting the water, the rest of her folding into it. The raffia doll dropped, floated, bits of pink oozed out from the raffia strands unfolding from the cork-ball head. Kari turned to white and pink and burnt shrieking, with steam rising from the water. Mal sent words like puss to Ruth across the enamel: 'you stupid friggin cow, you careless friggin COW,' while Kari stayed in the bath, pink and screaming. Till Mal remembered and lifted her out like a bit of salted garden slug. Put her down carefully before he knocked Ruth for six across the tiles. She didn't say anything, Ruth, just lay there looking at Mal while Kari tried to cry in a whisper.

'Come on, Bloss, no bath tonight.' Mal wrapped the blue bear towel around her, rubbed it side to side, up her back, on her legs, her arms. He dried her fingers and toes carefully, covered her in baby powder, slipped her pyjamas back on (bottoms first, then tops), lifted her over his shoulder, carried her back to the room she shared with Sarah. The room with the shining windows. He kissed her hair before he closed the door. Ruth closed the bathroom door, let the water out, watched it spiral down, left her hands dangling in the water. Touched the water to her face. She pulled the glugged up raffia strands one by one from the drain, the pink staining her fingers. The edges of the bath had pink streaks. Ruth rubbed at them with her hands until they were gone.

Six

The night dropped down suddenly, at half-past five. It was summer and everything, so no-one expected it to happen. They all said that, the whole town, for days, even years later – never expected it, no way, not a bloody sign in the sky. Jack was sprawled in the white lock-up, singing 'Come all Ye Faithful' through the bars. Calm it was, all calm and still and smelling of fresh and jasmine, like normal for October. Sarah pushed at the big shovel, digging a trench, *a moat*, around the prison. Making a castle for Jack, the king who would be invaded. Here was the plan: first, dig the moat. Sarah had to do that, there was only one shovel (except if you counted the yellow plastic beach spade, which really was for babies), and Kari's arms were sticklike, not for pushing or digging. The red hose would then be used for making the river around the castle. Kari sat on the third step, her callipers laid across her knee as she carefully taped them together with thick brown masking tape from the station. They were to be the drawbridge. Kari would be the soldier of the drawbridge, lifting and laying it across the promised river. Sarah would ride triumphantly across the calliper bridge and liberate King Jack. 'Joyful and triumphant, O come ye o cooooome ye to Be-eethlehem.' King Jack was the patient exile.

Kari noticed it first – she always did, she scented such things, storms, sunsets, battles – lifting her head and sniffing hard, breathing in deep. There was a crack from the paddock, like the stock whip but louder, harder. A crack then a thud, then a slash across the sky. Sarah stopped digging, staring hard at the Jacaranda branch fallen across the paddock fence, suddenly lit by that odd lightning slash. The shovel fell with a soft little thud on the grass beside her feet. Her face pointed to the sky, Sarah stared the storm out. Kari was like a baby, letting a squeal out, calling to Sarah. So they huddled together on the third step, watching this sudden mad fury batter at the garage door. Ruth swished out in the wind, her blue spotted A-line dress blowing up to her waist. She scraped Kari and Sarah together like bits of fluff, her call whipping away on the wind. 'C'mon, in, in, quickly. Now.' And in they went, pulled by arms, the red door banging behind them. They fly-wire was left screeking in the storm.

When the lightning started up properly – not just the odd surprising slash, but a round of cracks and booms – Kari pressed her face against the window. The red gum in the Fargate's paddock was cracking. 'It's gunna fall, the tree, the treeeeee, it's gunna fall.' There was a sound like the earth splitting open, and the top half of the tree cracked away, leaving the inside naked like a just-born thing. Out back, the white prison shuddered. Jack's voice battled with the storm, the metal roof shaking. Ruth fluttered on the edge of the door, a white-faced moth, *Poor bugger. Poor bloody bugger*, swinging and thumping through her head to the tune of the gale. 'Don't move!' The command flew over her shoulder and she was gone, leaving the storm poking its head in the banging door. Sarah pressed her nose to the window alongside Kari's, let her hand be held, squeezed back even. When Ruth staggered back in, Jack was hunched beside her. His flat face was Pekingesed up, yap yap yap. No singing came blurring out of his mouth though, no, just a stream of thank-you sounds meant to be words.

'Pranh clug hurgh hetch.' The wind and cold had knocked it out of him, the song, the words. He was half the size of Ruth, his trousers held up by his hand. Well, barely the size of Sarah, the way he was hunched up. 'Prenh cleth hurgh hetch?' Kari watched her mother push King Jack into the green armchair, the ugly one. His face contorted. 'Preh clug hrey CLEAH?' Kari scuttled around on the edges of the carpet square, waiting for his words to come back, however dim, however slow.

Ruth rested her hand on his shoulder. 'Sugar, Jack?'

The world broke through. 'Hroo.'

Ruth used a family cup and a teabag. She plopped the sugar in with a prisoner's spoon, left it on the saucer for Jack to stir. Kari climbed on to the big couch with Sarah, sat watching, like he was the telly. Ruth pushed a TV table in front of him, obscuring their view. Ruth bustled. She wrapped capability around her, and busyness, opened baked beans, made toast. Finished the shepherd's pie at the same time. She shone. King Jack crammed slices of toast in, grinning, singing, slurring out word-like creatures amongst dribbled baked beans. He had a paper serviette. The windows slapped in and out, bashing against the slap bang of close-by and far-off thunder. The red tablecloth flicked on to the Laminex table. Knives, forks, butter dish, brown sauce, salt, cracked down, sharp as the lightning sounds outside. 'Come and sit at the table you two. Today.'

Sarah backed into the kitchen, her eyes not leaving Jack. She looked spitty-eyed at the dish in the centre of the table, at the crisped-up mashed-potato lid, the scrape of cheese golden on the top. Looked back at Jack. 'I want beans, too.'

Ruth bit the inside of her bottom lip, pulled a chair out, 'eat what you can, then you can have some beans, good girl, eat up before your father comes home.' It was a regular litany, issued through Ruth's distraction.

He came in with laughing on him like the wind, Mal. Showing the storm who was boss, that's what he'd been doing. He scraped his chair out. Ruth scooped out piles of the pie, dolloped it on to a white plate. Left the table, ladled out peas from the Aluminium saucepan, passed the salt, set the plate at his right hand, bit her lip, sat on the edge of her chair. They ate on tippy toes then, all crinkling at the sound of a knife on a plate. Mal broke the quiet. 'Macka's shed roof blew off, poor bugger. Ha. Shoulda seen it, whole sacks were flying out through the top. Lost his new saddle. Poor bugger.' Ruth swallowed, smiled. 'And,' Mal looked magic-eyed at Kari, then across at Sarah, 'what do you think I saw flying through the sky tonight?'

Kari looked up at the steamed-up windows for inspiration, listened to the yowling outside: 'a witch?'

33

Mal grinned that grin, 'nup, witches are inside, I reckon. Cooking.'

Ruth let herself go to another place, thought about windows, cars, Macka's shed flying across the sky, anything.

'Saw a cat flying past me, whoosh.'

The quiet returned to the table. In the corner of the lounge, King Jack shcerracked. His body crippled over and convulsed, with that sound coming from his mouth, like a car starting, but human. Shcerrack. Shcerrack. His hands twitched on a slice of toast, beans squished in his fist, oozed down his arm. Sarah slid sideways from her chair. 'Leave it. No-one's been excused.' She left it, sat back silent.

'I couldn't leave him out there in this, Mal. He had to come in. What'd happen if he died? You'd cop it.'

Mal forked a pile of mince into his mouth, chewed fifteen times, swallowed.

'Shcrerrack. Prah celch. Prah celch.'

Ruth's chair tipped to the floor. Sarah looked fierce at her plate. In the lounge, Ruth slapped Jack hard on the back. And again. And again. She could feel his bones, could almost feel his liver, his kidneys, his spleen. His skin only just held everything in. 'Shcaa shcaa shceeeerack.' Jack gobbed up a perfectly formed ball of bean-coloured chewed toast. It landed neatly on the TV table. Jack's face folded up proudly. He coughed and slurped some tea. Ruth caught the toast-ball in the white paper serviette, dropped it in the pedal bin on her way back to the table. Mal's plate was empty. He laid his knife and fork carefully alongside each other, and: 'Outside.' Sarah's knife scratched the plate. She bunched her stomach up.

Ruth's face was pointing up, looking straight at Mal. 'He's not going out, Mal, don't make him, you've heard him, he's on the edge for flip's sake.'

Mal stayed still, just one fingernail flicking in and out of his thumbnail. 'He can stay where he bloody well is, you can sleep out in the lock-up where you belong.'

Ruth's face was hazy, bewildered.

34

'Don't friggin well try to do my friggin job. Sarah, get out move, go on, go to your friggin room, take your sister GO, as for you, ya slag, *out*.' Still no-one moved. Mal yelled this from his seat, the red plastic kitchen chair at the end of the table, his throne. There was room for only one king. 'Garn, piss off. You've got the keys, haven't yer? Seeing as you're so bloody good at gettin' in there and doin my friggin job, seeing you're so bloody attached to the place.'

Sarah meant her voice to be loud as the tree cracking, but it came out a huddled-in-the-corner whisper: 'Don't, Dad.'

He passed over her voice, stood up, did not see her, did not see Kari, did not see Jack. Ruth's small hands held the edges of the Laminex. 'Please, Mal, not with the kids here. I'm sorry, love. Please, Mal. Please.'

Please, Mal. No. No pleasing Mal, not now when he was un-pleased. Her hands scratched away from the table's edge as he pulled her by the shoulders. She said nothing, no sound came from her, no please, Mal. Her hands were on the floor, with the rest of her, falling sideways and down, with Mal standing behind her, pulling until she was a heap of Ruth at his feet, with which he kicked. She knew the tricks of silence, Ruth, how not to whimper or give in, how to think about Noosa and count the leaves in the tree outside and think *my face can see the window and can see through the window into the fresh garden and flower field beyond I can see the sunshine shining I can see the flowers through I can see the window I can I can see I cannot hear this yelling feel this kicking I can see the wind.*

Sarah used her finger to trace the white pattern in the Laminex, a squiggly diamond shape, all edged by waves, by foam shapes in white; she could run her finger along the foamy shapes. There was a groove near her finger, from a burn a long time ago, somehow, a finger-length piece of melted Laminex just there, just near her finger. Sarah could edge her finger along it, she could not hear the yelling then, could only think about the foamy shapes, the diamond shapes, the edges of the melt and that thud,

35

that thump, she could not hear, could only run her fingers there, along that melted ledge. Kari, weak and useless, was under the table, snivelling like a girl, like a spastic, a spastic girl. Kari yelped when the door slammed. In the lounge, Jack struck up the chorus of 'How Great Thou Art.'

They didn't see Ruth in the morning, but the door of the lock-up was bashed in around the edges and the rest of the Jacaranda had blown down. Kari and Sarah went to stay with Mrs Luciano, Wog's wife, for a couple of days, 'cause Ruth was ill from the storm'. Mal walked with them there, down the main road of Boolaroo and up First Street, stepping over broken doors and bits of shingles, dead cats, bicycles, trees. The Boolaroo school was closed three days for repairs. Everyone said it was the worst, absolutely the worst, gale they'd seen since 1953, and that was debatable. *The Chronicle* said that three people and an aboriginal had been killed by falling trees or sheds. On the night Sarah and Kari went back home after four days, Ruth cooked them baked beans on toast and made shepherd's pie for the prisoners – two bikers picked up for drag racing near the Point. Sarah wasn't hungry and went straight to bed instead.

Seven

Her name was Penny. She was fourteen hands – nothing really, piddly for a horse, she might have been a pony. A bay. And was she a gift to Sarah, or to Kari? It was Kari who had begged for a horse, though she wouldn't know how to ride if you showed her. Kari who sat rocking on the edge of the couch while Sarah snuck alongside, saying to that man, her father, 'will I ride too, Dad, will I?'

Penny. Gloss-coated and warm-breathed. Dark-eyed. Soft of lip and hard of hoof. On Christmas Day, Mal woke them both. Sarah first: 'Carn, mate, Santa's been, carn.' Then Kari: 'Where's my Blossom angel ay? Guess who's snuck in the window.' There was no need for chimneys in Boolaroo. They clustered – Mal, Ruth, Kari, Sarah – around the silver tinsel tree (Woolworths, twelve dollars ninety-five with the special offer of a musical revolving Santa for an extra eight dollars and forty-nine cents), scratching the caking of sleep from eyes, yawns falling from throats, Mal orchestrating the event. 'What's in that basket, Blossom?'

Kari, squealing; 'a black baby doll.'

The conductor, waving, 'And there? Meccano, that's right. Where else?'

Plastic typewriter, telephone, textas, gum-boots, clothes, Fuzzy Felt, toy pig, toy dog, toy toys, rocking horse. Enough. Sarah watched Kari growing fat on the cream of this, on the unwrapping and peering in, on the procession of cushions with gifts before her. Kari, clinking away in her callipered manger.

Sarah tugged at the pink collar of her Chinese girl pyjamas, watched Ruth scuffling at the edge of the tree. And Mal, turning the full beam of himself on Sarah, saying 'carn, mate, the big one.

37

Carn, mate.' Not, *'Carn, Blossom.'* No. *Mate*. Penny was always meant for Sarah – no argument. 'Carn, Mate, whaddya reckon there is outside eh? Dya reckon Santa's forgotten something?'

Sarah felt the twist of hope inside her, too frightened of its power to name it. 'Dunno, Dad.'

'There's something missing, isn't there?' Mal chucked Sarah under her arm, smiled over her head at Ruth.

'The star? There's no star on the tree like there is at school. Macka says you've gotta have a star so you can find your way back from the inn, like Joseph.'

'Yair, Macka says a lot of flamin things. He's got stories comin out his ears that bloke. Course we've got a flamin . . .' Mal looked up at the tip of the tree, his arm mid-flight to pointing, did a little jump, looked back and let his breath out, hands on hips. 'Bugger me. There's no flamin star. Ruth love, look at this tree, will yer?'

Ruth looked. 'Nope, no star on that tree. Not up top. Maybe it's fallen off, no, not on the floor. There's no star.'

'Well, what I wonder is,' and the magic was back in the voice and the hands and the eyes of Mal Sweet, 'what I wonder is, if we went lookin for a star, I wonder were we might find it? Corse, I can see we've gotta problem here, with no star. So we'll have to find it. We have to have a star to find the stable ay?'

Sarah could feel that bubble of mad swelling up up up inside her, that swallow of happiness catching in her chest. Her giggle-bubble fell out in words, 'we might have to look in the toilet,' and she snorted through her nose, hopelessly caught in that laughing. And no-one said, shush don't be a baby. Flying way up high, she called down at them, as an extra, 'we might have to look in our bottoms,' and Mal only laughed and Ruth only said, 'Yes, perhaps we might.'

'Righto. Everyone get yer star-hunting equipment. Slippers, dressing-gown, rope to catch it. Hup-two, hup-two.' Mal was the ringleader, handing out provisions like God, while Ruth flitted behind him. God's shadow. You couldn't see her at all when the light went away.

The cicadas were out already, chacking away in the sky, or the paddocks. Sarah tugged the arm of God. 'Dad, how will we find a star in the day? We did stars for Project and Mr Ambrose said stars couldn't be seen during the day, didya know that?'

'Yair, well, problem with Mr Cartwright is that he's only ever seen night stars not magic stars. Now we might just be looking for a magic star. Which case Mr Cartwright wouldn't know it if it jumped up and punched him right in the nose.'

'Boom. Biff. Kapow.' Sarah Batmanned her way down the steps, a star boombiffing Mr Cartwright in the nose. You could do that if you were a star.

Kari held the blue nylon sleeve of Ruth's dressing gown and leant just on one stick. They trailed, snakelike, down the steps, Mal at the front, then Sarah, jumping on uncallipered legs, then Ruth and the hobble-bobble Kari. 'We're off to find the sta—ar, the wonderful star of Mal's, because because because becaaaaaaause, if ever-a-wever a star there was.' Mal skipped sideways on the path, holding his pretend skirt out in front of him.

'Diddle da da dum dee.' Kari was the backing group. The music trickled over them all, shifted about on their bodies like sifting chaff.

Mal kept dancing, across to the door of the lock-up. He bent down, looked at the ground, looked under his legs: 'can't see a star here.' He lifted his arm, looked under the crook, 'nope, no star there.'

'No, in the sky, you have to look in the sky, Daddy.' Kari was astronomer. 'Stars like in the sky. Like in Sarah's project.'

'Not there, definitely no star there,' he tilted his head back, stared into the sky, then scraped at the sole of his shoe, 'nope, no star there either. We'll have to keep looking.'

They sniffed along behind him, turning this way and that, looking under rocks, up trees, even behind Kari's ear for the magic star. The garage door had been painted red for Christmas, and a metal bolt lay across its belly. Mal stopped at the bolt, twitching his nose, making his nostrils big small big. His foot pawed at the ground. Even Ruth had laughing coming out of her: 'Luvvaduck

Mal, luvvaduck. Yer mad as a hatter, I swear' and her eyes went soft at him.

'The star, the star!' It was Kari who saw it, tied to a stick at the top of the garage door. Wisps of silver tinsel floated out like flags in the heat, and the gleam of the sun against the foil star buckled their eyes.

'Well, if the star's here, this must be the stable ey? Whaddya reckon? We s'posed to go inside?'

The whole of Christmas was inside Sarah's belly. Kari could feel the sun in her legs, her hands.

'Well, whaddaya reckon mate?'

'It's the stable. We have to go in.'

Kari clinked behind Sarah, 'we have to go in to find the baby in the mongrel.'

'Yair too right Bloss, or the mongrel in the baby,' Mal's face had crinkles around his eyes.

There was just black inside the garage, deep deep shadow stretching way back to the end. All eyes squinted up, the bright of the sun making everything confused after it. There was a shape, there in front of them, and a sound like a humph, humph and then a clump on the ground. The smell of chaff, of hay, of sweat, of horse breath. The sound of a tail flicking. The shadow settled.

'Well? What's got ya tongue mate?'

She couldn't. She couldn't find it. Sarah's tongue was tumbling in her mouth. If she said, I love it my horse my horse, if he laughed, said, she's not your horse ya silly bugger, if he said, are ya happy with her she's yours ya silly bugger, if he said, if he said, why didn't he say, just say, oh god oh god oh god.

'She's yours, love. Garn. She's called Penny, but you can change it if you like.' Ruth pushed Sarah forward so gently.

Penny. Fourteen hands. Smelling of horse and breath and sweat. Mal pulled the doors wide open, let Sarah rest her head against Penny's belly. She was like gloss, and like oil and like the warmest thing ever, but firm too. Sarah's cheek moved up and down with the breath inside the horse.

'Righto, mate, can't mollycoddle her all day. When ya gunna

get on her?' Mal held out a brand new saddle, the leather oiled and shining. A white paper bow dangled on the front edge. 'It's about time you learnt to saddle up properly.'

Mal threw a green blanket over the horse's back, strapped stirrups onto the saddle. He stood behind Sarah while she buckled the straps beneath the roundness of Penny's belly, pushing his knee up to Penny's flank, pushing the breath out of the belly of the horse, murmuring at Sarah, like at the horses, 'that's the girl, that's the way, good girl, good girl. She'll puff herself up if ya don't push the breath out, that's it, now pull it tight.' Mal slipped the bridle over the horse's head, led her out through the double wooden doors, clipped across to the paddock. It was a special occasion, Christmas and the first day of Penny, so slippers were allowed on the grass. Sarah could climb on to the smooth shine of the saddle just in her Chinese girl pyjamas and even with bare feet. Only for this once, only for Christmas. Mal legged her up, hooking his hands together, making a step for her feet. And up. Sarah's leg swung high, like Mal's, over the back of the horse and she landed soft in the saddle, like Mal, just like Mal. Yeeha. She pushed the tops of her legs hard against the saddle, let her feet push against the stirrup while Mal bent down, shortened the straps on either side. *Perfect.*

'Now, start off on a walk, Mate, and I'll stick at her head just in case. I'm not leadin, I'm just stickin with you.' Mal let his hand rest against the bridle, not pulling, just resting, while Sarah gripped her knees, sat straight, chin up, hands loose, leant forward, all the things just right, just the way he'd said. 'That's the way, that's the girl, are ya ready for a trot?' Sarah gripped her hands, thought, *loose, loose, let her know who's boss* and nodded yes.

'Give her a slap on the rump, then, garn' Mal prodded Sarah. 'Garn.'

Sarah felt the gloss of horse flesh beneath her hand, the bounce of the slap. Penny's heels lifted faster, her back swayed. Sarah flopped about, pushing her feet into the stirrups, staring straight ahead, and up, and updown, updown up, up. When Mal trotted there was a rhythm, he made it with the horse, da da da da de dum, da da da da de dum. Sarah went dum de de dadadadaaaaaa dum plop dum. Penny kept changing the rhythms. 'She's being stupid, Dad. She's not trotting properly.'

'Yair, someone's not trotting properly in this paddock, wonder who that could be, ay? Slap her again mate, giver a real whack. Here, like this.' His hand swung up through the air and back, making a sound on the horse which stung. Penny's head jerked up, she pushed forward in a gallop. Sarah leaned herself far, far forward, her elbows tucked in like Mal's, her whole body curving into the horse; she was galloping, there she was with the wind and the roll of Penny beneath her and she could do it she could she really could. 'Right, pull her up, pull back, that's it, no not sudden, just, that's it, pull, pull, let her know who's boss.' Penny slowed smooth, so smooth you wouldn't believe it. 'Made for each other, I reckon. Yer gunna have to have yer first fall soon.'

'Me, let me have a go, Daddy, it's my turn.' Kari was perched like a kooka on the fence, rocking back and forwards.

'She's my horse, spastic, she's not everyone's horse. You have to ask me if ya want a ride and I say no. You'll break her. She's not a toy.'

'Sarah don't call your sister spastic.' Ruth's voice was automatic.

'Sure, you can have a ride Bloss, pass her here, love.' Mal held his hands out, let Kari be handed to him by solid-armed Ruth, lifted her onto the saddle. Kari called at them all, 'I'm up here if you're looking for me.'

'Give her a slap then. Atta girl.'

Kari's hand fell limply on to Penny's rump. Sarah, Boolaroo Christmas Champion, called from the fence. 'No you have to *slap* stupid, not like a poxy girl tap. Thwack properly.' Kari screwed her face up.

'You look like you're gunna do a poo.'

'Sshh, Sarah.'

Kari let her hand fly fly down with all every single bit of strength, hard hard hard. Penny stepped forward, walked slowly. 'I'm riding, everybody. Look.' Mal, laughing, swiped behind the saddle, a good firm slap. You could hear it like thunder, cracking around the paddock. Penny twitched and started forward, gallop gallop gallop. Kari's face turned back to Mal, her legs flouncing about like curtains. She tilted, a compass, down and down, sliding around the side of the saddle and down and down, and beneath the legs, between the legs of the gallop, and the unslippered feet there before the rear legs of the gallop, and the bang the bash of the hooves on the unslippered feet and the blood from the toe.

'She tried to kill me she ran me over I'm bleeeeding.'

Mal and Ruth ran together, Mal piling Kari into his arms. 'Sshh, it's okay Blossom, look,' he wiped at the blood, 'it's just blood, no crushed toe. Look.'

'She doesn't love me, she rode on me, I'm never riding her again, she did it purposely Daddy.'

'No, Bloss, she didn't know you were there. Look, it's just a little blood really isn't it?'

'But she did know, she knew I was there, I was riding. I'm never riding again.'

'Ah, Bloss, she didn't know it was you, you have to ride again, love.'

'She could feel me.'

'She thought you were Sarah. She didn't know.'

The star inside Sarah turned on its point, dug into her, burned. She slid off the fence, her bare feet hopping across the bindis on the lawn. She let the door bash behind her, she didn't care. One day, she was going to kill that stupid, that spastic, that sister.

Eight

CAFÉ REQUIRES MATURE LADY FOR TABLE SERVICE AND GENERAL
DUTIES, INCLUDING CLEANING FLOORS, TABLES AND WINDOWS.
CONTACT MRS ST CLARE, 53 4563. She read it again; MRS ST CLARE
53 4563. 53 4563. The number chuttled through her again, again,
again, getting louder and louder. No, it would be too ridiculous,
and besides, Mal. Ruth looked at the black phone, round and
glossed up, on the edge of the hall table. If she slid her chair
around and reached her arm out, leant kind of backwards, she
could reach it, the receiver could just fall into her hand, just like
that. But it would be – wouldn't it? – too ridiculous, and besides,
Mal. CAFÉ REQUIRES MATURE LADY FOR TABLE SERVICE AND GENERAL
DUTIES, INCLUDING CLEANING TABLES, FLOORS AND WINDOWS.
CONTACT MRS ST CLARE 53 4563.

The days extended long for Ruth, wrapped in the swirl of dust
mites and muteness, with the silence of the pauses and the waiting
for the evening storms. The long gap between the whish and
whoosh of morning noise – children's television (*Scooby Dooby
Dooby Doo*), popping toast, the brushing of shoes, the spilling of
juice, the fights over hairbrushes or crooked partings, the slamming doors, the swift exits and the battles of night – was a gap, a
hole in something, waiting to be filled in. In these times, the in-
between times, Ruth was invisible, unheard, untouched. She
scratched her arms, just checking that she was alive.

Ruth let her finger rest inside the circle on the dial, turning it,
feeling the cold of the metal, clicking her nail against it. Taptap,
taptap. The receiver was heavy in her hand, her sweat eased onto
the surface, slipped along it, made her palm warm. 53 4563. She
left her finger in the dial as it clicked back after each number,

holding it back so that the turn was slow. 5 ... 3 ... She could smell Mal's breath on the mouthpiece, could taste him if she closed her eyes.

'Yairs?' The voice was high, but kind of round. 'Yairs? Hullo? Hullo? Oh, for Heaven's sake.' Ruth waited until the woman on the other end – Mrs St Clare presumably – had plonked the receiver down. She held the phone on her lap. A slip of a laugh bubbled up. 'Oh for Heaven's sake. Indeed.' This was ruddy ridiculous. *Bloody* ridiculous. The laugh again, surprising her – where did this come from? She heard the voice again, saw herself, Ruth Sweet, sat trying to open her mouth, opening it and closing it, and – the laugh spurted out – no words coming out, she must have looked like a great flipping goldfish. Her head rolled forward and the laugh poured out like water, dribbling down her nylon floral blouse, pouring down her legs and across the floor in great big loud dollops.

At three-forty-nine PM, same as always, Sarah bashed herself in through the back door. Bang, stomp, stomp. And then the thwack of her school bag against the washing machine. The double plonk of her heavy Bartlett's black shoes dropping off, right then left. She waited for the set response, the beginning of the liturgy: '*Please* Sarah – do yer have ta bang so much?'

And Sarah, peeling her white-grey socks off, breathing in the sweat-dirt-sun smell and wiggling toes free, would call back: 'I *didn't* bang.'

'Well I could've sworn I just heard that door bang. Must've been Mr Nobody.'

'I always get the blame for *everything* around here.'

But no sound came. Sarah banged her bag at the washing machine just to make sure. 'Mum? Mu-uum.' She was tortoise-like, moving head first into the kitchen, swinging her eyes first one way then the other, letting her neck and then her body follow. 'Muuuuuum.' Ruth was by the phone, shining. 'Mum?' Sarah stood dead in front of her, poking her face into Ruth's light.

A shutter opened in Ruth's face. She blinked and giggled. Absolutely giggled. 'I've got a job, darl,' giggled again.

45

'Whaddayer mean, Mum? Whaddayer onabout?' Sarah's ears were burning.

'A job,' a chuckle fell out this time, 'in a café. My job.'

Sarah's head tilted about. 'But why? Whadabout us? Are you gunna run away?'

'Ohgawdno, darlin, I'm not runnin away, I'm just, I dunno.'

'Every day? Like Dad?'

'Not like Dad. Mornings only. I'll be home before your bell even rings. Whaddayer reckon?' She sounded like Mal, with that laugh in her voice. Weird, Ruth laughing.

'I reckon its weird.' A chucklelaugh bubbled out from Sarah's mouth, joined with the one falling from Ruth. The two laughs took off, danced on the floor. Ruth's mouth opened wide, cackling and cackling. HahahahaHaHaHAOhdear. Sarah crossed her legs, hopped about in the hallway, held her belly where the laughing came from, laughed and laughed and laughed until it was time to meet the bus from special school.

After Kari came in, carrying a mask made from a paper plate, Ruth dressed herself and cooked. Kari and Sarah took turns wearing the mask and singing along to *Adventure Island*. The kitchen steamed with everything that Mal loved to eat. Steak-and-kidney pie with honey carrots, baby jacket potatoes and cauliflower *au gratin* and passionfruit pavlova for dessert. Ruth held on, determined. He came in at 6.03 PM. Calm as calm he was, just walking in, sitting himself down, no flies on him, no sir. Ruth floated around him, all elegant in her navy straight skirt and white satinette blouse that showed the bit where her bones stuck out on her chest. She wore red lips. Oh yes. Sarah ate everything on her plate, did not kick her feet against the table leg, did not scrape her knife, just sat and quietly ate. Even Kari kept it down, not knowing why, only that she must.

'D'ya have a good day, love?' Ruth put his drink down, let her hand rest on his shoulders, then looked down at the floor and flicked her lashes up to his eyes. Sarah, watching, practised that look in front of the mottled mirror in her room for three days before she got it right enough to try out on Mr Cartwright. Mal looked across the Laminex at Ruth, looked at her eyes and her hand. Said nothing, looking at her red lips, watching her hips under the navy skirt. He watched her do the dishes, her hips moving back and side, back and side.

It was after baths, after prayers, after goodnight Kari and Sarah, that she took him to bed, peeled off her satinette and slipped the skirt down. She let her hands cover the bruises on her hips and thighs, he wouldn't like to see that, no, sir. Mal lay himself on the bed, watching her beg and let himself be hard. Ruth folded back the chenille bedcover and knelt above him on the bed. Her hands fluttered about him, not resting anywhere, just doing a dance. Mal watched and did not speak. Let her lower herself onto him, lay back and watched her breasts swing. Felt her beg, felt his power push and push and push and still didn't speak and still didn't cry out, didn't let the power out. He fell asleep on his back, his mouth open. Ruth watched him breathe, listened to his snores and said a kind of prayer.

On Wednesday, the day Ruth started work at Mrs St Clare's café (The Coffee Pot), she took baked beans and toast to Jack early. She was crisp in black and white (A-line skirt and button-through blouse), and all nerves and fumbles. The enamel tray slipped from her hands, one piece of toast sliding across the floor. 'Ohgawd struth, sorry love, oh me ruddy skirt.' Ruth touched a bit of spit onto her finger, rubbing at the edge of the black fabric. 'It's earlier than usual, love, just I start me new job today.' She was soft, shy with the unfamiliarity of the words, pronouncing them carefully as though they might break in her mouth. 'Me new job.' Gawd, she felt like a kid, just waiting for someone to poke her, point, say 'new job? You couldn't do a bloody job, ya great useless cow, you couldn't be good for nothin.' She'd waited for Mal to say it, to laugh, or knock her across the bedroom. To be shocked, or angry at least. But he was scary, scarier than hitting – just looked her up and down, said, 'fine, no skin off my nose,' and rolled over, went back to sleep. No guessing him, that Mal.

Jack crumpled the toast up in his hand, cramming it into his mouth, and drawing his face into a grin at Ruth. 'You're good, lady. Smart. Brave.'

She could see balls of toast bobbing about in his mouth, spit dribbling down his chin. Ruth held her hands together, kind of bit her lip. 'Ah, bugger off, Jack, ya great flippin charmer.' But on the walk to the bus stop she repeated 'Good, smart, brave' over and over and it helped calm the shaking in her legs.

The Coffee Pot was on the main street of Teralba, right next to John Brown Electrics (Mal had once broken a young Arab stallion for Brownie, nearly broken his own neck doing it). Inside was all purple carpet and round white tables. There was a tiny white vase on each table, with a silk – not plastic, silk – carnation in it.

'A little bit of elegance for our clientele.' Mrs St Clare was large and round with a high brown knot of hair, and an Englishey sort of voice. 'Be courteous to them at all times. To start with, you'll be clearing tables, delivering coffee and cleaning. As you progress, we can get you taking orders and even making coffees. It's quiet now, so give the tables a wipe over and then . . .'

'What about the windows? Shining clean windows are a welcome sight.' Ruth almost jumped at the boldness of her own self, just coming out with it like that, (*Good, smart, brave*) as if she'd worked here all her ruddy life.

Mrs St Clare puffed out, smiled at Ruth Sweet, said, 'You'll do very well here. Yes, then, do the windows. Lovely.'

Nine

For Sarah's eleventh birthday party, Ruth brought chocolate eclairs home from The Coffee Pot. She could serve eight tables in three minutes, never kept a customer waiting and could work the big shiny Italian coffee machine. 'Cappuccino. Vienna.' She practised the new words, explained them to the girls from Brownie's shop who came in at lunchtimes. 'Coffee with froth, coffee with cream, *café au lait*. That's French: coffee with milk.' The Coffee Pot was a kind of heaven, really it was. Twice a week, Ruth stayed an extra hour to clean the windows. Mrs St Clare had used soapy water before Ruth came along. Honestly. You wouldn't read about it. Soapy water. Ruth bought her own bottle of Windex, and sometimes used fifty-fifty water and vinegar. Sometimes, she stayed an extra two hours, her arms aching from rubbing up and across.

Mrs St Clare, impressed by the shining windows and carefully scrubbed tables, asked after the children, gave them treats, told Ruth she was an angel from heaven, really she was, 'you're absolutely wonderful. Wonderful. You've no idea. Really.' On the day before Sarah's birthday Mrs St Clare gave Ruth eight chocolate eclairs, ('How many are going to the party? Eight? Here's one each, no, I insist, really I do, now just enjoy it. Lovely.'). Ruth made a wishing-well cake, with chocolate icing and a green jelly pond and chocolate Freddo Frogs on the side and room for eleven candles all around the edges. It was beautiful. The most beautiful cake Sarah had ever seen.

On the morning of the party, Greg Winter's mum phoned Ruth up to say sorry; Greg was very ill and couldn't come to Sarah's party after all but they hoped all the boys and girls had fun. 'Boys and girls, ha,' Sarah, listening to Ruth pass the message on, stared at the floor, thought *girls are weak, chuck em in the creek*. Ruth hadn't even suggested that Sarah invite some girls to the party, what would be the point? Sarah was determined – girls would want dancing and dolls and playing at make-up, instead of proper games. Eight were allowed at the party, including Sarah and Kari. Without Greg Winter, that left seven: Peter Clarke, Macka, Steven Hill (even if he was as blond as a girl and sometimes scared of horses), Michael Luciano (called Wog, like his Dad, like his sister and like his Mum), and Ben Knight (mad as anything, could kick a ball to the end of the playground in one go). Plus Kari, plus Sarah. While Ruth ran about with crêpe-paper streamers and paper chains, Sarah was allowed to make chocolate crackles on her own. She watched the glob of copha, cold from the fridge, soften and collapse into almost-runnyness in the aluminium pan. She spilt Cadbury's cocoa all across the bench and down onto the floor, but no-one would yell at her, not even Mal if he came in from the station where he was busy putting papers into drawers. It was her birthday.

Ruth laid a table out in the yard and spread it with paper plates brimming over with sausage rolls, party pies, Cheesels, crisps, Lamingtons, jelly babies, the éclairs, Vegemite and peanut butter sandwiches and even fairy bread. There were small bowls of tomato sauce and paper cups next to bottles of lemonade and Coke and there was a big space left in the table for the wonderful wishing-well cake. Kari helped Ruth spread a white paper cloth over the table. There was a big rope lying on the ground to play tug-of-war and lassoing and limbo with. Mal was going to teach everyone how to crack a whip. Sarah's stomach felt tight and achey. She spread her arms out wide, like wings, and zoomed in circles around the yard, chanting, 'it's the day of my party, it's the day of my party.'

Kari clinked away from the table and wobbled around behind Sarah, joining in the song. 'It's the day of my party, it's the day of my party.'

Sarah stopped, bang, just like that, and let Kari crash into her back and fall. 'It's not your party, stupid, it's my party. Only my party.' Sarah felt the ache in her stomach again, felt tears for no reason just waiting to creep up and out.

Kari looked up at her, wide eyed. 'But I can come to your party can't I?'

Sarah's stomach and chest hurt, and stomping through her brain came, *I'm mean and horrible, I'm mean and horrible.* She pulled Kari up though, and wiped the dirt off her hotpants. 'Of course you're coming, silly. You're the only girl at the party.'

At half-past eleven, Ben Knight ran through the front gate. His grown-up sister waited at the edge of the footpath until she saw him waving his red parcel at Sarah. She waved at Ruth across the yard, then walked off fast, towards the Penny's Head. Sarah was suddenly shy and held the corner of the table, embarrassed by the offering held out towards her by the skinny Ben Knight. Catching her awkwardness, he dropped the present onto the table and kicked his feet on the ground.

'Thankyou what lovely wrapping are you Ben? Have a drink you're the first one here lovely to see you Sarah offer Ben a drink thank him nicely unwrap your present remember you're the hostess.'

Sarah was breathless from Ruth's list of instructions. She tore at the red tissue paper.

'I chose it.' Ben bounced on his heels, watching her rip away to the brown plastic of a hand gun. 'It makes a proper bang.'

Sarah tried it, twirling it about her fingers like in the movies.

'Hey Sarah! *Vrroooooom.*' Steven Clarke zoomed himself towards the table, his hands circling on an imaginary wheel. 'Race ya.' A brightly wrapped square thing landed on one of the plastic chairs and a swirl of bodies vroomed across the yard. Sarah held her gun proudly in the air, like out the window of a car.

After everyone had arrived (Macka was late because his dad was too drunk to drive him from Teralba, so he had to get the bus with his mum), Mal came out of the station and lined them up to learn to whip crack. Steven Hill said, no, he didn't want to

51

do it, Peter Clarke kept tripping over the whip and Macka nearly caught Sarah on the leg. They played Cross Over Red Rover and tug-of-war before Ruth flicked the paper cloth of the table and called out *'lunch.'* They crowded around the table, picking at the plates and spilling sauce down shirt fronts, until Mal emerged at the back door, calling, 'lights out everybody,' and holding the big plate with the wishing-well cake on it. The eleven candles flamed up around the edges. Sarah looked at the ground during Happy Birthday to You, while Mal sang loudly, 'you look like a monkey and you smell like one too,' and laughter spurted up all round the table. Sarah got to eat the chocolate Freddo and make a wish (she closed her eyes and pretended, she knew it wouldn't come true so there was no point anyway). When Mal said 'did ya wish?' she sat on her crossed fingers and said yes.

She could feel that pain in her stomach again and between her legs felt wet, like she'd accidentally done a wee. She slipped sideways from her chair and walked carefully across the yard to the toilet near the garage. She slammed the wooden door behind her. She was bleeding. There was blood between her legs, dark and red and shining. She stared at the stuff. Blood.

Sarah stuffed a wad of toilet paper between her legs and walked bow-legged to the back door. Ruth was coming out, a plate of fresh fairy bread in her hands. 'Mum.' Sarah waved her mother's face close to her own, her voice the smallest whisper. She wanted to cry and her mouth was twisting over the words. 'I'm bleeding. Between me legs. I think I'm on me rags.'

'Oh gawd, come inside.' Ruth pulled Sarah by the arm, yanking so that it hurt. 'Yer only eleven, for flip's sake, how can ya be on ya rags?'

'I can't help it, I didn't mean to.' There was some strange rage coming from Ruth, Sarah was catching it, and it got wound up with her fear. 'I just looked and there was all blood.' A tear had begun to slide down Sarah's face. Oh, that was terrific. Just useless, just like a girl. 'You're hurting me.' She could hear the sound of her voice, coming out all whiney and snively.

Ruth pulled her into the bathroom and leant against the door. 'Let me see.'

'Muuu-um.' A bright burn was creeping down Sarah's face. It was all new and shameful.

'For gawd's sake, Sarah, just let me have a look, I can't tell if it's yer rags if I can't see, can I? Good girl.'

'See?' Sarah held out the wad of shine-covered toilet paper to Ruth, shocked again by the deep redness of her own blood. She thought about the kittens in her wardrobe, their redness and shine.

'I dunno how it's happened this young, I was thirteen before I got mine. Right. Well. Nothin we can do about it.'

'What do I do? I'm all wet. It's horrible.'

'Yep. You're a woman now and there's nothin you can do about that either.'

'I can. I'm not. Oh god, it's just disgusting.'

Ruth reached into the small cupboard and pulled out a thick pad – 'it's called a sanitary towel: peel the back off like that, yair, that's right, now press it down into your knickers, press, that's it. Comfy? You'll get used to it. When you change it, just wrap it up in newspaper, pop it in the bin and put a new one on. Come on. You'll need to watch your running around for the rest of the party, my girl.' Ruth paused and softened. 'It's not that bad, Sarah, sorry love, I'm just surprised, that's all.'

Sarah tried not to notice the huge wad between her legs, tried not to pull at the pad when she got outside. There was a game of breaking going on, with the rope. If she ran with that thing stuck to her knickers she knew it would slip sideways and slide out and then it would be all bloody at her feet and she'd have to step over it and pretend she hadn't seen it and she didn't know where it came from but everyone would know. She sat with her legs crossed while the boys lassoed each other, and then watched them play chasies around the paddock. Kari sat with her, watching. Now and then Sarah slipped into the outside toilet and pulled her knickers down beneath the bare globe, staring at the red globs nestling on the white towel. She poked her finger into the jelly-like blood and watched it move. She ate three slices of the wishing-well cake and five chocolate crackles while the boys had another game of tug-of-war. Macka ran over to the table and prodded her in the back. 'Why aren't you playing?'

Sarah stared him out. 'Don't want to. Don't feel like it.'

'Scorse yer a girl and girls can't be strong.'

'I beat you before, stupid. Anyway I'm not a girl, I'm a woman.' She tried the word out, just testing it for size.

'My dad says all women are sluts.'

Sarah stared at Macka's small brown face before she stood up and swung her arm at him, her fist bunched up as tight as she could get it. She heard the crunch of nose and felt the wetness of blood between her fingers. Macka was bent over, blood gushing from his nose and covering the ground. 'You've broken my nose, you bitch bitch bitch.'

The tug-of-war stopped short and Ruth dragged Macka inside. 'Come on, I'll clean you up, it's not broken, be a strong boy, come on don't be silly stop crying. Keep playing, boys. Sarah get inside.'

Sarah watched her feet go one in front of the other over the grass and up the back step. She held her fist together, trying to feel the power in her hand. But the ache had spread to under her arms, the pad was slipping away and all she could feel was blood oozing down her leg.

Ten

It was Sarah's idea to go to the docks. There wasn't a particular reason, just that she would start high school the next week and everything seemed stupid. All Ruth wanted to talk about was being a lady and growing to be a young woman, and Mal was just gone. All through the holidays, he never showed Sarah how to lasso properly, or let her go with him to the new paddocks for breaking. Kari was allowed, she was young enough to sit on the fence and be held by Smithy or Blue. Since she'd punched Macka's nose and made him bleed, Mal called Sarah too rough for a girl and said she'd have to be a young lady now. Ruth suggested bringing girls to the Boolaroo house to play.

'I don't know any girls and I don't like them anyway.' Sarah sat on the edge of the steps, not moving anywhere, no way.

'Aw, love, you must know some. You can't be a tomboy all yer life, can ya? Come on.'

'I'm not a tomboy. I'm just me.'

'Listen love, yer a young lady now, a young woman.'

'Well why isn't Wog a young man? He isn't is he? No, he's a boy.'

'Well it's different with girls, love.'

'Oh god. I hate you.'

'Sarah...'

'Well, I do.'

'Ssshhh. Your father's coming.'

Everything went quiet when Mal walked up the steps. Ruth held her arm across herself, until Mal tapped at her with his boot. 'Carn inside. I wanna talk.'

Sarah's mouth tasted like blood. She sat on the step, with

the cement getting slowly warm under her bum and mozzies screeching around her face, until the sun started being fierce and Kari banged through the back door. Sarah shifted to make room for her sister on the step. 'Are they fighting?' She didn't know why she was asking this, Kari wouldn't answer straight anyhow.

'No, it's quiet, very quiet.' Kari's hand slipped into Sarah's and stayed there.

Sarah didn't want to stay, didn't want to be stuck there all day with talk of ladies and girls and women and changes. She squeezed Kari's hand hard, turned to face her full on: 'd'ya wanna have an adventure?'

The docks were noisy and big. Bigger than Sarah's dreams. Bigger than she remembered from the one day visiting them with Mal, holding Mal's hand, hiding her face in the back of his big palm. The edge of the dock wasn't like the edge of the creek or even the lake. It was sudden, a big cement kathwop, ending like a smack in the face.

All the way in, on the bus (paid for with two-cent pieces from Kari's pink pig money box) Kari had bounced on the high back seat beside Sarah going, 'are we nearly there yet? is it far to the docks? are they big dya know your way I have to go to the toilet.'

Sarah had stared straight ahead, didn't even say shut up. She took her shoes off, just because. The bus driver took them right up, right to the docks. Sarah and Kari bustled about the banging crates and loud yells of the docks, walking walking walking, a part of the noise and shapes of big men in blue singlets. The knees and thighs of the big men were at their eye level, walking closer to the smell of salt and fish and then a metal stair ladder going up like the beanstalk. Up to the clouds, and up. Joining onto a boat. A big shining blue and white boat. As big as the world. They stepped back, dizzy, from the edge. Looked up to where the boat really, truly touched the sky. Way up there, up top, up front, was a flag. Big and flapping away up there. Not like the flag Sarah had waved when the Queen came to the Royal show. This flag flapping away was nicer, like a picture. White, with a big red circle smack dead in the middle.

A brown hand, small and hairless, patted Sarah's shoulder. She looked up to the brown face, flat and small like the hand. A voice, not like the loud banging voices of the singletted men, saying 'you lost hey? What you looking for, Sailor?'

Sarah stared up at the neat face. 'No, we're not lost. We're looking at the boats. We're allowed.'

Kari nodded beside her and agreed, 'we're allowed.'

'Allowed hey? Not runaways?' the white legs of his trousers flapped in the wind, like the flag on the ship.

'No. We're not runaways.' Sarah took a breath and crossed her fingers in her pocket, 'It's an excursion. For a project. About ships. We have to look at all ships. For the project.'

A flat white grin crossed his face: 'ah. Ah yes, now I am seeing. A ship, hey. We take you to a ship – just for a little, hokay?'

Sarah and Kari followed the brown man up the high stretch of clanky stairs. The metal burnt crosses into Sarah's bare feet. They clattered behind the brown man, calling 'whasyername?' So that he wouldn't be a stranger. His name was Sim, like Simmo from Marmong, who's black Arab stallion had got lost in the big gale. They could follow Sim up and on to the big blue and white boat, take a ride from him even, now that he wasn't a stranger. The stairs went up and up and did a twist on themselves. Kari rocked about, holding on to the edges. Another brown man came out of a door. They made bird sounds at each other, he and Sim, and laughed. Sim touched Sarah's shoulder, saying, 'yes, small for a sailor but good, hey?' Laughing. Not like the laughing in the paddock, loud and thwacking, his laughing was soft, inviting. More brown men, like bugs under summer stones, came running running running from small doors on either side of the stairs. And all jabbering like birds, quick and high, cacking-clicking at each other.

A light switched on behind Sarah's eyes; she tugged at Kari's arm: 'It's a language. Like Spanich.' She wriggled her hand into Sim's hand and looked up at him, proud: 'I know Spanich. Johnny

O'Keefe sang "Everybody Loves Saturday Night" in Spanich and I could sing the whole thing with the record. Dad said it was just like the real one. Senorita sin sinitty sin, hey-ey, senorita, senorita.' She danced around him, clicking her fingers, while Kari clapped her hands and crossed her legs and squeaked laughter.

Sim opened a big heavy door. Inside, dark and heat smacked Sarah in the face. Kari squished herself in behind Sam's legs. There were more brown men, yelling over the big sound of grinding and growling. Sim waved a man in blue trousers over, and made more bird sounds at him. 'Drink girls, hey?' He leant down, put his mouth near Sarah's ear, 'Thirsty, yes?' He nodded and Kari nodded with him. Sarah concentrated hard, remembering what Mal had told her about Spanich, then called up to Sim, 'Si. Si.' He did a half frown at her, then nodded. They sat in the engine room, hot, smelly and noise-filled, swinging their legs and being invited into the soft laughing. The drink man came back in a stream of unexpected light from the door, carrying a black tray with small white paper cups lined up on it. He held the tray in one hand, like Ruth at The Coffee Pot, and took the little paper cups off with the other hand. There was sweet green cordial in the cups. Kari drank hers in one gulp and then burped.

'Are you like Spanich?' Sarah tapped the hand of the drink man, her legs bashing against the wall.

A soft laugh, 'No, not Spanich. Japanese.'

Something slid together in Sarah's head. Japanese. Click. 'Is that like Jap?' Sim's eyes went wide, startled, 'yes. yes, Jap hey. I guess so, I guess Jap, hyeh hyeh.'

Inside Sarah's stomach everything went black and thick and tumbly. Her lips felt glugged-up like early morning eyes, thick with sleep. She spilt her cordial on the wide white trousers of the Japanese sailor as she ran, grabbing Kari's hand, calling, 'Run, run.'

Kari swung her legs out to the side, leaning over, twisting about as she ran, pulled by Sarah. Her callipers' heavy clinking echoed by the metal stairs. Sim was behind them, calling 'Sorry, hokay? Hokay girls?'

'Run harder.' Sarah pushed her legs in front of each other, running to the sound of, 'Stupid. How stupid could I be?' going over and over in her head. She yanked at Kari's arm, dragging her down the steps and down. Kari's legs buckled and bent, they were no use at all. Sarah turned around, so that she was going backwards, and slipped her hands under Kari's armpits. Kari stuck her legs straight out in front of her, like two wooden pegs. Sarah had to slow down a bit, trying to stop herself falling from the weight of Kari pressed against her body. But no-one followed, it was only the sound of Sim's voice that drifted down the stairs.

Puffing hard, on the cement of the docks, Sarah put her hands on Kari's shoulders, like Mal. 'They would take us to the jungle on this boat, burn us and starve us.' Kari's mouth looked too small and shaky, and her eyes were runny from tears. Sarah tried harder. 'I saw a photo of Dad once, in the button box. His shoulders were sticking out and bones poking through his front. He didn't look like Dad. It was the Japs that did that.' Kari didn't smile, didn't do anything and Sarah even kissed her before she said, 'Come on, let's go home.'

In among the legs on the dock they smack-crashed into some blue police legs.

'Lost mate?' A proper man's voice, gruff like Mal.

'Yes,' Sarah said this time, 'yes, lost.' Trembling, that the Japs might follow them, find them, steal them away to the jungle. Yes, lost.

'What's yer address?'

Not thinking about trouble, Sarah squinted up at the policeman, 'we own the police station in Boolaroo. That's where we live.' She made herself stand straight up, forgetting that they had run away for an adventure, forgetting that Mal didn't know. 'Mal Sweet's kid, that's who I am.' Because she had not forgotten that, who she was.

The policeman, Mick Pery from Toronto, walked between Kari and Sarah, holding one hand each. His mate was slumped in the white highway patrol car, dazed by the sun. Mick opened the back door, pushed Sarah and Kari in and shoved his mate on the shoulder. 'Mal Sweet's kids, got themselves lost. Reckon Mal's gunna have a word or two to say. He's got a flamin temper.' Kari squealed all the way back to Boolaroo, flushed up with the fast of the highway patrol. Sarah stared out the window, busy with the sick in her stomach.

In the station, Mal ran fast across the room to Kari, picked her up and turned her around in the air. All soft he was, inspecting her like a new bridle. 'Are ya orright, Bloss? I've been worried sick.'

Kari wriggled in his hands and shone back at him like the sun. 'We went on the bus and the boat.'

Sarah stood on the outside edges of her feet, counted the tiles on the floor and waited for him to notice her.

Mal held Kari right into his chest. He flicked his voice over his shoulder at Sarah, 'ya should know better, yer sister could've been hurt.' There was fire in his voice. Sarah looked up from the tiles, remembered nineteen was what she was up to in her counting, and stared hard at the side of his face.

He stayed looking at Kari, like Sarah was a fly on the window-ledge, not quite bothering him yet.

The mad sick in Sarah's stomach bunched up tight, then cata-pulted out with: 'We ran away, no-one even knew and we were on a Jap boat, they gave us green drink and made me laugh and I liked them and I want to go and live with them. With the Japs.'

Mal pushed both of them, Kari and Sarah, up the back steps of the house. 'Where's ya friggin mother?' Kari had begun whim-pering, quietly, like a puppy, and Sarah ran beside him, yelling into his side 'it's not her fault, we ran away, no-one knew.'

Inside, Ruth looked at his fire, and fast-walked upstairs to the bedroom.

'Don't, Mal, don't.'

Kari did a clink-run behind her, grabbing her arm. Ruth pushed her arm out, forcing Kari back. 'Stay with yer sister.' Ruth was short, sharp and as fierce as Mal, but Kari kept clinging.

Sarah yelled again 'leave her, leave her, she didn't know,' and then hid against the wall.

Mal was close behind Ruth, following her to their bedroom door. He threw words over his shoulder, 'this is yer mother's business.'

Ruth looked strong and almost not afraid. Kari wouldn't fall back, kept clinking along beside Ruth, determined to protect her.

Sarah's rage bunched up in her stomach again and the fear of Mal pushed her along the wall, to the door of her bedroom. 'It's Kari's fault, not Mum's. It was Kari's idea.'

She slammed her bedroom door shut behind her but even through the wood Sarah could hear Ruth screaming and screaming with the hard thuds of Mal's punches. Kari was yelling 'Get off get off off off off,' her callipers clinking as she ran across the landing.

There was the sound of more punches, more of Ruth's screams, and Kari, clinking and yelling 'Stopstopstop' and Mal saying 'get off ya stupid bitch, get out the friggin way.'

Then a big sound of Kari's scream and a tumbledown sound and Ruth calling out 'no no Kari no' and a thud like a tree against the wall. The screaming stopped then.

The silence echoed round Sarah's head all night.

Part Two

Eleven

Ailsa Craig was named after a memory from her mother's honeymoon. Catching a glimpse of a solid island in the middle of an estuary, the woman had asked for its name. Ailsa Craig, meaning fairy rock. Caught by the romance of it, she quickly conceived, and poured the name on her daughter's head. Ailsa Craig was both rock-like and island-like, with not a trace of fairyness about her. She ran her nursery, 'Miss Ailsa Craig's Romper Room', with rallying cries of 'routine, regularity and responsibility.' The playtimes, storytimes, snacktimes and naptimes, were carefully regulated and controlled.

A high fence surrounded the garden, bright with a mixture of wattle and lavender. Red-and-blue painted horses, on long rockers, were lined up in a perfectly straight cavalry next to the red metal climbing frame. The large Federation house had been painted a clean white inside and out, and the partition walls knocked down to make two large rooms, with a tiny kitchen at the opposite end of the building to the inside toilet. Pots of paint were lined up neatly on Laminex benches, higher than the reach of four-year-old children. 'Okay, everybody sitting up straight, hands on knees.' They were well trained for school life at Ailsa's Romper Room. 'We'll have Blue Group going quietly. QUIETLY thank you, to their worktable please.'

As Ailsa boomed her voice out, a small cluster of three- and four-year-olds stood up, hushed up, and crossed the room to a low hexagonal table covered in a blue plastic cloth. A tin pot, covered in daisy-printed plastic, was set in the middle of the table, filled with thick paintbrushes. 'Very good, Blue Group. Yellow Group, your turn. Tina will be helping you, and if Red Group will go to their work table, Felicity will collect your paints for you and help make your masks.' Felicity nodded her new, bobbed haircut and waved a paintbrush at her group.

'Blue Group, Tina will be taking care of you for the time being.' Ailsa Craig (never merely Ailsa, always Miss Craig or Ailsa Craig), tilted her head in Tina's direction. 'Tina. Come over here. That's a good girl.' Her voice was deep and raspy like sand. 'Tina, keep an eye on the blues for the next session, I'm interviewing for the rest of the morning. Good girl.'

This was Tina Dolan's first job. Her dark freckles were a legacy from years spent on the beach in Conoundra, where the Queensland sun had also burnt into her mother's face. Margaret Dolan had been operated on just the year before. The sun had bored so deep that Margaret Dolan's nose was removed. Tina left Queensland two weeks after her mother returned home with an artificial nose conspicuously powdered brown and the rest of Margaret looking somehow worm-like without her tan. Tina wanted somewhere cold, somewhere wet and hostile to the sun. She decided on Melbourne and caught the morning Smith's bus to the coach station in Gympie. The bus to Melbourne broke down, so she settled for Sydney instead. She read *The Sydney Morning Herald* on the coach, and Miss Craig's advertisement for qualified and unqualified workers jumped up and smacked her in the face. She'd been the first one to work with Ailsa Craig in the brand new nursery, which had a waiting-list of sixty before the doors were even opened. Tina always wore a hat and carried a bottle of Baby Blockout in a black cloth beach bag. After three months, Tina knew the routine of Miss Ailsa Craig's Romper Room.

'So. Miss Sarah Sweet, is it?' Miss Ailsa Craig held the heavy wooden door open for Sarah. 'My office is this way.'

Sarah held her breath and watched the wide back of Ailsa Craig, rock woman. Her heels left marks in the purple carpet. Sarah held tight to her straw bag, gripped it in front of her like a shield. A splash of laughter dribbled out from the front room as she passed, a girl with high red pigtails ran past the doorway. 'Did you have trouble finding the place?' Miss Craig held the door open for Sarah, stood aside so she could enter.

'No, no problems. Well, I got a taxi, that made it easy.'

The door swung shut as the rock woman stared hard at Sarah, a crease across her forehead. 'You don't drive?'

Sarah gripped the straw bag tighter, only five minutes in the door and she was blowing it already. 'I don't have a car at the moment.'

Miss Craig pulled a vinyl-covered straight-back chair out from the wide desk. 'Have a seat.'

Sarah could feel her legs shaking, could see the black cotton of her skirt moving. She gripped her thigh muscles, tried to breathe, tried to relax.

Ailsa Craig sat opposite her, separated by a long expanse of desk, and rustled through the papers in front of her. 'Right.' Finally, the woman looked at Sarah. 'You didn't finish your Certificate, so it would be an unqualified post, you do understand that, don't you?'

'Yes, of course.' The fabric in Sarah's skirt was jumping up and down now. She held her bag firmly on her lap and looked at her hands. Veins sticking out, long fingers. Freckles.

'And why?'

'Well, I am unqualified. I didn't finish.'

'No. Why is it that you didn't finish?'

Sarah squeezed her leg muscles harder, harder and harder. 'Personal problems. It was very difficult to study, it seemed wiser to withdraw.'

'Were you ill?'

'Yes. Yes, I suppose I was. Yes, I was.'

'Family?'

'I'm sorry?'

'You stay with your family.'

'I don't really have any family.'

'First Aid?'

'Yes. St John's, Red Cross and Bronze lifesaving.'

'I see. Why did you leave the Surrey Hills Nursery?'

'To do the Certificate. To get myself qualified.'

'But you didn't.'

'No. I want to work with children. Very much.' Thinking: *do I? I must be frigging mad.* But smiling anyway, teeth tight.

'Have you worked on a group system before?'

'Yes. At Surrey Hills.'

'How many?'

'Six per group.'

'I see. What do you see as the most important aspect of this work? For the children I mean.'

Sarah looked at the neat lines of the woman in front of her. 'Discipline. Children need to be clear about who's in charge.'

An almost-smile slipped over the woman's face. 'Routine, regularity and responsibility. That's our motto. It's never too early to start. Do you agree?'

'Yes. Absolutely.'

Ailsa Craig scraped her chair back. 'Fine. Start on Monday.' She held the door open. 'Yes or no?'

Sarah wobbled as she stood up. 'Yes.'

'Fine. Come and meet your group before you leave.'

Sarah held the slit on her skirt closed as she walked towards the door. Her head was swirling and her stomach was full of something like sick. She pushed her hands against her legs while she smiled, lips together. Breathed deep. 'Lovely.' The sick in her stomach twitched.

'Straight ahead, first right. You saw them as you came in.'

Sarah smiled again, opened her palms outward. *Ohmygod, ohmygod, ohmygod.*

The room was large, airy. The hexagonal tables were covered with paint, sheets of paper splattered with colour were spread across the walls, held with thumbtacks. 'Right, that's Tina, you'll meet properly on Monday, don't chat now, she's busy on the floor. Felicity is a qualified worker. We don't have chat on the floor, we keep busy and we keep to the routine. Snacktime is next. The blue group will be yours. Come with me.' Miss Craig half-pulled at Sarah's arm, leading her to the small blue table.

Sarah knelt down, got herself close to the five small faces sitting about the table, sending away the ache inside her. *Be good. Be kind.* 'That's an exciting painting.' She pointed to a yellow spot on a blue page and looked at the blond boy painting around it. His arms had the soft roundness of infancy, his skin was still luminous. Sarah wanted to touch his skin. See if her finger left a dent. She touched the page instead. 'That's lovely and bright.' Keeping her voice low, like with the horses. Soft and low and calm. She touched her face, recalling loud voices, only yells and shouts. The ache again, inside. *No. Quiet.* She pointed to the edge of the page. 'Is that the sun?'

The boy looked at her, affronted. 'No, that's my cat.'

The dark-skinned girl next to him pushed her page in front of Sarah, pointing to a blob of green and red. 'That's my mum. She's dancing. Are you our new lady?'

'Yes I am. That's lovely dancing.' Sarah leant across the table, turning the picture around.

'What's that on your arm?'

Sarah looked down at the top of her arm, exposed by her jacket slipping away as she leant across. Her hands felt sticky, her face hot. She glanced up at Miss Craig. 'Oh, that's a bruise. That's from bumping into walls. Aren't I silly?' She pulled her sleeve down and felt her face burn.

The girl painted a blue spot on the wild red dancing, she looked up at Sarah, 'that's my mum bumping into a wall, isn't she silly too?'

Twelve

There were boxes on the landing, littered amongst the plastic flowers. Sarah held her black skirt up while she stepped carefully over a slightly crushed crimson gladioli. She had never seen Messrs Whiley and Crow, largest suppliers of DISCREET AND PERMANENT OFFICE FAUNA in Sydney. For some reason, the glass doors through to their grey showroom were always closed when she came in through the double-bolted doors of the Sun building. The only evidence of their existence, apart from the regular pools of flowers and boxes, was the stained wooden plaque at the entrance to the building: third plaque from the top, fifth from the bottom.

There were seven plaques on the right hand side of the wide door, battered squares with black letters etched into the wood. The building was almost always locked – WHILEY AND CROW, SENIOR AND SONS (LOCKSMITHS), JORDAN'S DEBT COLLECTION and the drum maker on the third floor, were around at odd times, no guessing them. But the others – MARCUS ESTATES, BLUE ANGELS, FASTRACK COURIER SERVICE, BOLDPRINT, TEMPLE DESIGN – they were ghosts. Really, you could imagine dead bodies locked behind one of the thick metal doors. You wouldn't smell the rotting flesh through the doors. The names were still there, on the plaques, but there were no sounds in the building. Never were, not even from the drum maker, and you'd think you'd hear him. His doors had been open once and she'd seen inside, but he wasn't there. It was a ghost-building. Everyone had gone.

Sarah didn't have a plaque. Of course she didn't. FLOOR FIVE, LIND & SWEET – BASTARD AND BLUDGER, INC. Sure. Oh no, not bludger any more, no way. Carer. Carer indeed, she'd nearly punched the lights out on some guy at Circular Quay, who'd shoved in past her to get on the bus. Bastard. And the squelching in her guts around those kids, like at Surrey Hills. Why should they have it so soft and quiet and easy and safe? But wanting to make it like that too, wanting to make it safe. She felt herself go soft inside, but thought instead about that woman. Ailsa fucking Craig. She was like a machine, just bang-bang-bam, one question after the other, like she knew what was what and Sarah didn't have a clue. Ailsa Craig had stared long at the bruise on Sarah's arm, and raised her eyebrows for a second, Sarah could have sworn she did. The grille to the lift was open, concertinaed back in small folds. The tiny glass window on the inner door of the lift was wet from someone else's breath. Sarah leant against the vinyl-covered wall and felt her stomach lurch up with the creaking of the lift. Sounded like it had asthma.

She saw his feet through the little window. First the block of floor coming into view, then Robert's feet – his black boots and tatty laces. Then his legs – those horrible grey track pants. She could see two green garbage bags next to his legs, with clothes tumbling out. His face came into view, that stupid goatee, the too-big nose and too small lips. She held the inner door closed for a minute, after the lift had stopped. Stood staring out at him. He stared in, didn't try to push the door open. She watched him grow grey through the fog of her breath. She drew a line through the mouth-shaped steam. He did nothing. Nothing. Just stood there, smug and smart-assed, staring in. Sarah was encased in glass, she could hear nothing, feel nothing. If she concentrated really hard, she could feel a small wedge of hate nestling at the bottom of her stomach and she could will it into life.

She closed her eyes, focused on the hate, fed it. Imagined his goatee covered in toast crumbs, the way he'd looked this morning. His always bloody rightness. The wedge grew, and was a beautiful thing. It was all she had, that anger. She opened the door and slid the grille back. When Robert stepped back to let her out, she could see the rucksack on his back.

'I'm going. It's become, you know,' he slipped his hands through the straps of the rucksack, 'I dunno, ridiculous. It's gone too far. Hasn't it? Too fucking far. I'm going.'

'You said that already.' Sarah tried to stare him out, tried to will him down.

'Well. Um. Oh, fuck, I don't know what to say.'

'Try "sorry".'

'Sorry? What for Sarah? What the fuck for?'

Sarah rolled her sleeve back. 'For almost losing me the job.'

Robert's goatee moved from side to side. 'You're unbelievable. Unbefuckinglievable, ya know that? You wouldn't have made it to the bloody interview if I hadn't woken you. Look, I don't want to fight again. I've had enough.'

Sarah breathed on the rage in her belly, blew the flames into life. 'You should have said that last night. You wanted to fight then.' Oh shit, her eyes were beginning to leak again. She squeezed her eyelids together and dug her nails into her palms. The tears edged down her cheeks, but it was still just fury she felt. Robert's hand touched her shoulder and she felt herself lean into him, saw herself open her eyes and look right into his face. 'Don't go. Please. It'll change, it will.'

His chest rose with his breath. There were tears in his goatee, glistening in the hairs, and one teardrop just tinkling on the end of his nose. Sarah was side-tracked, fascinated, waiting for it to drop like an unexpected bit of snot onto his *Town Like Malice* T-shirt. 'I can't. I have to. It just doesn't change. It's been too many times.' His hand flicked up and wiped the tear from his nose. 'I'm sorry. So ya got the job.'

'Yair.'

'Great.'

'Yair.' It was going, the wedge, she was back to that numb again. Robert was a hazy shape in front of her.

'Well,' he picked up a garbage bag in each hand, 'I'm sorry, Sarah. I've left forty bucks for the gas bill.'

'Oh, Mr bloody generosity himself.'

He stepped forward, trying to pass her. 'Please Sarah, just let me go.' Tears on his cheeks again.

'Where are you staying? Tell me.' She hadn't noticed herself doing it, but her arms were spread out, each hand gripping a side of the elevator grille, a bar to him going.

'I can't tell you. I don't want to tell you.'

'Don't go, Rob, come on, we've made up before.' She pushed her hips towards him and leant back into the crook of one arm, so that she was draped across the elevator door. If there wasn't the rage, there was at least this. She pushed herself up and forward, one hand reaching his cheek, her hips reaching his. Her arms twirled up through his hair. 'It'll be okay, come on,' she was whispering in his ear now, she was the girl in the film, she was Vamp Queen.

'Oh, fuck off, Sarah. Just don't. Okay? Don't.' He pushed her back, her head colliding with the wall.

She didn't feel the snap inside her, she was still kind of numb, even though her hands were suddenly clawing at his face and she could hear herself shrieking at him. 'You bastard bludger frigging asshole.'

The garbage bags dropped to the floor and Robert's hands waved about his face, trying to push her claws off. His brown leather jacket fell out. Sarah ducked down, down under his hands, down to the brown leather jacket. 'That's mine.'

'Bullfuckingshit. You gave it to me. You – get off Sarah. Leave them.'

'I want to see what else you've got in here of mine. You're not going with half my wardrobe.' She was kicking at the door, dragging the garbage bags behind her. 'Open the door for me.'

'Give me my stuff. Leave it. Just give it to me. There's nothing of yours in there, why would there be?' Rob's arms went round Sarah's waist, yanking her back from the door. 'Oh, you savage bitch.'

Clothes spilt out, dribbling between the door and elevator, mingling with shredded green plastic. Sarah tore at the bags, tossing his clothes across the hall. She rubbed two white T-shirts into the dirt of the hallway floor and spat on his only sheet, which had holes in it anyway and had come from St Vincent de Paul and might as well go back there. Robert's boots scuffed in amongst the clothes, then kicked at her hands. 'I'll have you up for assault, you bastard.' She'd got that shrieking in her voice again, it was weird, just weird, listening to herself. 'You could break my fingers.'

Robert was laughing, Sarah could see the chip in his third-from-the-front-tooth. His teeth were yellow near the gums. 'Assault, my ass,' he pulled his foot away, began piling clothes into his arms, stuffing them back into the plastic.

'I wouldn't assault your ass if you paid me, Lind. In your bloody dreams.'

'There's no way you could have me for assault, ya know you couldn't. You wouldn't. I can't believe ya would.'

'What if I already have? What if the cops are on their way?'

'Then I'll fucking well wait for them and tell them the fucking truth.'

'Do ya think you could get one sentence through your mouth without a fuck in it?'

'Where did you learn to be such a hypocrite?'

'Copper's daughter.'

'Bullshit.'

Everything stopped for a moment. Sarah looked up at Rob's knees. 'Yair, bullshit. But it sounded good.'

The laughing came from both of them. Rob's lips pressed into a thin line, trying to hold the spurt of laughter inside his mouth. It trickled out the corner. Sarah pulled the sheet to her face, her back shaking. It was all right, it would be all right.

Robert sucked the laughter back into his body. 'So.'

'So what?'

'So are they coming?'

'Who? The cops? No, they're not.'

He knelt down, his feet on his blue check shirt, and put his face near hers.

'You can't keep doing this, Sarah.'

'I won't. I promise, no more. I swear Rob, I really do.'

He put his hands on her shoulders again. She waited for the it-will-be-all-right sign. He let breath out through his mouth, loud. 'No. I've had enough.'

'I still could press charges, if I wanted.'

'Sarah, I hit you once. Once.'

'Once is enough. No man has the right.'

There was a laugh like a shock wave, zigging out from his mouth. 'The cut in my stomach is still healing, my hand is still blistered, and I've got bruises all over my back. What am *I* gunna do? Press charges? I don't fucking think so. I've never hit a woman, ever. But you ... I don't want to hit you again. I don't want to hit back. But I'm not gunna be your fucking sucker anymore. Give me my stuff.'

He scooped the sheet, the T-shirts, the undies, into the shredded bag and wrapped the plastic-like rope around the fabric pile. The rucksack opened as he leant over, and a sea of MAD comics, *Direct Action*, and dirty clothes slid out of the opening, over his head and covered the hallway floor. 'Fuckfuckfuck. Keep them. I don't give a monkey's green shit. And you can keep the fucking jacket, ya pinched it anyway, didn't you?'

He stepped over the paper and laundry sea, swam towards the elevator.

Sarah rocked herself, an armful of odd socks in her arms. She watched him push the door, unbalanced by the armful of shredded plastic and dribbling clothes. A pair of green Y-fronts got caught in the grille door, and obscured his face as the elevator went down.

Sarah watched him disappearing and crawled forwards, yelled down into the shaft: 'Who's going to help me with the rent?'

There was no answer.

Thirteen

The flat was large without Robert, the silences screeched in Sarah's ears. She turned the cassette player up full ball, so that the sounds of Eurythmics and XTC got blurred and scratched by the volume. The nights stretched into boredom. She didn't wonder what he was doing, but threw bottles of Coke onto the street way below, vibrating with the smash of glass on concrete. Ultimo was full of other warehouses like the Sun building, so the streets were empty at night, except for the passing of traffic. Cars full of people with lives. Sarah drifted about, staring down at the phone box on the street, wondering who she could ring. Robert had turned up during her second week at college, and somehow absorbed her. It was what she'd wanted, something loud and booming, like her, something full of fire.

There had been two friends from Surrey Hills nursery, Nikki and Sandra, girls who bored Sarah with their excitement and optimism. They gushed over children, both of them. When Sarah left Surrey Hills nursery for the red brick of North Ryde Technical College, Nikki followed. Sandra wept for both of them, swearing to have weekly, no, *daily*, meetings at the Hopetoun Hotel. Sarah met with them for the first week, let Sandra pay for the Bacardi and Coke, asked after her group at the nursery – but mostly sat silent. After she met Robert – after he *appeared* in her life like a sign – she stopped pretending to be interested in either of them. When she saw Nikki in the college refectory, Sarah stared past her at a spot on the wall and waited for Robert to finish his photography class. There were no other friends; the sex and the rages with Robert took her life up, left no room for anything else.

Robert dropped out of his Art course after six months. Sarah lasted until halfway through her second year. The night before her term exams, Robert got drunk and broke the record player. She stayed up all night, calling him a useless frigger, throwing plates at his head, and hitting him with the buckle of his brown belt. At five a.m., she locked Robert outside, naked, and fell asleep on the floor. She woke up three hours after the exam had finished and never went back to the college. She threw the Dear Miss Sweet letters in the metal bin, unopened.

So now, there was nothing. Just the smashing of Coke bottles, the scratchiness of copied cassettes played too loud on a ten-dollar tape player. And in the daytime, Ailsa Craig's Romper Room. Sarah would wake mucky-eyed and dry-tongued, the smell of unwashed sheets in her nose. Most mornings, she would remember to wash herself, and sometimes to eat. There were crackers in the kitchen, tea bags and instant coffee. She planned to buy milk, but kept forgetting. Other things came up and took her mind away. She buried herself in the noise of the nursery, the busyness of cut and paste, painting projects, cutting fruit for playlunch, mats out for morning naps. Sarah wanted to lie with them, curl beside the small bodies and rest on the roundness of them. Wanted to rest on the safety of their lives.

On the train to Wahroonga each morning, she counted the stops and tried to fill her head with new things, tried to find new rememberings. Thought about how to make egg-carton chickens and puppets from socks. Allowed small hands into hers through the day, let them rest there, let herself find rest. Just sometimes, hated them – the owners of small hands – for their safe lives. In the afternoons, she got off the train at King's Cross, drank coffee at the crowded corner café, Posie's, for hours, until she was hungry enough to buy a kebab for dinner. She ate on the street, or by the fountain, or sometimes, walking home through the back streets of the Cross and Darlinghurst. Glaring at the men who littered the streets.

Weekends were a problem. The emptiness of the warehouse flat was amplified, it echoed around her, XTC and The Smiths bouncing off the walls and into her face. She tried sleeping as much as possible, rolling over and over, pulling the pillow over her ears, blocking the light out, trying hard not to think. But her body itched, ready to move and be awake. She walked to the Cross or the Quay, swinging her arms, pushing her legs forward, striding out with that familiar chanting in her head, *I'm not like my sister, I'm not like my sister*. She didn't notice it these days, it hung about on the edges of silence or muffled the corners of conversations. She fed pigeons and seagulls with packets of cheese Twisties, let flocks of birds gather round her. She was Sarah Sweet, protector, defender, benefactor.

On Sundays, the Quay shook with the rumblings of people, trains and ferries. Once, a shrunken grey man, hunched up, and with a face creased like, who? someone from Sarah's far-away memory – the one she tried to put away – dangled a Big Bird puppet on a string, making the bird tap dance to the tune of 'Summer Time', played on a red plastic kiddies' tape deck. He was terrible, but he creased and grinned, sang in scrawling words through his scrunched-up face and Sarah threw fifty cents in his knitted hat, calling herself a stupid stupid sucker.

The best place was by the water, or sometimes, on a ferry. She caught the ferry to Manly or Cremorne, sat in the wind and watched gulls hovering over her like angels. If you got a return ticket and sat away from the crew, you could stay on the boat all day, back and forthing across the Harbour – and why not? It filled the hole while the waiting was going on.

Sarah was paused. The numbness was a warm blanket, enfolding her. She couldn't hear bangs or crashes, barely noticed the loud sounds of bottles smashing. When people pushed past her on the street, she let herself be shoved aside, did not feel the contact of arm on arm, body on body. She watched herself constantly, placed herself in mind-films with tears and screaming and blood and everyone saying sorry and kissing and fucking afterwards. Hate, she could feel hate, or sometimes rage. If she concentrated hard enough. Waiting for the boats across the Harbour, she watched the clocks and let herself be full of hate for the black suited, pony-tailed men who clockworked past each other.

The clocks at the Quay were high on the wall, lined up next to each other with round faces and large wooden hands. One row marked ARRIVALS, the other DEPARTURES. After each ferry left, a short man in a blue suit would climb onto a step ladder, holding a long stick-with-a-hook, which he would wave vaguely about, until the hook caught a hand and tugged it to the right time.

Sarah was waiting for the Manly ferry the first time she saw Zan. The clock stayed still, the short man did not come out with his hook-on-a-stick, but stayed stuck behind the ticket sellers' glass. Sarah dug her nails into her palms, glared at the glass pane, at the idiotic incompetence behind it. No point in expecting any-bloody-thing, not really. She folded her arms across herself and stared at the high clocks, trying to count in her head. *One cat and dog, two cat and dog.* It didn't really help, but it filled the gap in her brain between rage and boredom. Pigeons crammed around the feet of passengers, smacking their beaks fiercely on the cement. Sarah bought a packet of Twisties from the news stand and crushed a handful of them in her hand, scattering the pieces around her feet. She licked the crumbs from her yellow fingers.

The wingbeats were drumlike, filling the air around her. Amazing things really, just scented out food, or saw it, or what? Found it, anyhow, and could swoop on it so quickly. Usually one who hovered around the edges, fearful of the competition, waiting for a chance. The air smelt of them, turned white with their breast feathers. One hovered, fluttering mid-air, waiting for the chance to peck. Sarah was a statue amongst them, the circle of pigeons shoving and pecking at each other. Their beaks hammered. Except for the mid-air hoverer, a small bird, scruffy about the neck and with a twisted leg. A spastic bloody bird. Sarah spat at its stu-pidness, its pathetic weakness, fluttering around up there, doing nothing, getting no food and waiting until someone was sorry enough for it to feed it. Still, she lifted her hand, to throw some crumbed up Twisties into its path. Protector, benefactor, despiser.

The bird flew back and up, away from the food and towards the wooden clocks. It flapped about, nearly hitting the Fibreglass ceiling and dashing itself against a far window. The pigeons on the ground went on scratching about her feet, cleaning the rest of the crumbs while the spastic bird flew like a panic up and around, hurting its own self all over the bloody place. Sarah just watched, just stood there, waiting. Something would happen, it would die, or be knocked stupid, or something. She was trying to make it safe, that was all, and it wanted to hurt its bloody self.

Neither dead or knocked stupid, the pigeon settled on one of the clock arms. The weight of the bird body swung the arm down, so that the twelve-ten ferry to Taronga Park became the twelve-thirty ferry. As the time changed, the bird fell off the clock, swooped on a scattering of crumbs, and flew away. A laugh, low and slippery, but big, came from behind Sarah. A woman's laugh.

'That was like watching fate move.' She was tiny, not like her laugh at all. Barely up to Sarah's armpit, and thin as thin. Hair everywhere, big Medusa hair, swirling about. Big lips, too. Small face.

'Sorry?' Sarah could feel her face frowning up. There was something happening in her stomach, an anxious wave steadying itself for assault.

'The bird. Like fate. A woman's about to get on that ferry, right, for a rendezvous, it's urgent, she's meeting her lover, they're running away together. It's their only chance. She comes along, notices the ferry doesn't leave until twelve-thirty and wanders off for twenty minutes. Misses the ferry. Her lover sails on without her. Gets killed when a storm blows up, or makes the plane, which gets hijacked. Never seen again. Woman number one spends the rest of her life dead guilt-wracked and unhappy. Tragedy in Manly.' Something soft and other-country about the voice. English?

'Planes don't leave from Manly.'

'Ship then.'

'I don't think so. Romance and Tragedy in Manly? No. I can't see it.' The wave in Sarah's stomach was turning to a warm flow. A laugh, of all things, a *laugh*, was spreading up and across her chest.

'Don't spoil it. I was almost overcome with grief for a moment.'

80

'Poor woman.' There that did it, the laugh rose up and swam out her mouth, down, down to her shoes. The sound of a train shuffled loudly over it.

'Oh shit.' The woman turned her head to look at the electronic train board. 'See ya.'

There was a whirl of hair and skirt. Sarah watched her push past a suited inspector, squeezing herself up the escalator. Bits of paper fell out of the woman's cloth bag as she ran. Cinderella. Sarah let the warm be there in her belly and chest, then passed the guard, picked up two of the scraps of paper. A pink one and a white. Nothing. Rows of numbers, additions and subtractions. No words at all, not even one. But still, the laugh, bubbling around in there, some weird alien creature. She'd forgotten about that – about laughter.

Fourteen

And then it was winter. Sydney was drenched and grey for days at a time. The Harbour swelled and Sarah bought a coat but did not stop her ferry crossings. She stopped smashing bottles and spent the nights instead staring at the fall of rain on the window and reading *Beginners' Guide to the Tarot, the Runes and the Palm,* just for fun. Her head swam with signs and portents. On the train to Ailsa Craig's Romper Room each morning, she looked out for the Queen of Cups and The Fool. Wondered how she might recognise them without their costumes. Ailsa Craig's routine was soothing in its way. Sarah had no feelings for her group (blue group), only sometimes was amazed at the smallness of their bodies. She laughed dutifully and tended wounds with soft noises, but all through a sweet distraction. That cotton wool numb, letting nothing get in.

During the rain, cars and taxis came to the nursery in the mornings and afternoons, delivering and collecting and protecting from the wetness. Lunch times at the Romper Room were dripping and overloud, with steam rising from cramped bodies. The children crammed inside the playroom, eating sandwiches off plastic plates while the television blared out *Romper Room* and *Playschool.* Sarah sat in a circle with her group, singing along with 'The Wheels on the Bus'. Afternoons took on a different quality in the nursery, voices yelling over rain, bright yellow raincoats ending on the wrong bodies. 'Who didn't hang their coat up this morning? What is this on the floor, Matthew?' Ailsa Craig made order from disorder, managed to have children lined up, neat and clean.

Only half-way through the season, winter felt like it had lasted forever, would never stop. Sarah's head was hot with the day's muddle, ready to sleep on the train back to the quay. The weekend loomed with wet, empty ferry rides and the shadows of the black-and-white portable television she'd bought from Paddy's Markets. Something to cheer her up, but it sat squat in the corner of the flat, on whenever she was there, with ugly shapes hazing around in static. It was okay with music on though, like a music video show. Even the news looked half-way interesting with New Order being scratched out alongside it. A multi-media experience.

Still, the end of Friday was dull with lack of expectation. Sarah welcomed parents, pushed children toward them, said yes, he's much better with his sharing now, isn't he, oh, no, I think she's playing very well, how nice that he's recovered, yes see you on Monday, have fun, have a nice weekend, have a lovely time. Wondering if they noticed her absence in these conversations, her complete lack of interest in their children's games/bowel movements/sibling bloody rivalry. Not to mention their neatly filled weekends. Almost done, almost empty, the white rooms of the big house beginning to settle. Tina waving off the last of her group with high-pitched sweetness, beginning to wipe the traces of sticky hands from the benches. And now, the tugging at Sarah's arm, the simpering beside her. The putting on of a patient face.

'I've got a headache.' The small hand was damp and warm in Sarah's hand. 'Where, Rachel?' Sarah knelt down, put her face close to the child's, waiting for the girl's finger to point to her eyes, temple, neck. Or perhaps, worn down by the noise and wet of the afternoon, her ears. Sarah's own head thrummed with the residue of young shouts and full-volume TV. 'Where's your headache?'

'In my tummy.' Rachel turned her round face to Sarah's, her mouth screwed up in pain.

'Headaches don't grow in tummies, do they? Where do head-aches grow?'

'You're laughing.'

'I'm not laughing. No. Are these laughing lips? No, these are sad lips. But do you know what you can call an ache in your tummy?'

'A tummy headache.' The rounded eyes looked up at Sarah and, full up with tiredness and ache, the face collapsed in on itself, flooded. 'You *are* laughing at me.'

Sarah sucked her breath inwards, made her voice almost a whisper. 'I think you're a tired girl. Is Daddy coming to get you?'

The girl's tears grew suddenly into shrieks, pouring over Sarah's words. The white rooms, empty now of children and parents, echoed with her sobs. 'I'm *not* tired, I'm sick.' The words were barely comprehensible through the snot and screams and hiccups.

Sarah's fists balled up, the warmth of fury beginning to creep up her body. She held her lips hard together and made her arms go limp, to stop the desire to shake the guts out of Rachel, shrieking there on the floor. Her shoulders tensed, ready to pick the child up and throw her across the room. She pushed her eyelids hard together, squeezing her eyes shut. The screaming stayed, outside and in. Oh god, oh god, oh god. Everything inside her was turning soft, crumbling. *Shut the frig up*: Mal's voice bounced about in her head. She could see herself, just for a moment, as small as Rachel, flapping her hands in terror. Trying to be small, silent, invisible. But never enough, never small enough, never invisible enough.

Rachel was still sobbing, huddled into Sarah's lap. And there it was again: the wanting to shake the child, hit her, scream in her face; 'no-one made it okay for me'. And the wanting to scream at herself for never making it okay for Kari.

'Problem?' Tina's pale face was drawn into a concerned shape, the lips pushing outwards, the eyebrows gathering in close. It was a look that went with the job.

Sarah called herself back, gathered her face together. 'Rachel's Dad should have been here half an hour ago. She's got a little belly ache – isn't that right, sweetheart?' Sarah made her voice soft, like Tina's, tender and light. The child was shuddering to a stop, easing into a whimper, eyes beginning to droop. Sarah stroked the small shoulder. 'I'm not sure how to play it. Her Mum doesn't drive.'

'I could call her at home – if he's held up in the storm he could be ages. This one's not in a state to hang about, is she? We could get her a taxi. Miss Craig won't be back today, we can explain on Monday. And when he turns up – assuming it's before midnight – I'll send him on. No problem.' Capable bloody Tina.

'Go on then. Thanks. I'll go in the taxi with her and then come back to clear up.'

While Tina phoned for the taxi, Sarah rocked Rachel, going coo-coo-shhh-sshh-there, that's all right now, good girl, that's the girl, thaa-at's the girl – a familiar song from somewhere far off.

'That's it, tha-aat's the girl.' Sarah held the soft body. Looked down at the face, round and smooth, staring up at her. Calmed and comforted. Trusting. Sarah felt some unnameable thing move inside her, way down, way down deep. She pulled songs and thoughts of tea and taxis to her mind, pulled the numb blanket over her shoulders, over her belly, over the twisting nameless thing. The flash of her own small self, screaming and uncertain, and the other too-small body, unprotected.

Rachel had drifted into a snuffly, post-hysteria sleep – her cheeks two burning pink circles – by the time the sound of a taxi horn cut smoothly through the rain. Sharp little stabs danced up and down Sarah's arm as she tried to move it, lifting the child up without shaking her awake. Impossible, of course. Rachel's eyes opened as soon as Sarah stood up. There was a silent moment, while Sarah held her breath, waiting for the screams to start again. She painted the gentle smile, the I'm-here-taking-care-of-you look and turned her face to Rachel, cheeks still pink from sleep. 'Time to go home now, time to see Mummy.' Perfect. There was no response from Rachel, she was dozed-up and had forgotten. 'I'll be back in five, Tina, thanks for your help.' Sarah sent the call over her shoulder, back towards the little kitchen. A rattling on the door interrupted, blocked off her words.

'We're coming.' Taxi drivers hated waiting even a second, for flip's sake. She could see a bulky shape outlined through the mottled glass of Ailsa Craig's Romper Room door. The pouring of the rain bevelled and bent the shape, made it wriggle itself into inhuman forms. He obviously had his face up against the glass though, trying to see in. Rachel slid down to the floor, a neat little lump, while Sarah opened the door with one hand, speaking loud over the wwwshhhh of almost-sleet. 'Sorry to keep you waiting.'

'Daddy.' Rachel catapulted herself toward the door.

'No, *I'm* sorry. Hello sweetheart. There was a crash on the freeway, terrible hold-up. Is that taxi outside for you?'

'Ohmygod – it was. Never mind – I'll come out and tell him to go – see you on Monday, Rachel, be a good girl, no problem, Mr Betts, have a lovely weekend yourself, drive carefully, yes it's a real storm isn't it? Bye, you too Rachel, bye.' She held her jumper over her head as she walked with them down the drive, feeling her face lashed and waving them into a long blue car. The 'Engaged' light was shining on the taxi roof, a dull glow fuzzed up around it, the yellow light melting into the rain. Sarah stepped into a gutter full of water, on her way round to the driver's side of the cab. She could see the steam on the inside of the window, and the shine of the meter through the haze. The window rolled down as she raised her fist, ready to tap. She stopped the swing of her hand before it collided with the face inside the car. Big lips. Medusa hair. A punch of recognition, right there in the guts.

'Taxi? I didn't have a name.' It was, it was that same woman, with the laugh and the voice bigger than her body. Even sitting there behind the wheel she looked teensy, like a kid driving her Dad's car down the driveway. It was weird, but for some reason, Sarah's mouth dried up. Everything seemed swollen around her. The woman didn't recognise her – why should she? – although Sarah wanted to touch her hair, say: remember that laugh, remember you made me laugh?

'Yair, sorry,' – the words were coming out in a creak – 'she's just gone. The little girl I mean. I mean, yes, we did order a taxi, it was for a little girl, but he came. Her dad. That's who we were waiting for.' Her hair was stuck to her face. She wanted to laugh at herself, she was that ridiculous. 'So we don't need one now. A taxi.'

The door opened and the woman ducked her head down as she peered out at Sarah. 'Hey. Howyadoin?' That was it, the updownupdown voice. 'Remember me?' The hair shivering about, a grin in the voice.

'Umm, sorry?' Sarah stepped back, slapped her hand across her body, felt caught out.

'We met. No, we didn't really meet. I-saw-you-saw-me kinda deal. At the Quay. That bird? Remember?' And the voice was beginning to slip into a half-giggle, a nervy kind of one. It died away, the hair being twirled about a small finger. Then quieter: 'I'm sure it was you.'

'It was. Hi. Are you English?'

'Yair. Sort of. I'm Zan.'

'Are they connected?'

'What?'

'Being English and being Zan. Do they go together? Or is being Zan something different from being English, like Irish?'

That laugh again, wide and long. 'So where are ya going? You'd better get in before you get drenched. Before you get more drenched.'

'We only called a cab for Rachel. I usually get a train.'

'I've come over from Cremorne for this job.'

'I'll get my stuff.'

She left the door open, gathered plasticine models and squished them together, making one delicious blob. Stuck it in the crafts cupboard, swept plastic cups into a pile and ran them under the cold tap, watching the water spray out. She ran to the small office like a mad thing, calling farewells to Tina, grabbing her bag and trying not to think of the cost of a cab from Wahroonga to Ultimo. Bloody hell, she was a madwoman, she really was. But she wanted to laugh again and felt the pins and needle stabs travelling up inside her body.

Fifteen

Water poured down Sarah's neck, waterfalling along the back of her head and into the stream of her collar. Felt reckless. She opened the front door of the taxi – the passenger side – and swung herself in, feet last. Mud dripped onto the floor of the car, water splashed from her body onto the seat. 'Sorry. Mud. Water. Sorry.' And just that laugh, Zan's laugh, folded up a bit this time, and the warm start of the engine. The headlights cut through the grey of the rain as the car turned, a neat round slice dividing the road in two. Sarah held her breath in, pressed her hands into her lap. Tried to press, hold, contain everything: her whole bursting self, hold it in. Zan was neatly packaged beside her, small hands placed evenly on the wheel, hair spiralling down across her shoulders. Red-brown hair. The breath of them both was loud on the inside of the car, drops forming on the windows from steamy breath. The stallion madness which had shoved Sarah into the car was suddenly shy and gone. Words bubbled up, seemed too strained or too stupid, and then hid away again. The silence stretched and stretched and stretched.

Sarah stared into the window, tracing the line of a water drop with her eyes. When the drop reached the bottom of the window, flattening out into the rubber rim, she turned her head. Looked at the side of Zan's face, looked at the meter. 'It's still on nought – you forgot to put the meter on.'

'We'll live.' The big lips shone in a smile.

At least there were words trotting about in the taxi, the crackling of snapped ice. Sarah's aloneness laid a weight on every word. Hope flickered in her ribs, for what? Words, the passing of time, someone to ride ferries with? A substitute for the dull attentions of Nikki and Sandra or for the time-passing qualities of Robert. The hope of somehow, catching the burning life and zing of Zan, absorbing it into herself. She'd learnt this: that if she bit on the tip of her tongue and let a hissss wriggle through her brain, that burn of hope would go, would be snuffled out. And that was a good thing. Hope was just awkward.

Still, even with the hiss travelling through, and the bite on the tongue, that thing flickered in there, a hotfire dance.

Zan's hands had nails bitten down past the tips of the fingers. Even the fingers looked gnawed at, bits of skin hanging off, showing bright pink muscle-flesh underneath. Sarah was drawn in by them, those fingers, it was like picking a scab. Or gawking at a car-crash. Just horrible, but too hard to resist. The hands on the wheel were close together, the two index fingers pointing fiercely in at each other. The thumbs, small and sausage-fattish, pressed at the wheel under the fingers. Fingers and thumbs red from the contact. And all those chewed-up nails and fingers. The fingers were short, didn't make it all the way round the wheel. On the index finger closest to Sarah, a scrape of dried blood edged around the bottom of the half-sized nail.

The redbrown hair swished out with the turning of Zan's head. 'Oh, don't look at my hands. I bite my nails. And my fingers. Horrible isn't it? Except it's really nice. To do, I mean. It's not nice to look at, that's the problem. But, oh man, have you ever bitten a nail off?'

'Not one on my finger.' Sarah shoved the tough into her voice.

'What, someone else's finger? That's a bit rude isn't it? Was the person wearing it at the time?'

'Not by the time I'd finished.' That mad mad laughter again, diving up like a wave. Sarah felt like a wild rodeo man. Yeehah. Her laugh met up with Zan's, and grew large.

'Okay. You've wasted yourself girl. Seriously.' The left-overs of a smile still bobbed about Zan's face. Mouth, eyes, cheeks. 'Wasting the joys of nail-biting on someone else. Really, really seriously. Just try it, it's like, oh, it's just a huge release. Go on. Seriously. Look.' She reached over, and grabbed Sarah's hand.

89

Pushed it towards Sarah's mouth. 'Get your nail between your teeth. Like this.' She put a stubby finger to her mouth, showed her teeth and growled, tearing away at a small piece of loose skin. 'Yair, well, I haven't really got any nails to get at, but you have a go.'

Sarah pushed a nail between her teeth and pulled hard. Gripped with her teeth and pulled away with her finger. It was like smashing bottles, it really was. A little wait, a pause where you have to pull harder, then shhhrrrred, the rip of the nail. And the trophy, a moon shaped bit of dead cells. Interesting, but not enough to fill you up. 'It is, you're right. It's great.' But she spat the half-moon away.

'So you live in Ultimo? I didn't think anyone lived there, I thought it was all warehouses and falling-down offices. Move it, you bastard.' The taxi swerved past a red Mini.

'I live above a warehouse with a few falling-down offices in it.'

'For real? Brilliant.'

'Do you live ...? I mean where? Do ya live this side?'

'Share a house in Surrey Hills. Not for much longer though. I'll be bloody homeless next week.'

'Seriously?'

'You bet seriously. Bunch of guys, didn't know any of them from Adam. You know, answered an ad in the *Herald* and all that. Been there four months – oh, piss off, you wanker, big car, small dick – sorry, I get a bit aggro when I'm driving. Yair, four months. I needed somewhere permanent to get this job – I was in a hostel up till then. So the house is fine, cool. Then one of the guys – Andrew the apeman – tries to come on to me. I say thanks very much no thanks I'm a lesbian no offence, not you, I'm just not into men, get me? No, he doesn't get me. Thinks, one, I must be joking, or two, I need a man like him to set me straight. Finally get it to click for him that it's not going to happen, and he's morally bloody offended. The three of them have a house meeting, decide they don't like the idea of having a dyke in the house. Bad for their image. So, that's it. Gave me ten days to find somewhere new. Can't say fairer than that.'

Sarah wanted to say, ohmygosh-I've-never-met-a-lesbian-before-what's-it-like? She bit on her bottom lip, to stop the words gushing out, in case the joke fell flat.

'Anyway, so that's it. Haven't found anywhere. And I don't want to go through that again, know what I mean?' Just for a moment, Zan's face, all the bigness of it, looked small and break-able. 'Pass me that bag will ya? There, underneath the seat. Ta.' She scrabbled around in the brown cloth bag, looking updownup between the road and the bag, driving with one hand, scrabbling with the other. The scrabbling hand emerged with a blue tube. Small, L-shaped, with a metal container poking out of the top. Zan put it in her mouth, pushed the metal container and sucked her breath in. And again. A breath whooshed out of her mouth. 'Asthma.'

Miss Sneed, a history teacher at Booragul High School, she had asthma. A little round pulpy face she had, that woman, and always out of breath, always holding onto the edge of the desk or leaning against the blackboard. She'd run once, in the teacher's three-legged race for sports day. Had to be taken to hospital afterwards. Two weeks of unsupervised history classes. Asthma. Sarah looked down at her hands, at the newly-bitten nail, and back to the window. Zan was as small as a child; Sarah felt big, strong beside her. Able to protect.

Outside, the edges of Darlinghurst were looming into view, the electric colours of the Coke billboard making the rain red. Small figures climbing about beneath the lights. Sarah pressed her face close to the glass of the window. Drew a line through the steam puffed it up again and wrote *asthma* in squirly letters, then rubbed it out. 'What will you do?' She kept her face staring out, away from Zan.

'Something will turn up. Usually does. What's that?' She wound her window down, tapped Sarah on the arm. 'Look, there.' There was the round bleep of a car-horn behind them. 'I'll go round again.'

Sarah pushed herself back in the passenger seat, turning her head, twisting herself about to see, to get a glimpse of the thing, whatever the thing was. The tires of the taxi shrieked in a skid. Sarah pressed her feet against the glove box and was not disturbed, was not concerned. They came back onto the overpass.

'Wind your window down so you can see. Can you see? I'll try and slow down.' They were in a stream of traffic, pushing them forwards.

Sarah let last bits of rain slip down onto her hair, let the wind slap at her face. There was a pigeon, smack bang in the middle of the road, its head snapping about, cars missing it on either side by finger lengths. 'Ohmygod it's stuck there. Legs must be broken. It can't move. Poor thing.' She was Sarah Sweet, defender of pigeons.

'I'll have to stop. There's a car behind me, I'll let him pass.'

'You've got half of Sydney crammed up your bum, ya can't stop. Go round again.'

Sarah's ears ran, dizziness swelled. The taxi swerved, skidded, went round again.

Zan tapped her fingers on the wheel. The pigeon outside looked small, wet. Sarah imagined terror in its eyes. She didn't want terror in there, in the car with her. 'What'll we do if we manage to pick it up?' The ringing in her ears got higher, louder.

'Take it to the vet.'

'It's probably got lice.'

'We can't just leave it.'

'We can't stop.'

'We can't.'

'Just go. Just leave it.'

Another car horn sounded, headlights flashed. Sarah closed her eyes as they drove away, past the bird, past the overpass, past the Cross. Dared the dizziness to just try it. That always worked.

The rain had stopped, settled into an easy drip, by the time they got to Ultimo. The winter light was beginning to go, the grey slipping into black. Two pony-tailed Suits got covered in puddle water when the taxi stopped. Black splotches across the double breasts. Poor buggers. Zan left the engine on, leant over to open the door for Sarah.

Smiled, and looked small. 'Take care. Shame about the bird, hey? Sometimes I think those things are a sign.'

It was, of course it was. An omen. A test which she, defender and protector, had failed. Zan was puffing on the blue tube again. 'Listen. Zan. If you want, you can, it's only two rooms not counting the toilet and shower but ya could, I mean if you want, you could sleep in the big room, not the bedroom, I've got a couch, I mean, ya can move in, I mean stay, crash for a while. Until ya find somewhere.' Sarah wanted to grab hold of that puffer thing and squeeze some breath from it. She waited. For an answer to her offering, her answer to the Sign.

Zan switched the engine off and leant across, put the tube in the glove box. 'Are you serious? That's lovely. That's really really kind. Just until I find somewhere. Thanks, I will.'

Sixteen

Queen's birthday inbloodydeed. Still, it was a holiday; a weekend and an escape from sticky hands and endless questions. The drummer downstairs was in, that was weird. Sarah could hear him, rattling away on those giant chimes he had. An occasional thunder of timpani. The one time she'd peeked inside the half-open doors of his studio she'd seen rows and rows of huge drums, electronic things, and metal chimes. Loads of metal chimes everywhere. But she'd never heard them being played, not before now.

The black-and-white portable squatted in the corner, casting shadows about the room. *The Barclays of Broadway.* Fred and Ginger were blurred bunches of static jumping about the screen, accompanied by the occasional chime downstairs. Sarah swept the floor with a dustbrush, scrabbling about on her knees, and brushing the dirt onto a sheet of the *Sydney Morning Herald*. Personals. Sarah plonked herself down in the pile of dirt she'd gathered, squinting at the tiny words. Who the hell were these people? She rubbed dirt across the floor, smoothing it into the cold tiles with her bare feet.

The traffic outside Sarah's window was slow, just the occasional sound of a truck passing through on its way to, where? Somewhere interesting. Zan hadn't given a time. Just said she'd bring her stuff over after work. Settle in. Just for a few weeks. Until she found somewhere. It was ridiculous, the trembling in Sarah's body, the desire to put flowers on the scarf-covered cardboard box by the window. On Saturday, she'd been into a second-hand bookshop in Glebe and bought *Short Stories by Kafka, The Female Eunuch* and *A Nietzsche Reader*. She stood them upright on the cardboard-box table. Stood back, considered. Shuffled them, placed them casually on top of the television, laid them flat, messily sprawling on top of each other. Ridiculous. She put New Order on the Toshiba cassette player, and used thumbtacks to hang a batik sarong – bought from god-knows where – across the window. It made the light in the room deep and browngold, casting rich shapes across her legs as she lay down on the sofa, arching her back to avoid the sticky-out spring. Her feet hung over the edge, but Zan was short, she'd fit.

The pot plant in the toilet had been dead for weeks. Sarah stuck bits of smashed Coke bottle in the soil, making a shining glass surround to the brown plant, and tied broken mirror to the dead wooden stem, with fishing line she'd found outside the plastic-flower suppliers downstairs. Pretty, almost. There was no shower or bath: just a plastic pipe, for a washing machine, attached to the chrome taps over an aluminium sink. It made it a pain in the head to wash, but you got used to it. Or Sarah had. Got used to straddling the drain in the middle of the floor, shivering as the thin stream of water poured down her arms, breasts, legs. The tricky bit was turning the water on when you were in the right position – standing on the drain – otherwise water splattered about the grey walls, wetting clothes and towels. You had to sort of lean on one leg, holding the edge of the sink with one hand, and the pipe in the other, then quickly let go of the sink and grab the taps as you fell forward, turn them on and shove yourself back to standing. On the days she could be bothered, it was a kind of morning exercise.

She heard the sound of the downstairs buzzer humming through the building, cutting over a bass drum sound from downstairs. Even expecting it, even after waiting for the sound, it made her chest tighten up when she heard it. She'd only heard the buzzer pressed once before, once when Rob had forgotten his keys and stood outside pressing and pressing and pressing the black button at the front door. This time, the loud snore-like sound came only twice. One long buzz, one short. She needed three keys just to unlock that huge front door. Keys which were always on the television. No. Or next to the double mattress that she slept on. No. On top of the rust-stained bar-fridge. No, no, no, no and no. Sarah threw bits of newspaper around, dug about in the plastic rubbish bin, looked under the couch. She accompanied herself with a steady hum, a regular beat of fuck-fuck-fuck-fuck-fuck-fuck-fuck. Didn't notice that the boom of the bass drum downstairs had ceased playing along. Didn't care. She ran to the top of lift shaft, yelled down, 'I'm coming hang on hang on' and ran back inside. Fuck-fuck-fuck-fuck-fuck. Pockets. Check pockets. She didn't have any pockets. Bathroom. Check bathroom. Sink. Soapdish. Pot plant. That was it, the keys lay in a smug little heap underneath the dangle of broken mirror. Sarah grabbed them up, dirt catching beneath her bitten thumb nail, and ran.

The lift was two floors below, Sarah could see it. Parked outside the drummer's room. Faster to run downstairs than wait for it to crank up. She yelled down into the lift shaft again, 'wait a sec, I'm coming' and heard it echo back into her own face. She ran down the stairs two at a time, only making it down half a flight before she knocked Zan for six.

'Thanks for the welcome.' Zan had fallen backwards and ended half-sitting half-standing, leaning against the backpack which poked over her head. It looked like she could fit inside it, it really did. She had that smile again, and the laughter easing out of her mouth. All the big life fitting in the small-sized body.

'Oh bloody hell, I'm sorry – couldn't find the keys – how did ya get in?' Sarah was breathless with the rush and the laughter.

'Some guy let me in.' Zan shook her head and did a smile-grimace.

'The drummer.' Although they were a full floor above him, Sarah whispered the words.

Zan's mouth formed an O. The way they were going, they were going to end up standing there all day, whispering and making signs to each other.

'Come up. I'm at the top.' Sarah grabbed hold of Zan's hand, yanked her onwards and upwards.

Zan dropped her pack in front of the lift, said 'hang on' and unzipped a side pocket. Pulled out the asthma thing, took a deep gulp. Press, gulp, press, gulp. Stood up and swung the pack onto her back. 'Okay. I'm all right now. Take me to your parlour.'

'Is that it? Have ya got any other stuff?' Sarah led her into the big room, pointed to the couch. 'Your bed, Madame.'

'No, this is it, I'm afraid. Did you say that guy was a drummer?'

'Yair, I've never seen him.'

'He didn't say a word to me. Like something out of the Addam's Family. I'm standing there, right, and the door swings open, I put my big grin on my face, cause I think it'll be you, right, and this six-billion-foot man is standing there. So he looks at me, I look at him. I say I'm here for Sarah, he points upstairs, and walks away. That's it. Not a word. But a drummer? Wow.'

'Have you got a sleeping bag? Today's the first time I've heard him at all, he's not usually here. No-one is. Maybe he's deaf.'

'Yair, I have, shall I dump it here? He heard me say Sarah.'

'Maybe he reads lips.'

'His eyes were about three feet above my mouth. No, I think he's just, you know. Just like that. Doesn't want to talk. Had an early tragedy – saw his mother killed, right in front of him, has never been able to talk since. So you have to have sympathy for him, I suppose. What sort of drumming does he do?'

'Dunno, he's got some chimes and stuff. I saw them once. And some big drums.'

'I fancy doing that.'

'What, playing drums?'

'Maybe. Sort of, be in a band, sing and play percussion. Be a hoot. Wouldn't you want to?'

Sarah rubbed at the floor with her foot. Thought about it. 'No.'

Zan bounced onto the couch, her legs swinging. 'What do you want then? Do you know there's a spring sticking out of this thing?'

'I don't want anything. Ummm. Cup of tea maybe.'

'No, come on. What else?'

Sarah wanted not to play. It was stupid, it was like the stupid wish game kids did on their birthdays, or crackers, or mandarin segments. Wishing and then looking like suckers. She wanted to want nothing, but that sounded stupid too, so she didn't speak, just let silence hang like a fat ripe moon. The chiming started up again.

'How did you find this place?' Zan held her hands out and looked at those stubby fingers.

'I used to live with a guy here. He was sort of the caretaker at first. When we left college. We had it rent free for a while. Then they said they didn't need a caretaker but we could pay cheap rent. It was easier to stay.'

'What happened to him then?'

'He was a bastard.'

Zan nodded at the floor, looked at the plastic watch on her wrist and jumped up. 'I have to go. I've got to take the cab back. Thanks for the bed. Really, I mean you don't even know me. I could be a killer. So, I just slam the door behind me? Great. I'll be back in a couple of hours, is that okay?'

And then she was gone. Sarah switched the portable on. Hazy pictures of men shaking hands in front of a big clock. A woman in a suit. Sarah let the pictures drift over her and lay on the couch. Sideways, avoiding the spring. Zan's rucksack was propped against the couch, just there in front of Sarah's hand. It was blue, with its metal frame poking up at the back. Sarah ran her hand across the top, across the bump of nylon zips. She sat up, leant forward, unzipped a pocket. The right-hand pocket. Her face was hot. She pulled her hand out quickly, as if from fire. Looked towards the door. Held her hand against her body. Waited. She stayed like that for a while, pictures of suited men and women in tight dresses moving about the darkening room. She pushed herself forward, sometime later. She sat herself, cross-legged on the floor, in front of the rucksack. Unzipped the top compartment and pressed her face in close. Everything smelt fresh. White things were neatly folded, not scrunched up. She didn't touch them, closed the lid, zipped it. In the left hand pocket there was a loofah. *A loofah.* That pocket had already been opened.

Sarah shuffled the bag across the room, leant it against the wall under the window. She looked out of the window, to see if anyone had seen her being so weird. There was no-one, who would there be? She was five storeys up in a deserted warehouse block. She lay down on the couch again, spread the cover from her bed over herself. Closed her eyes and let her head go heavy. Her feet, her legs, her hands tingled, went limp. Dropped. Her mouth opened. The air weighed down on her face, pressing. Her face, falling deep, deep, deep into the couch. The air pressing, her mouth going soft.

When the buzzing zoomed into her sleep, she made it into a huge bird, swooping down with a giant beak, an open beak, swopping down onto the small people running on sand, the screech, and the beak, open and letting out the loudest screech, the most endless screech, the why-won't-it-just-stop-screeching screech, people running on sand, the air heavy, thick on her face, and the bird swooped and it swooped and it swooped. Sarah ran on sand, her mouth open, her arms out, then climbing up into the air, up where the air was thinner, up in the air, her mouth open, screeching, screeching.

It was her own cry that woke her up, so that she jumped, bashing her head on the wooden arm of the torn couch. She opened the window, head still heavy and mouth sticky, and threw the keys down to Zan on the footpath. Zan waved, called 'cheers', then disappeared into the doorway, away from Sarah's view. Then the chug of the ancient elevator and the tapping on the flat door.

'It's dark in here – were you asleep? I'm sorry Sarah, I woke you.' Zan smelt of cold air. She sliced through the television-lit room like a lamp.

Sarah shielded her eyes. 'No, it's fine, no worries. I just – oh, flip, I dunno what happened. Is it late? I've got to go to bed, I'll see you in the morning. Ummm, I moved your pack, it's over there.'

And Sarah backed herself out of the room, into the other room, the room with her bed in it. She climbed onto the mattress in her clothes and lay for hours in the dark with her eyes open wide.

Seventeen

Sarah woke to the sound of the elevator clunking. Her face was damp, there was a patch of spit on her pillow. She walked into the big room on her heels, hobbling, old woman-like. Zan's sleeping bag was rolled up, tucked next to her pack. The sleeping bag was blue, like the rucksack. There was a note on the couch: *Thanks again for the bed (Slightly more comfortable than sleeping on a tree branch). I'll be back about 7 tonite – don't worry if you're not in, I'll wait (or wait for the spooky drummer to let me in!!!) I'll bring some bread and stuff. Don't you eat breakfast???* Sarah opened the window, stuck her head outside. Rain. She heard the echo of the door slamming five floors down and watched Zan emerge, holding the cloth bag over her head and running towards Piermont Road.

Sarah splashed water on her face and rubbed her hands over her slept-in clothes. Made them presentable. Brushed her hair on the bus and bought an apple from the market guy at the Quay, to clean her teeth with. The train was squeezed full of bleary bodies, recovering from the long weekend. Sarah's head jumbled and she concentrated on her body being weary. By the time she got to Wahroonga, she was ready to sleep again. The drowsiness kept her enclosed from the pressing and pounding and pleading of those small sticky bodies. At lunchtime she drank a cup of coffee and rested her head on the cool pine table in the nursery kitchen. The day drifted on around her.

Sarah wandered home through the Cross, walking slowly, counting steps in her head, not wanting to be home early, not wanting to be waiting. At the fountain, a wide-faced man and a small boy threw bread at the seagulls. Light shone off the metal frame that buckled around the boy's body. He had a high-pitched squeal, he let it out, the squeal, each time a gull swooped for a glob of bread. Piercing it was, like a siren. Right there in her ear. Sarah stared hard at him, squealing and squealing there, when all she wanted was peace. Some quiet. The boy was dribbling over his callipers and laughing and hiccuping. Sarah closed her eyes against the sun. The squealing stayed in her ears. *Stop, get off off off.* She could hear the sound of callipers clinking, feel herself small, hiding. Quiet, just wanting quiet.

She opened her eyes and made a stone-hard face back at the man smiling at her. She left them both squawking. All the way through the back streets, fury jumped about under her feet. She walked hardfast but took the long way round, right through Piermont, almost a two-mile detour, walking and walking and walking. By the time she got to Ultimo she was wet under the arms and almost empty again.

Zan was waiting outside the Sun Building with two white plastic bags on her lap. She was hunched over, curved like a comma on the step. Her mouth spread across her face, matching the curve of her body. She dipped in and out of the plastic bags, waving her hands about like Lovely Victoria from *The New Price is Right*. 'Bread, Milk. Tea. Cherry Cheer. Peanut Butter and – ta daaa – for your appreciation and enjoyment, ladies and gentlemen: Fa-laaa-fel roll. Thank you, thank you, thankyou.' Her hair flapped about as she bowed to the traffic.

The last of the fury slipped off, disappeared into the lanes of cars. Zan was like a bubble, changing things, making them glisten. The bread smelt warm, the falafel oozed out their smell. 'Ohmygod, that's fantastic. I'm starving.'

'Me too, I had to stop myself scoffing them both before you got here.' Zan held one of the wrapped rolls out to Sarah, then spread her skirt across the step. 'Picnic? I don't think I can wait any longer.'

They hunched together, Sarah edged in on the mat of Zan's skirt (long, wide, wild tartan checks) and pulled at the bread, dipped it in peanut butter. They tore at the kebabs, chilli sauce dribbling down chins. A car horn tooted and Sarah waved a bottle of Cherry Cheer in the air. Yelled: 'Get your own, ya yobbo' with a mouth stuffed full of falafel.

When the rolls, half the loaf and most of the peanut butter had been eaten, they walked round and round the block playing Hopscotch and Step On Cracks, Break Your Mother's Back. Until way after the street lights came on. Until way past dark.

The drummer was in again. His door was open and a shiver of cymbals came sounding through when Sarah and Zan giggled past. Zan hummed the tune from *The Addam's Family* and Sarah slapped at her hand. Upstairs, Sarah boiled water in one of the two brown pans that Robert had left. There was a two-ring gas flame and a camping stove, left by the last caretaker. Zan sat on the floor, L-shaped, her legs stuck straight in front of her. 'I didn't know if you had tea or what, I couldn't see any.' She leant forward, watching Sarah.

'No, there's some cruddy coffee, that's all. Here. The cup's pretty cruddy as well. Sorry.'

They watched blurry re-runs of *Get Smart* and *My Favourite Martian*. Zan stayed on the floor, her back pointing up straight and stiff looking. Sarah lay out on the couch, watching Zan's hair. A memory of small hands covering her eyes from behind and brushing her hair, soft, pulling the hair back and letting it fall. Then another one: small hands flat on the sheets of a bed and Sarah brushing at the hair spread on the pillow. She wanted to lift Zan's hair, that was all. Just to lift it, feel the weight of it, and then let it fall back onto her shoulders. The black-and-white haze flickered over Zan's head, making her hair electric. Zan sat still, absolutely absolutely still, watching the shadows on the small box. Sarah watched the colours on Zan's hair, and let her hand float out, a skin-balloon, so, so light, let her hand float and land, watched it land, there on Zan's head, watched her own hand stroke Zan's hair.

Zan turned her head, looked at Sarah and patted her hand. Like patting a horse. Taptap, like that. The mouth filling her face in a smile. Taptap, and then her head facing the television again. Sarah held her legs and arms tight, lay on her back, her hands folded

102

on her belly and breathed only through her nose, trying to keep it quiet. Something sharp stabbed into her bum.

'Oh, flip; how did ya manage to sleep on this spring?'

'I don't think I did, really. I think I spent most of the night with my legs like this.' Zan bent her legs, pointing her knees at the ceiling. 'Sort of worked, but I felt knackered this morning.'

'I think I'd just got used to it. I've only just noticed how annoying it is.'

'Listen, I'm not complaining, if it's a choice between a poky spring or the poorhouse, there's no competition. Mind you, if you've got some spare blankets I could lay them out on the floor and sleep on that – like a super-advanced Futon.'

'I've only got what's on my bed. But listen, if it's really annoying ya could, I mean I'm not being weird or anything, but I mean, well it's a double mattress, I only use one side, I mean, ya could, I'm not, you know, you could sleep on the other half. If it was really annoying you. I'd sleep on one side, you'd sleep on the other.'

Zan's mouth had gone tight, almost small. 'What do you mean, you're not being weird? I don't get you.'

'You know, I'm not, you know.' Oh god, oh god, oh god. Sarah's face was full of flames, her tongue was nailed to the bottom of her mouth.

'No, I don't. It sounds, right, like you think if you share a mattress with me I'm going to jump on you. What's this *weird* business? Because I'm a dyke, Sarah, this does not involve me getting my kit off with any female who happens to be within a six-foot radius of my feverish hands. Honestly.' Zan's voice had gone deep, her words were coming out sharp and clipped.

'I wasn't, that wasn't what I meant. At all. I just didn't want you to feel obligated.'

'To what?'

'I don't know.'

Sand had filled the whole inside of Sarah Sweet's body, right up to her nose and mouth, right down to her toes. Sand grated under her tongue when she spoke, rubbed against her eyelids when she blinked.

'I'm sorry Zan. I'm really sorry.' She didn't know what for, what she was sorry for. Her head seemed to be sinking into the sand.

'Okay.'

They sat frozen for a while, soft sounds of some late news show not even blurring the edges, just bumping against them. Sarah slid off the couch, sat in a matching right-angled shape next to Zan. The sand was grinding against her, making a rough tingle. Her shoulder rubbed against Zan's cheek. It felt soft and fiery. Sarah could see the shape of Zan's lips from the side, poking forward in a round shape. Red, purply red. Different to the rough edges of Robert's mouth. Sarah wanted to try, taste, test. She put her hand under Zan's chin. She didn't need to pull Zan's face towards her, Zan turned. Looked straight into Sarah's face. Sarah could feel the sand, dry, dry, dry, behind her lips, could see the wet, the water behind Zan's lips. She leant forward, softly, trying not to spill the dry sand from her mouth, waiting for the water from Zan. There was a burst of a trumpet from the television. Zan's lips were soft. Wet.

'What is this? What's going on?' Zan's lips pulled back, opened and closed like dry hard things. Sarah's tongue, still dry, couldn't move. She couldn't lift it. Zan folded her arms across herself. 'Is this curiosity Sarah? Tried sour and now you want sugar? I'm not a bloody experiment.'

Shame kaboomed around Sarah's body and she flicked the sand away from her tongue. 'It's not that. It's not. I just. Please.'

Zan looked towards the door, the TV shapes jumbling on her cheek. Her hand went to her mouth, her lips gnawing at the little finger. Sarah touched her hand. It was soft. A tear edged it's way down Zan's face, down the side of her nose, crept down to her mouth, across, on to Sarah's finger. Zan was small, tiny, weak. Sarah was strong. Sarah leant into the tear, into the lips and pressed. There was the softness and the wet warmth inside. Sarah closed her eyes and let it all blow over.

Eighteen

Moments of beginning loomed large – always – in Sarah's head. They were moments with a sharpness, an edge which was lost afterwards in the dullness of day-to-day. She could still recite the words spoken to her on her first day of kindy: ('Who's a big girl today, Sarah Sweet?'), and recall the ritual acted out on her first day of high school (tearing at a plastic bag, chewing at strips of paper, deep breaths, tight chest) – but the years in between were shadow-like: unformed, unseen by the human eye. First horse ride, first train ride, first party, first swim, first kiss. Bright and large and clean. First kiss of Zan, first taste of a woman's mouth. Too sharp, too bright. It cast shadows on the wall.

Strange though, how quickly the easing in happens. The first moment cutting slices through everything, and then, then what? Everything settles doesn't it? The first morning, still sharp. A strange shape in Sarah's bed, the bones of a thin back pressed against her stomach. Soft skin, the fierce strangeness of long hair in her face. A gentle awkwardness over orange juice and cold tea. Mouths tasting of morning, not quite fresh. But still, the newness made it almost-fresh. You know, the way it does.

For a few days then, perhaps a few weeks, Sarah's tongue stung with the taste of salt, sugar, tea, lemonade, chocolate milk, bread, everything, absolutely everything. She touched children at the nursery softly-softly on their foreheads, blowing air onto the tips of their heads, to cool and soothe them. Even when they needed no soothing. The white flash of the sun bouncing off the Harbour burnt her eyes, but sweetly. Sounds were sharp in her ears: seagulls screrracking, wind jumbling about through trees; the slide of the train on the metal sleepers or the rumbling of car

105

engines transfixed her. She saw the old busker at the Quay, that useless old bloke with the Big Bird puppet and plastic tape player, and her whole body swelled with some raw joy. She gave him a five-dollar note and smiled back at him when he folded his toothless face up in a grin. Everything was shiny, for a time.

Even after the first weeks of waking with Zan's body next to hers, Sarah counted over each second like a rosary. She woke before dawn once, torn from sleep by small yelps from Zan, caught in a nightmare. Zan's body was smooth next to Sarah's. She curled like a worm, Zan, her legs tucked under her. She turned, straightened, pressed close to Sarah. You could feel the line of the bones under the skin. Sarah turned on her side and shoved up so that she could be breast to breast with Zan. Amazed at that: the sameness and the difference. The softness of round breast against hers. Was that how she, Sarah, felt? Even with Zan's slight bumps, her almost flat chest, Sarah was willed into fascination. Wanted to suck on them, be fed. The nipples red and arrowlike. Harder than Sarah's, and more red. Sarah watched the light grow on Zan's body, lay with eyes wide open for hours with the sun slowly filling the room. Mapping the differences. She watched Zan's eyes twitch beneath the lids, noticed the lie of the hairs squinting out beneath the armpits. She pulled the cover back, ran her eyes and hands down and across Zan's legs. Soft skin and the tangle of brown-red, like a face beneath the belly. Zan kept the whimpering up and made little brushing movements against her face. Sarah did not wake her, and in the morning, did not ask what the nightmare had been about.

Zan had nightmares often. Sarah stopped being woken by them. Some nights, Zan tried to stay awake, rolling her tongue over Sarah's body or talking in her ear. Like a mozzie, buzzing about. Sarah lay beside her saying yes, yes, yes. Letting her eyes drop slowly closed. 'Yes, mmm, go to sleep now.'

Zan tapped and prodded at Sarah, tried to finish conversations started days before, or to tell jokes with only half-remembered punchlines. 'What do you call a dyslexic, atheist, no hang on, an insomniac, agnostic, dyslexic? Umm, hang on, wait, someone who lies awake all night wondering if there really is a god. Oh shit, no, I mean, if there really is a *dog*. Oh damn.'

And that itself became a joke between them: that Zan never recalled jokes, always laughed at them fresh like the first time. She said it was deliberate, she like it that way.

They held hands on the street, ate meals which Zan cooked, and spent weekends wandering the Quay or drinking at Posie's Café. Most afternoons, the black-and-white taxi skidded on the drive outside Ailsa Craig's Romper Room. Things were taken for granted. Once, caught up in the beginning of spring, Sarah had breathed in salt and wind and wrapped her arms and legs about Zan, on the Manly ferry. She held her mouth against Zan's, sucking deeply, probing. The sun bathed their heads, ran down across their bodies, melting everything between them – the air, the wind, their skin. Zan was laughing into Sarah's mouth, her hands squeezing hard. A pale fat man tapped fast and firm on Sarah's shoulder and said that that sort of thing was an embarrassment and to keep it for their own sick living-room and, anyway, if they didn't stop they would be let off at Cremorne with no fare refund and have to find their own way back. Zan had drawn blood from her fingers she bit at them so hard, between squirts of the blue puffer.

Zan carried the asthma puffer with her everywhere, tucked in the canvas bag. That bag, it was always on Zan's shoulder, it dropped down her arm sometimes when she was running. It was over-full all the time, Zan had to scrabble around in it for change, or pens, or bits of paper. Sarah's hands fisted up, watching her dig about for tiny items. Zan would squat down on the street, she didn't care, pulling tissues, pads, god knows what, from that bag and placing them on the footpath. She'd find the puffer eventually, go 'Ta-daaa,' as if she'd done something really bloody clever. Then suck. Squirt the stuff in the tube – Ventolin, it was called – down into her mouth and eventually say, 'it's okay now.' As if there was ever any question that it wasn't going to be okay.

The asthma came when Zan moved too fast, ate too much or got upset. Sarah had a birthday. Zan was driving all day and too

107

late into the night. So Sarah drank the bottle of vodka on her own. Threw the bottle at Zan when she finally did come home. Not really at Zan, at the wall behind her. Zan ducked and grabbed her puffer, first thing, as if it was a bottle or a breast. That was only once though, that yelling and smashing. Mostly it was good. Good and soft and full of Zan's laughter and half-forgotten jokes. Even so, Zan kept sucking at that puffer and chewing at those nails of hers. The fingers were chewed way down, they were always pink with blood. Bits of skin and blood would stick in Zan's teeth. Sarah wanted to hit her or at least yell that it was stupid, it made her look dumb and stupid. She didn't though. She blew air through her teeth, or clicked her fingers, or slapped at Zan's hands. Sometimes, said *don't*.

There was a dark-haired old waitress at Posie's who had seen Zan sucking at the Ventolin and said, 'Oh what a shame. My daughter has asthma. Horrible thing. And you're such a nice looking girl and everything, except for your fingers of course, shame about them too, really. Have you tried Stop 'n' Gro? I tried that and it worked wonders.' She held out her fingers for inspection. Short fat sausages with red nails stuck on the end.

'I like them like this.' Zan waved her stumpy fingers in the woman's face.

'It's probably because of the asthma, though, because you get nervous.'

'I don't get nervous. I like the feeling of biting my nails, that's okay isn't it?' Zan was smiling at the woman, as if she wanted to be her friend, as if it mattered.

'Anyway, it isn't actually any of your business. Just bring us the bill.' Sarah was fed up with the talk of stumps and nails and fingers.

'Well, I'm sorry.'

'It's fine. How old is your daughter?' Zan twinkled at the woman, smoothed the ripples, made friends and wanted the whole life story. Leslie, her name was – and she and Zan had talked about nails and asthma and it had taken ages.

Sarah and Zan had run for the last train after that, screaming down the escalators, shoving people out of the way. Except Zan had to stop, pull the puffer from her bag, and she was breathing hard and saying she couldn't keep running like that, she was so sorry, and Sarah told her to stop acting like a bloody spastic cause that's what she was going on like and she wouldn't know what it was like to be spastic if it smacked her in the face. And that was the truth.

Nineteen

Sarah couldn't breathe. Her face was squashed flat, and her nose buried in something thick and smooth and smelling of smoke. Someone had tied her lips together and nailed her tongue to the bottom of her mouth. She tried to push her jaws apart, open her mouth and let air in there, but nothing happened. She tried again. Open. She couldn't remember what it was that ever made her mouth, or eyes, or hands, obedient to her brain. It was all so bloody complicated. Dry and sticky inside her mouth. If she stretched out her hand, she would find some water there somewhere, she was sure of it, but her hand didn't twitch.

The smooth thick pile of hair in front of her face moved, drew away. Zan rolled over, put her face close to Sarah's. 'I feel like shit.' Zan's voice was a thin croak. A waft of beer-gin-cigar hit Sarah in the face.

'Mmmm.' That was it, all Sarah could manage. Her head was heavy and her stomach seemed to be spinning.

'Water. I need some water.' Zan crawled across Sarah. Her hands patted about on the floor. 'You stink, by the way.'

'Mmmpissoff.' Sarah lifted her hand and grabbed at the glass of water.

'Piss off yourself. Let me have some first.' Zan's throat moved as the water poured down. She closed her eyes and gulped, more and more. 'That feels better. I'll get ya some more. Don't move. Not that there's much chance of that, you poor thing. Oh sorry.' A laugh fell out of Zan's mouth as she tripped over Sarah's leg. She kicked gently at Sarah, at her back, and half fell onto the floor.

Sarah listened to the neat pat of Zan's feet on the floor, the slight squeak of the door. The sound of the pipes filling with water, and of water coming out of the taps. Water. Sarah tried to work up some spit in her mouth, desperate for some liquid in there. Zan was taking ages. The taps being turned off, always that clunk as the water stopped flowing. Pat-pat-pat of Zan's feet. The slosh of water. And then the slap of a wave in Sarah's face, water running down her face and soaking into the pillow. Zan's laugh ran down onto Sarah's body.

'You bitch.' Sarah's mouth was unstuck, her eyes fresh and clean. A red plastic cup, a kiddies' cup – where had that come from? – lay on the floor beside the mattress.

'You looked so thirsty, I thought you needed an instant hit. Anyway, I didn't think you'd wake up if I didn't drench you.'

'What makes you think I wanted to wake up?'

'I wanted you to. I don't want to be alone in my hangover.'

'Oh god.' Sarah rolled on to her stomach, pushed her face into the pillow. Soaking wet and cold. 'Oh bloody hell, Zan, it's freezing now. Get off. I don't want any more. Stop it.'

Zan sprinkled more water across Sarah's back. 'Come on, get up. There's a glass here for you. Seriously. I won't do any more.'

Sarah sat up, took the glass and poured a mouthful of water into her mouth. Waited, smiling, before she spat it out, spraying Zan's face and chest. Zan ran for the bathroom and fell on the water which had dripped across the lino floor. She lay face down, her naked back shaking with laughter.

'Stay there.' Sarah slid off the mattress and stepped carefully over Zan's body. 'I'll get a towel.'

There were two eggs in the bar-fridge. One of them was cracked and stuck to the cardboard carton. Sarah tugged, leaving a Tasmania-shaped bit of shell behind. She crossed the room holding the egg carefully in her hand. Zan lifted her head. 'Don't you dare. Oh, don't Sarah, I'm really feeling queasy.'

'What? I don't know what you're talking about.' As the eggs, both of them, cracked in Sarah's hand and squelched onto Zan's back. It felt great, the cool yolk bursting beneath her fingers. Zan was rolling on the floor saying nono don't, but the laughter was

111

tripping from her and tears were streaming down her cheeks. Sarah rubbed at the egg, letting her hand slide about in the mixture of white and yoke covering Zan's back, and sides, and breasts. Zan turned on to her back, stopped laughing, stopped saying nono no. The white and the yellow blended together, became a smooth pale even colour, sliding about on the small roundness of Zan's stomach. Sarah rubbed, circling the small breasts, rolling the red nipples between her fingers, watching them shine beneath the wetness of the egg. She ran her hand down the slide of Zan's belly, down to the tumble of red. The hair stiffened and formed peaks, caught together by the egg-glue. Zan trembled and trembled, then was still.

The egg dried in mud patterns, tightening, then cracking, on both of their bodies. 'This is seriously egg-on-my-face – oh god, I'm witty.' Sarah rubbed at the drying mixture, forming scab-like lumps on her chin. She peeled at her skin, flicking yellow balls onto the floor. They sprayed each other with the laundry pipe, letting the water squirt out fast and hot. Zan rubbed at Sarah with a scratchy towel, padding under her arms, between her toes, lifting her breasts and getting under. Sarah leant back and let herself be rubbed clean. Her head still swam from a night full of too much gin. 'Let's go to the Cross, have breakfast at Posie's.'

'O-woo-oh, breakfast at Sweetheart's, o-woo-ooh.' Zan belted the tune out in Sarah's ear, her voice fresh and bright for a hangover day. But it had to be said, so Sarah said it.

'Don't give up your day job, darlin.'

They walked to the Cross, moving slowly through the sun and buying Coke and orange juice to keep them going. The night before had been loud, with some band in the Kardomah Café thrashing away at Velvet Underground covers. Two guitars, a skinny boy singer, a mini drum-kit, and an out-of-place double bass. Most of Zan's pay had gone on the endless trips to the bar, blurring out the noise and sweaty bodies. They'd yelled in each other's ears, bobbed about to the music, lost each other in the crowd, found each other again and staggered home, yelling at strangers. Sarah had told a line of people in a queue for a taxi that Zan was the only woman she'd ever loved, and who could blame her, hey?

The path outside the Kardomah was covered with cans, bottles, empty chip packets, needles and condoms. In the daylight, the whole place was boarded-up and looked dead. You didn't notice the grey paint or the peeling pseudo-gothic columns at night. Zan wrapped her fingers through Sarah's, pulling her towards the fountain. They pushed past a swell of tourists – the Great Aussie Tours bus was parked across from the New Orleans Bourbon and Beefsteak Bar – and headed up the Darlinghurst road, saying coffee coffee, give me coffee.

Pigeons were clumped all over the fountain, pecking at the ground and at each other. Two fat pigeons were scratching and pounding at the neck of one scrawny bird. Feathers and blood flecked the cement, mixed in with breadcrumbs and bird shit. Most of the birds had white dandruffy stuff gathered all around their beaks.

Zan started to dig around in her bag. 'I've got some crisps in here I think.' Her hair fell over her face, muffled her words.

'Leave them. Don't feed them. They're just scabby pests. Come on, let's go. Come on, Zan.' They made Sarah feel sick, those birds with lice and scabs and blood-stained feathers. Useless creatures. They passed the taxi rank, the spot where Sarah had declared love before a group of strangers. There was a patch of vomit just near the Taxi sign. Sick rose up in Sarah's throat and swam down again.

That dark-haired waitress was on duty at Posie's. Leslie. Warm as anything though, always smiled and gave them an extra serve of coffee. Never mentioned the puffer. Another girl was on as well: new and young. Two waiters as well, running about the place like chooks with their heads off, honestly, the place was so crowded you could hardly let your breath out. The smell of bacon and coffee floated around at nose level. Zan waved her arms about, ordering sausages, bacon, toast, tomatoes. Sarah could hear saliva lapping about in her mouth. She waited to see the spit dribble down Zan's chin. Ordered coffee. And orange juice. Raised her eyebrows at Zan. Excessive Zan. A slow familiar tide was easing up Sarah's body. Bunching up in her stomach like sick, and rising, a tightness and a sharpness. When the new waitress bought their tray out, Zan zoomed her smile at her, said hi, is this your first day; and the girl shone at Zan, she really did.

'Oh, this is heaven, it absolutely is, you have to have some. Go on – just a bit of toast then? Oh bugger, I'm a slob and a half.' Egg yolk squirted across the table and on to Zan's lap. 'I'm obviously big with eggs today.' Zan reached her hand out across the table, the warm did not fill Sarah Sweet.

The noise from the street drifted in with the open door. Two hands and a black double bass case edged into the café. A head peered around from the side of the case. Black hair, thick eyebrows. The case shuffled forward. Bumped into two women trying to leave. They stepped sideways. The case stepped sideways. They stepped forward, the case stepped back. Finally they all squeezed around each other, in a tight semi-circle, and the women hurried out through the door. The face behind the case emerged, followed by a body, tall and bony. 'It's that guy isn't it, from last night, look, yair it's him, the bass player.' Zan was sitting forward on her seat. Sarah tried to look casually over towards the door, but Zan was waving at him, calling him over. She didn't even know him. 'I thought he was great, shove over, he can sit with us, there isn't anywhere else look, it's crowded out in here.'

'He might be meeting someone Zan.' Sarah's face was burning.

'Yair, us.'

And he was, apparently. Chairs were scraped back as he squeezed past, holding the huge case in a close hug. 'Hi, are you inviting me to sit here? Thanks. I'll lean Dolly over here.' He leant across Sarah, resting the case against the wall and sat down opposite them both.

'Dolly?' Sarah tried to curl her lip, the way Elvis did.

'Well, you know, for luck or something. It's just nice to have a name for it.'

114

'We saw your gig last night. It was great.' Zan pushed her plate away. Flashed the big-lipped smile at him.

Sarah dug her nails into her palms. 'Well, what we saw of it was great. We were pretty pissed. Zan was saying earlier that she didn't remember a thing.'

'Neither do I, to be honest. Never mind. Hey, I'm Eric.' He looked at Zan.

'No, I do remember you. You were dancing about near the stage. I'd recognise that hair anywhere.'

Sarah's stomach rumbled. Eric poured sugar into an empty cup. 'Hungry hey?'

'I'm Zan and this is my lover, Sarah.' Zan's hand was squeezing at Sarah's knee under the table. Kneading, trying to soothe.

'Great. Cool. Lovers, hey? Great.'

Sarah wanted to practise the sneer again.

'Do you guys want coffee? I'm desperate, I've just finished.'

'Just finished playing? No. Really? Oh no, don't take that away, I'll have the last bit of toast.' Zan grabbed at her plate and snatched the toast.

'Zan hates to miss out.' Sarah made her voice soft. The kneading stopped on her knee for a moment. Zan stared across the table, at Eric.

'Don't we all. Yair, the Kardomah closed about seven-thirty, then we had to pack up and load the gear. It was our last gig, too, so we had to get the gear back to Newt's place. He owns most of it.'

'Last gig? What a shame. What's happening? Sarah, do you want that orange juice, only I'll have it if you don't.'

'Long story. Newt's going to New Zealand basically, so we're without a lead singer and his gear. Plus we're all on each other's backs now anyway. It gets to that stage, you know, where every-one's just getting at everyone else.'

'So what now?' Zan chewed at the fingers of her one hand, left the other squeezing away at Sarah's knee.

'Dunno really. First thing is get somewhere to crash, I've been crashing at Newt's, so I'm up the creek when he goes. Then, dunno, get another band together. Or maybe hitch up to the Territory. Depends.' His eyes went glassy, staring over Zan's shoulder, but moving about really fast.

Zan reached for Sarah's hand and squished the fingers together. Raised her eyebrows. Meaningfully. Sarah let go of the hand and reached for her coffee.

'What?'

'What what? What do you mean what?' Zan wrapped her arms around herself, as if she was cold.

'What were you squeezing my hand for? What do you want?'

'I don't want anything. I was squeezing your hand because I love you.'

'Oh, please, not while we're eating.' Sarah puffed her cheeks up in a mock vomit.

'Anyway,' Eric put his cup down with a clatter, 'I'm gunna head off. Just needed a quick one. Take care. Might see ya again, hey?'

'Yair right. Listen give us your address. If we hear of anywhere – to crash, yair? – we could let you know. And listen, if you want to get another band together any time, I'm your woman.' The red-brown curls falling into the plate of bacon rind and cold egg white.

'Right. Yair, I'll do that Zan. Catch you both, hey? Oh, here's a buck for my coffee.' He reached for the black case and wrapped his arms around it, began inching back to the door.

'Eric. Eric.' Zan was on her feet, her voice shooting through the whole café.

'Leave it, Zan.' Sarah tugged at her arm.

'Your address.'

'Oh right, forget my head and all that, hey? It's Fifteen Wordsworth Road. I'm there until the end of the month. Pop round. Hey, everyone in here knows my address now. Oh, what the hell hey, you might as well all pop round. See ya.' The door banged behind him.

'Wow, that's brilliant isn't it? A band. I'll bloody well follow that up. And what's wrong with you, grumpy pants?'

Sarah held her breath for a moment and pushed Zan's hand from her leg. 'Nothing. Let's go home.' She touched Zan's hair, wrapped it around her hand. Stopped herself saying you-get-everything-I-get-nothing and said instead: 'I'm just hungover.'

Twenty

'He could though – couldn't he? On the couch, he'd have to put up with that bastard spring, but he looks tough enough.'

Sarah stared deep into the eyes of Maxwell Smart, private spy. If she stared hard enough, it would look – wouldn't it? – like she was not hearing, could not hear. She edged closer to the TV. Smart's lovely assistant Ninety-nine was in trouble.

'Except he'd have to stay on the couch, even if it got unbearable. Or he could bring his own bedroll. No room in our bed for strays.'

Maxwell disappeared. A woman in a white nightie riding bare-back in the middle of the night and eating a chocolate bar. Sarah watched her and listened. Zan tapped and tugged and prodded and would not let things be.

'What do ya think? Sarah?'

'No way.' The woman in the nightie kicked the horse to a gallop and rode off with the chocolate wrapper dangling from her hand. 'No way in this world.'

For days, Zan was restless, lion-like. She paced in front of the lift, swinging her hair. She played Violent Femmes on the tape deck in the corner, and sang along loudly, waving a glass in front of her face for a microphone. At night she stared at the ceiling. Sarah did not ask about her staring or her pacing, she knew what these things were about. She knew that Zan had tried to open the drummer's door with her taxi identification card. The door did not open, Zan's card broke in two. Zan watched *Countdown* and MTV and sang along with the words and said doesn't that look fun. Sarah stayed silent, watching the small screen.

Late Saturday-night video clips were interrupted by women in

118

nighties dangling chocolate from their delicate little hands and women curled up in their satin-sheet-covered beds, sucking on huge slabs of chocolate. Zan chewed and chewed on her fingers, taking skin and paltry bits of nail into her mouth, and swallowing. 'Have we got any cocoa? Only I'd kill for a hot chocolate, I swear I would.' More skin into her mouth, more pink muscle showing on the short fingers. Sarah watched, pulling her lips together, breathing out loud enough for Zan to hear. 'Oh *man* I would love some chocolate. Isn't there some cooking chocolate or something in here?' The cupboard doors were opened, plates, empty margarine containers and brown tea-spoons were pulled out and dumped on the floor. 'Whass this then?' She sounded like a send-up of one of those stupid English cops with the big high hats. What wankers, honestly. Zan was holding up a jar, filled with something brown and crumbly looking. She stuck her nose in, took a sniff. 'Nah. Something rotten.' She stuck the jar on the fridge though, didn't throw it out or anything. 'Less go get some chocolate, yair? Come on Sarah, get some, get up and go get chocolate.' Zan stuck her fist out before her, warrior woman. 'I am Zan-hunt-down-chocolate-for-my-woman. Ooga.' Sarah was caught in a fierce hug, the breath squished out of her in one go.

It was only on the way back in, loaded up with chocolate bars, chocolate slice, chocolate milk and chocolate mousse from ZIPPEEZE ALL-NITE SHOPPE, that they noticed that Whiley and Crow, 'discreet suppliers of plastic office fauna,' had discreetly left the Sun Building. Sarah held the door open for Zan, giggling with chocolate-fever, then did the customary double side-step shuffle, to avoid the pile of boxes always outside the heavy door of Whiley and Crow. Her feet edged around, trying to feel the edges of the boxes, and felt only floor. There were no boxes, and no plastic flowers. 'Did you notice if the boxes were about the place yesterday?' Sarah prodded Zan's arm.

'Mmm. Have some Dairy Milk, oh I love you chocolate-oh-chocolate-of-my-heart. What are you asking me? No. I didn't. Hey – they're gone. Wow, no boxes. It's like a new space in here. I don't know though – I didn't notice that they *were* here yesterday.

119

I haven't noticed them for ages come to think of it.'

'I have never, absolutely never, seen this place empty before. It's weird. I didn't notice it yesterday either.'

'Doesn't matter. They didn't give us a spoon for the mousse, the bastards.'

'I wonder if they've shoved all the boxes inside or just left.'

'Let's go upstairs, Sarah.'

But Sarah was poking about, private spy. She pushed at the door, turned the handle. Green carpet, covered in scraps of green and pink plastic. One armchair with the stuffing dribbling out on to the floor. A notepad on the floor. Nothing written on it.

'They've skipped bail, Ninety-nine.' Sarah squeezed the words out the corner of her mouth.

'Wow. Oh check out this space. This is brilliant. Totally brilliant. Completely perfect.'

'Completely perfect for what?' Something slithered up inside Sarah's guts, an uneasy serpent.

'A squat. Check it out – there's no way in the universe anyone is coming back here. Mr Plastic Flowers has found new lime-green pastures.'

'They could be back.'

'No way, Sarah, they've skipped the country. Obviously Mr Plastic Flowers was discovered to be smuggling black cockatoo eggs inside those plastic petals, so he's fled back to the hills of Wales, taking his lovely assistant, Miss Felt Grass, with him. Poor Mrs Plastic Flowers and her two children, Bill and Ben, have been left behind. They are, as we speak, driving to Alice Springs in a Mac truck, which she stole at two AM last night. So they won't be back. We've got ourselves a squat.'

Sarah closed her eyes for a moment, imagining Zan the taxi-driver, careering along Pitt Street, reeling stories out for the suited ladies in the back seat. The irresistible teller of tales. 'We don't need a squat, Zan, we've got a flat. We're okay.' And still, that twirling sickness inside, as if she, Sarah, was being hurtled down the back streets in the back of the cab, too fast, not sure who was driving.

'Eric needs one.'

'Someone else will take over. They'll have let the place out again.'

'Who'd rent it? The place is deserted. Even if they did – what's the problem? He sees them coming, gets his gear and leaves. Simple. Haven't you squatted?'

'No.' Feeling simple herself. 'He's probably found somewhere by now anyway.'

'Fine. We can only offer. I mean, it's too perfect, the timing is *immaculate*.'

Sarah watched herself, her lip pushing forward into a pout, her arms folding. Her foot kicking at the floor. 'Why do you want him to move in so badly anyway? Why do you want to see him so much?'

'There's a room here, he needs one. A fellow human being. Are you sure you don't want any chocolate? C'mon.'

'You're avoiding it.'

'What?'

'The issue. Why you want to see him so badly. Just tell me the truth.'

Zan stared hard, slowly unfolded Sarah's arms. 'What are you saying, Sarah?'

'I'm not saying, I'm asking.' She could hear it in her voice, that heaviness, like a stupid baby. Honestly.

'Asking what? What's the problem?'

'There isn't a problem. I don't have the problem anyway. You're the one who's so mad desperate to get your eyes on Eric.'

'I'm not. Is this about, no, I mean, you don't think – do you?'

'I'm asking.'

'You don't get it do you? This is an experiment to you isn't it? Isn't it?'

'What?'

'Me. Being with me.'

How had this been turned around? It was supposed to be Zan being questioned, but everything had swung about. Nausea was swelling in Sarah's belly. 'You're not an experiment. I just want to know why you're so keen to have him here?'

'That's exactly what I'm talking about. You think I want to get off with him, because you don't get it, you don't get the fact that *I don't fuck men.*' She was yelling right in Sarah's face, as if it was all Sarah's fault. Her hands were on Sarah's arms still, just resting there. When Sarah opened her arms, pushed them out and apart really hard, Zan went flying. She fell in a muddled heap on the floor. Her breath came out in short puffs. She scrabbled around for her bag, breath shorter and shorter, couldn't find her puffer. Sarah just watched, just stood there like she wasn't even a part of it, watching while Zan leant her head in her knees and breathed really hard and then put her hands on her chest and slowed her breath down. The breathing was loud, like a storm. Something slid into Sarah's head: wind outside, a foot kicking, Laminex table. Trees falling and the sound of *please, please, please.* She put her hands against her ears, she would not listen.

Everything went quiet. Zan picked up a plastic leaf. 'If he starts another band, I want to be in it. That's it. Simple, nothing else. I mean, look at it – it's too ridiculous isn't it? He needs a space, there's a space here. I need a band, he'll start one. I'd be mad to ignore it, it's' her voice notched into American talk show and she shook her hands about, 'a cerrrrazzeee coincidence.'

Sarah's mouth twitched.

'Here, have a leaf. Come on,' Zan stood up and touched Sarah's hand. 'Don't be silly with me, Sarah. I don't deserve it. Okay?'

Sarah nodded. All the words had slipped down her throat.

'Anyway,' Zan was bright again, like everything was really, really fine, 'it's good for the karma. Find someone a home, the good turn will come to you.' Right.

Everything zoomed along then, happening too fast for Sarah to keep trace of. She was pulled along by Zan's grin and her own jumbled misery.

Zan was out the door in a whirl, Sarah a limp rag behind her. 'Zan, it's one o'clock in the morning. We can't go round there now and say, oh hi, howyadoin, we've found a cosy little home for you.'

'Yair, we can. Better late than too late.'

They caught a taxi to Wordsworth Street. Zan was full of action, full of warrior-woman. Sarah was full of a stale fury, hobbling along saying: yes, that's fine let's get a taxi, oh no, I'm fine now, not cross, no, I understand now. Etcetera. The door of fifteen Wordsworth Street was open, lights on. A red couch, a single bed and a stainless steel sink were piled on the verandah and some twelve-bar blues were blasting out on to the street. Too loud for door-knocking to be heard, so they headed down the hallway, towards the noise. Intrepid explorers.

In the room at the end of the hallway were: Eric, his bass, an amplifier and some guy with a guitar. Bare light-bulbs and lots of noise. They kept playing, smirking across at each other. The guy on the guitar mumbled into a microphone on a stand: 'my baby's goin, my baby's goin down to New Orleans, I feel so bad.' Zan squeezed Sarah's hand, her eyes shining and shining. The bass stopped in a sudden thump. Eric waved at Zan and Sarah, tapped his friend on the arm and yelled, 'stop, man.'

'Hey. Pull up a piece of floor. Ya here for a jam?' His eyes were darting about all over the place, like that time in the café.

'Maybe. Found anywhere to crash?' Zan kept hold of Sarah's hand, pulling her down to the floor.

'Nah. Bummer, hey?'

The guy with the guitar – long legs, thin arms – laughed through his teeth. 'Havya looked for anywhere mate?'

'Nah. Bummer, hey?' Eric plucked a note on the bass. Sarah let a compulsory hahaha float over in his direction.

'Well, boy – we've found you a squat. Brilliant space, downstairs from us. Bring your own bed, but no rent. You can't say fairer than that.' Zan did a hostess-with-the-mostest flourish.

'You serious? That's excellent. Hey, this is Eric.'

'I thought you were Eric?' Sarah did the lip-curling sneer.

'I am. We both are. He's little Eric, I'm big Eric. And look,' he pushed little Eric next to Sarah and sat himself down on the other side of her, 'this is a Sarah sandwich. Between two slices of Eric.'

Sarah didn't mean to laugh, it just slipped. So Zan and both the Erics thought everything was just fine, and everyone laughed like at the end of an American sit-com.

'So, Zan, are ya gunna have a jam with us? I'm not gunna hike my stuff over there now. Where is it anyway? Maybe it isn't my kind of area.'

'Ultimo. I'd take what I could get if I were you. What, a jam now?'

'Now or later, doesn't matter. We've got the gear set up though, now's a good time. Thought you wanted to get a band together?'

'Yair, I did. I mean, I do. I think I do. I want to have a jam though, sure. Give me the mike.'

'Excellent. What about "Knockin on Heaven's Door"?'

Sarah lay down on the floor, listened to Zan belting it out. Even with her eyes closed, she could see the shadows of Zan dancing about in front of the light. The shadow grew bigger, the light shrunk and the music grew far away.

When she opened her eyes again, the sun was up, her back was killing her, and Zan was still singing.

Twenty-One

Intimate Strangers. Zan thought it was a great name for a band, though she couldn't remember how they'd found it. A chance comment, perhaps, thrown across the room during that first rehearsal in the area formerly known as the offices of Whiley and Crow, some commentary on the nature of these people joined together by, what? A guitar, a double bass, a few microphones, a keyboard, three amps and a bunch of leads.

Big Eric had arrived at the Sun Building like a skinny Pied Piper. Little Eric bought his sleeping bag along with his guitar. Big Eric introduced his mate, Gravy, as a keyboard player and sequencer who needed a crash pad as well. There was some guy with them who had a shaved head, one long eyebrow and a bed-roll; no-one seemed to know his name. Posters advertising old gigs at the Kardomah and the Lansdowne Hotel were stuck to the walls with Blu-tac. The guy with the eyebrow got carried away and Blu-tacked a box of matches, a banana skin and a clock to the door: called it urban art. Sarah sat bunched up on the stairs, counting the mattresses as they went through the door. A girl with a chain in her nose arrived with a fold-up camp bed, smiled at Sarah and said, 'hi, is the squat through here?'

That night: squawks and squeaks and mismatched melodies. Zan twirling about with a microphone, her hair streaming about, her voice punching into walls. The girl with the nose-chain sat on one of the mattresses banging out rhythms on a kettle. Sarah sat against the door, doodling on a notepad like she had better things to do and better places to be. They all said Zan was great, yair, excellent, yair, really, really cool and Zan bopped about and wrapped her arms around Sarah, smiled at Eric and said, 'yair, let's do it, let's get a band together, why not?'

The days were stretching out more and more, Summer was inching slowly in. The nights were lighter, and filled with the endless rehearsals of Zan and her bloody band. There was a jasmine tree outside Ailsa Craig's Romper Room and Sarah picked small flowers from it, breathed in the sweet smell while she walked back from the Cross in the afternoons. Zan sometimes picked her up, but mostly, no, if she wasn't driving she was busy rehearsing, or writing obscure whirly lyrics, or learning words or tunes. She did a cover of 'Femme Fatale', bunging on a German accent and pulling her hair over one eye, but she kept forgetting the words and giggling when she should have been looking sultry. That was the word Eric used about her, sultry. 'Zan's excellent, hey? Really sultry.' What the hell was that supposed to mean? Sultry? Please.

The weekends arched out again, slippery and lonely. Sarah drifted about the Quay, caught ferries, shooed pigeons away. Threw a rock at a seagull once, when it swooped too near her chips. Zan stayed in, rehearsing and rehearsing, like it mattered.

Sarah got back to the flat one night and found candles lit up all along the stairs, all outside the elevator. A little line of candles leading to the door of the flat. Filled with candles. Burning and burning. On the television, on the fridge, on the floor, on the window ledge. There was a sarong spread out on the floor and a bottle of wine and two plastic wine goblets and plates and the smell of freshly cooked curry and Zan with her hair tied up and wrapped in a sarong herself, with oil and incense making the place smell like the jasmine lady on a mat of pearls, zooming in straight from Sarah's dreams.

Zan fed her and there was no music playing and Sarah had to go and spoil it all saying, 'how nice of you to fit me into your busy life,' and asking how the band could bear to be parted from her for even one night. They slept back to back that night, a cold wedge of bed between them, instead of all tangled up and warm, the way it should have been.

*

126

Big Eric was weird, that was the other thing. His eyes always flicking about the place, like too many thoughts in his head. Side to side they went, his eyes, and downwards pointing. You'd swear he was about to pull a gun on you sometimes. And all the time saying stuff to Sarah like, 'hey, Sarah, I think it's really cool, you know, about you and Zan and everything, you guys really dig each other, hey?' Dig? What a joke.

The band had thirty-five minutes' worth of songs and Eric was saying time for a gig, hey, gotta getta gig guys, gotta getta gig. Sarah sat in on the rehearsals sometimes, bobbing her head along and smiling as if she really could give a shit about the Intimate bloody Strangers and their crappy little songs. Gravy and both the Erics kept saying how fan-bloody-tastic Zan was, how absolutely frigging amazing that she'd turned up at just the right time. And she was, she was pretty fan-bloody-tastic. Her voice travelled like her laugh, it shot out and around, slapping people about the face. She'd stand there looking really, really tiny, then – wham – she'd open her mouth and this huge great walloping wall of voice would come flying at you. Everyone thought it was great, just great. They called Sarah their mascot, or sometimes – laughing their heads off – Chief Groupie. Sarah laughed along, there didn't seem to be much choice.

There was never a rehearsal on Wednesdays. Zan drove late, so Sarah took the slow walk home, stopping off for a kebab at Posie's. As if she'd never met Zan, as if things hadn't changed at all. She was tired; the endless drone of the nursery wore her down. It was almost half-term and there was a sense of panic and rush in Ailsa Craig's normally well-ordered Romper Room. Enrolments for the next year starting already. Inspections by hopeful parents, everyone perking up, looking their brightest, doing their damnedest. Sarah rested her head on the brown Formica, put her forehead on the cool table-top. Hard and soothing. It had no resistance, no give: it was tough, that was the comfort of it. 'Hi luv. Girlfriend not here today? Shame. She brightens the place up, I reckon. Oh bugger, not that you don't brighten the place too – sounds like I'm playin favourites. Ya both brighten the place up. Like fireworks or somethin. Anyway, whaddaya-avin?' It was dark-haired Leslie on duty, trying for waitress-of-the-year, but sounding like one of those mothers saying, 'No, I love you both the same, the exact same amount.' You could never believe those mothers. They were obviously lying or they wouldn't have to say it. Did they think kids were stupid or something? Honestly. *She thought you were Sarah, that's why she trod on your foot Bloss.* Sarah shook away the memory.

It was dark by the time Sarah left Posie's. She walked back through Darlinghurst, telling an old guy in a longish green coat to fuck right off, when he tried to flash his dick at her. Oh yair, and what was she gunna do, scream? Run? It was hardly frightening. Stupid prick.

Her hands were still clenched in tight little balls by the time she got to the Sun Building. Big Eric was sitting on the steps, lighting a badly rolled cigarette. 'Hey, number one groupie, howyadoin?' Smug as shit he was.

'Oh piss off, Eric, I'm not in the mood.'

He dropped the cigarette and blinked, as if she'd thrown water on his face. 'Whassup? Fighting with Zan?'

'What is this, an interobloodygation? I'm just not up for stupid jokes right now, okay? I've been surrounded by screaming kids all day and some geriatric wannabe just tried to show me his shrivelled wonder, and I need some rest. Is that good enough?'

'Hey, Sarah, man, I'm really sorry. Oh man, that really sucks.' His voice had gone all soft and whispery.

'It's fine. It's not a problem, okay? I just don't want any more hassle. I'm fine.' But for some reason, she wanted to put her face on his knee and cry. Stupid.

'Hey.' He held his arms out wide, like an ad for Happy Families.

'Get out, Eric, I don't want a hug. I just want a cup of coffee. Since when did you smoke anyway?'

'I don't. I'm just testing it out. Come up to the squat, I'll make you a drink. Everyone else has gone over to Paddington. Some gig at the Markets.'

Upstairs, he boiled water in the ancient electric jug and scrambled about looking for coffee. Sarah sat small and folded in, at the end of one of the mattresses – impossible to tell who it belonged to. She waited for him to start on about how fantastic Zan was, how excellent their first gig would be, how cool it was that Zan and Sarah were so into each other. He was just quiet though, his flicking around, looking past Sarah.

'What's the time?' She took the hot mug from him.

'Nine-thirty. Why?'

'Just wondered.'

'When's Zan get home?'

'Dunno. About tennish.' She blew on the coffee and sipped. Stared at him, at his skinny arms. 'It's stuffy in here. Come and sit near the door. Let the air in.'

He followed her across the room, to the double mattress near the door. There was a sleeping bag crumpled up at one end. 'So, do ya wanna talk about it?' He was playing this super-nice guy, as if he cared.

'I said no. Talk about something else.' She didn't even want to be there, drinking coffee with him. He stank of cigarette smoke.

'The band's going really well. Everything's coming together, hey? Zan's voice is excellent, hey? And she can write too. The guy who does the bookings at the Kardomah is keen to hear us, I've played there heaps before, hey. Reckon we might get to be a support for the Dugites. Be an excellent combination. They'd love Zan, I reckon.'

It was like his voice was just droning on and on and seeping into Sarah's brain, his words and voice just slicing in and he wouldn't stop and all she wanted to do was just to shut him up to tell him to stop talking about it, she didn't know she didn't care she'd had enough of all the talk, there was that zooming in her ears again like the sea was inside her head and she leant in, she zoomed in and she was going to just put her hands on his mouth, that's all, just to stop him, just shut him up, that's all she wanted to do, but instead of her hands it was her mouth and that was it she didn't know how to stop then and she would show him she would show she knew a thing or two she was good, she was as good as, as good as anybody, not invisible and somehow wanting to hurt Zan hard for no reason, no reason at all, and she flicked her tongue around and she sucked and licked his lips and the inside of his mouth which stank of smoke and she could feel him growing breathless and hard and she could feel a kind of victory beneath her skin.

Eric had pushed her head back against the wall and was pressing against her. She slipped her hand down, trickled it like water down his chest. Unzipped, unbuttoned, undid. Wrapped her hand hard, kept her mouth on his and kept sliding, slow and slow, and soft, then hard and fast, and quick, slow, slow, quick. He was groaning inside her mouth saying, you're fantastic and shoving at her with his hands, reaching for the band of her jeans. She pushed his hands back, half pulled away from him. She had her eyes open, could see the watch on his wrist where he gripped the edges of the mattress. Nine fifty-five. She slowed down.

Zan appeared in the doorway as Eric came, spurting across Sarah's hand and across the mattress. Sarah wiped her hand on the sleeping bag, and said sorry, Zan, I'm really sorry. Eric tried to smile at Zan, all casual and hip, but his dick was hanging out like a dog's tongue, he had stains across his jeans and his smile was coming out crooked. Zan didn't say a word, just looked at them both then walked away. Sarah heard the clunk of the elevator and that was all.

Twenty-Two

For days, for almost a week, Zan slept on the couch, never minding the sticky-out spring. Sarah tip-toed around her, holding her breath, holding out for an explosion. Zan left early in the mornings and came back late at night when Sarah was lying on her back in bed, expecting Zan to just stay away. Zan could drive off into the night, couldn't she? She could stick her thumb out and get out of there, head off to anywhere. Zan could, if she wanted to, stick two fingers in the air at Sarah and head off to a better someone, somewhere. She should have, that's what she should have done, if she had sense, if she had guts, if she cared about herself. Sarah lay on her back, stared at the ceiling and let the thinking circle her head. Zan didn't yell, didn't talk, didn't throw anything. Sarah couldn't tell what she was thinking, and it wasn't fair.

There were giant panda bears on sale at the Quay. A whole stall was devoted to them. A sign hung above the stall table proclaiming STUFFED TEDDIES, BIG AS THE KIDDIES. FUN! FUN! FUN! A peace offering, yes. Sarah crept up on them, an intrepid hunter of wild pandas. They must have been five-foot tall, seriously – stuff being as big as kiddies, they were as big as Zan. Blue and red ribbons tied around their necks, you could choose which one you wanted. Thirty bucks, but Sarah needed a seriously big peace offering.

There was a copper behind the stall, a shiny young constable in neatly pressed blue. Sarah hesitated, confused. A smaller sign was propped at the front of the table: HELP THE POLICE YOUTH CLUBS – GIVE YOUTH A CHANCE. Sarah's mouth went tight, police bloody youth indeed, as if they needed any help. The scrubbed-behind-the-ears constable grinned at her – it made his ears stick out. Sarah looked at the big clock at Wharf Number Three. Seven-fifteen. Shops would be shut. She pulled out her wallet, grabbed at a red-ribboned bear.

'Prezzie, ay?' The young cop sounded like a bloated mosquito, buzzing about with his Darwin accent.

'No.' Sarah handed him two twenty-dollar notes and shuffled her feet.

'Ah, well, least ya know yer helpin a good cause, true, ay?'

'No, I don't. I just want the bear. If there was somewhere else to get one, I would, but it just happens that I'm in a rush.'

He fumbled with the change, red spots marking his cheeks. 'Okay luv, I'm just, well, I dunno, we're helpin the youth of Oztraylya, now that can't be a bad thing, can it?'

'The youth of Australia would be better off without you lot. Thanks for the bear, don't bother wrapping it. Bye.'

He looked about twelve, honestly, and his whole face was bright red by the time she'd stuffed the change in her wallet and picked the bear up in a hug. Poor bloke. Still, better to find out while he was still young that he was in a bastard's job. As if he didn't already know.

The bear kept slipping out of her hands and bumping against her knees as she walked. She stopped at the little kiosk near the bus stop and bought a notepad for forty cents, wrote *This is a Sorry Bear* on a sheet of paper and tied it to the red ribbon around the panda's neck. The bus driver asked if the panda was her boyfriend, she said, yes, he was more interesting than most men, haha bloody ha. When she got to the flat, she leant the panda against the door, nearly squashed him while she tried to find her keys. An envelope had been pushed under the door with *Zan* on it, in backward sloping writing. Sarah sat on the couch, slid the envelope behind the panda, and watched a crappy adventure film about a woman in a canoe who fell in love with an axe murderer. Then there was some talk show, then a fuzzy awards ceremony for something or other, then something else and something else. She was falling asleep on the panda's shoulder when the door finally clicked open. Zan switched the light on, read the note around the bear's neck and sat on the floor. On the other side of the room, far away from Sarah.

'It's a sorry bear.' Sarah sounded like a kid, she could hear it in her own voice.

Zan sat and stared, like a statue.

'Oh fuck, Zan, I'm sorry. I'm really sorry. It was an accident.'

Zan raised her eyebrows and made a sucking sound with her teeth.

'I don't know what happened. It just happened. It just. Look, what can I say to you? I didn't want to. It wasn't like I wanted him or anything.'

'Did he make you?'

'No.'

'No. Exactly.'

'I don't know. I get, I can't help things sometimes. I get. Out of control. I'll try. I will.'

Zan pointed at the bear. 'Is that supposed to make it all right?'

'No. Not all right, just, I dunno, better maybe? Can't it be better?'

'No, I don't think it can be better. It's not like something that can grow back.' Zan slid a bit forward, leant closer towards Sarah. 'You need to know that if anything is, like, remotely okay between us, it's not because you bought me a bear. You can't buy my forgiveness like that.'

'I just wanted to show you how sorry I was. Am.'

'Right.'

Sarah sat. If Zan went, she'd tell her to take the bear. Or she could throw it out the window and see it splattered. She felt a tear squeeze its way down her cheek. Good. 'Please?' She moved closer to the light, just enough so that Zan could see the tear. She hoped the light picked it up.

Zan rubbed at her legs, as if she was cold or numb. 'I love you, but it's not, I can't, I don't think I can.'

Sarah squeezed her legs together and held the breath in her throat. Zan was staring down at the floor, picking at the skin on her fingers. Sarah watched. *Say it say it say it. Say no.*

133

Zan looked up, back at Sarah, back at the stupid bloody stuffed panda, sitting there with a red ribbon around its fat neck. 'Things happen, I guess. I mean, these things do. Happen. I can't just give up. Not if you don't want to.'

'I don't.' But there was a ball in the pit of Sarah's stomach, heavy and thick, and Zan looked crumpled and too thin. Spineless. Sarah rubbed at her head, pushing the words away. She pulled the envelope out from behind the bear. 'This was under the door. I didn't open it.'

'I should bloody well hope not. It's got my name on it. Eric's writing. I'm not sure I want to open it actually, I don't feel very warmly towards him, strangely enough.' Zan tore at the paper and pulled a sheet of brown paper from inside. She read it in silence and sat for a moment, staring at the note. She crumpled the paper, held it in her hands. Chewed at her finger. Reached for her bag, took a puff of Ventolin. Sat.

Sarah was itching inside. Trying to look glazed, staring over Zan's shoulder like it didn't matter, like she didn't care. Zan sat, said nothing, the paper crumpled in her hand. Sarah itched, said nothing. The itch grew. Finally: 'What? What did he say?'

'Um. He wants. Um. He said. Well.'

'Sorry?' Grovelling bastard.

'No. Not really. Sort of. He does, he does say sorry. In passing really. We've got the gig. At the Kardomah. With the Dugites. I could really stuff him up if I said no.'

Say it. Say no.

Zan squirted more Ventolin into her mouth. 'I think he's a bit of a bastard, but then so are you. I'd be mad to say no. It'd be a bastard of a thing to do. Anyway, I want to do it. Supporting The Dugites. I'd be mad not to.'

'Right.' Sarah smiled across, her face tight. 'Great.'

'And I suppose the bear could be a mascot. Or something. Thanks.'

Sarah passed the police youth clubs' stall at the Quay the next day. The shiny young policeman was there again, trying to smile at Sarah as she stomped past on the far side of the path and dived into a card shop. Postcards of Sydney in summer covered the walls and big birthday cards saying BIRTHDAY WISHES FROM DOWNUNDER. Yair, right. There was a neon pink card beneath the birthday cards, with blue writing on the front. HELLO in big scrawly letters. Inside it said: *long time no write, just thought I'd let you know I was still alive.* Why not? The young boy behind the counter grinned at Sarah and said, Have a Nice Day as she paid for the card and four stamps.

Sarah sat in the front carriage on the train and leant the card against her knees. She looked at the card for a long time before she wrote *Hi mum*, and underlined the words *just thought I'd let you know I was still alive*. Underneath, she wrote *Love, Sarah*. She sat with the card on her lap for ages before she added, *I'm well and happy and working in a nursery in Wahroonga (very posh). It's run by this dictator woman called Ailsa Craig. Seriously though, its fine. Sydney is good*. She stared at the woman sitting opposite her, then: *Please take care of yourself*. She wanted more, but the words weren't there, weren't anywhere. She stuck the envelope in the letter box outside the Wahroonga train station, quickly, then ran the rest of the way to the nursery: chasing out thought.

Twenty-Three

There were posters outside the Kardomah, with a big picture of The Dugites in black and white, and PLAYING HERE scrawled across. Below the picture, in small black letters: WITH THE INTIMATE STRANGERS. It had even been listed in the *Sydney Morning Herald* daily gig guide: KARDOMAH CAFÉ – THE DUGITES DOING WHAT THEY DO BEST. SUPPORT – INTIMATE STRANGERS. TONIGHT. 9.00 PM. Zan trembled all over when she read it, showed it to Sarah. Read it over and over again. Out loud. She spent the whole day making siren noises in her throat, going ahhhhhh on different notes and massaging her throat. As if she'd ever 'warmed her voice up' before, as if she was some sort of prize bloody champion. Sarah massaged her back and said yes-everything-will-be-fine-they'll-love-you. Eric bashed on the door at five o'clock and stayed outside the door, yelling, 'we've godda go and do the sound check, yair? Come on, Zan.'

'Are you coming with me?' Zan grabbed onto Sarah's hand, squeezing hard.

'I'll seeya there later. What would I do?'

'Help with the sound check. Help unload.'

'Move it Zan.' Eric bashed harder.

'Please? I'd like you to be there.' Zan ran her fingers along Sarah's palm.

'I will be. I'll be there later. When you start playing. No, before you start playing. I'll give you a hand with stuff then. There's no point in me just hanging out for hours while you guys go, blah, blah, check. Dooya want me to bring some food?' Sarah Sweet, nurturer.

'Umm, no. I don't know if I'll feel like eating. I'm too, I mean,

I feel like I'm ten years old. I'll see you there then? About eight?'
Zan touched her lips against Sarah's, light as anything.

Sarah sat, for ages, just staring at the wall. For no reason. Just sitting there. At first, she was busy listening to the sounds of Zan and Big Eric and Little Eric and Gravy all leaving. She could hear their voices, echoing up and around. Then the heavy bang of the door downstairs, then nothing. Just quiet. She dug her nails into the skin of her palms, harder and harder; checking to see how hard, how far, how much she could hurt. She washed her hands afterwards, and splashed the metal-cold water on her face. She tried to put Zan's jeans on, pulling at the zip with a coat hanger and ripping the zip away from the seam. She left them scrunched on the bed and put a stained brown dress on instead. Outside, it was already dark and the air was cool.

The New Orleans Bourbon and Beefsteak Bar was around the corner from the Kardomah. Bursts of laughter and tinkling glass sounds swept out onto the street, in front of Sarah's face. She could hear a piano playing something old. She stood outside, listening, until a group of women in stilettos and short skirts pushed past her, giggling. One of them had HEN written across the back of her jacket, in pink neon. Sarah stood in their path until the Hen pushed her onto the road. The piano was louder than the sound of the traffic. Someone honked as she crossed the road. Inside the bar, it was all bearded men and cigar smoke and signs saying COCKTAILS UPSTAIRS, IN THE PIANO BAR.

More bearded men in the piano bar and a grand piano in the corner. The boy behind the bar looked about twelve, all scrubbed up and clean. 'Whiskey thanks,' she felt old and wise and Lauren Bacallish next to the boy's clean face, 'no ice.'

'What sort?' Maybe he only looked young because of all the beards.

'Sorry?'

He was smirking at her. 'No preferences then. House.' Smartass.

Sarah sat on a seat, leaning against the wall, alongside the piano. She could see his long fingers, and the jar full of coins on the piano lid. He didn't sing, just played, and his fingers moved

137

really fast. He stopped playing and Sarah looked at his face. Sunken eyes, something missing. Eyes not looking anywhere. She looked harder. Oh, blind, he was blind. People were applauding. Sarah clapped one hand against her leg and tried not to spill the whiskey.

'Sounds like there's a few of you here tonight. Great.' His voice was nice. Smooth, like the whiskey. He had a mole on his face and hairs grew from it. 'I don't get paid, so feel free to add to the tip jar. It's right there in front of me, ask someone to show you if you're blind.'

Sarah wasn't sure whether to laugh or not. He started playing again, a slow one this time, all gentle chords and soft touches. Someone without a beard asked him to play 'Hotel California' and he laughed but played it anyway. Everyone sang along. Then they wanted more songs to sing along to, so he played 'Blowin' in the Wind' and 'The Rose'. Sarah got another drink and didn't sing along. He played a honkey-tonk version of 'Lola-La-la-La-la-Lola', and all the beards and some women in pastel jackets started bopping around each other and waving their arms in the air. One of the beards edged closer and closer to the piano, waving his arms up and down, dancing closer. And closer, until he waved his arm in front of the tip jar and knocked it on to the floor. He danced about for a few more moments before he knelt down and came back up without the jar.

Sarah watched him dance away to the edges of the crowd and thought about yelling, Stop Thief, but didn't. Instead, she watched him walk casually down the steps, finished her whiskey and followed him outside. She pushed him lightly on his back as she passed him; that was all.

The blonde girl sitting behind the table at the Kardomah couldn't find Sarah's name on the door list. 'No sorry. Sarah did you say? Can't see it at all.' There was a thump of indistinct noise coming through the closed door, so the woman had to yell.

'Zan should have put my name down. Are you sure?'

'Zan? Hang on – oh, are you with, wait a sec – sorry, you *are* here. Wrong list. I thought you must have been with The Dugites.

Go on in. Intimate Strangers've nearly finished though.'

She could hear Zan's voice as soon as she pushed through the door. Belting out. She pushed forward. Excuse-me-excuse-me-excuse-me. She knocked someone's drink from their hand and pushed on forward, until she could see Zan. Everyone was watching her. She was too small for the microphone stand, but she'd wrapped the lead around herself. Her eyes were closed and Sarah could see the sweat on her face. Could hear the gravel in her voice as she let out a long loud low note, shook her hair out and said, 'thanks very much, we've been the Intimate Strangers, you've been a great audience.'

A great audience? She sounded like an American showman. Still, there were some yells of 'more, more' in amongst the chants of 'Du-gites, Du-gites.' Zan was shining in the middle of the applause, her smile a bright slash. The clapping slowed as the lights came up. Sarah waited until the taped music came on before she crossed the empty dance floor. Zan was on the stage coiling a lead around her arm. Sarah reached her hand out.

'Hey. Oh, it's you, I just felt something grab at my ankle and I was hoping it might be an obsessive fan. I thought you must have missed it, I was looking for you. Where were you at eight?'

'I was late. Long story.'

Zan looked at her for a moment. 'Okay. Anyway, you made it. They really liked us didn't they? It was so much *fun*.'

Big Eric grinned at Sarah, all blustery-cool, took the microphone stand away and said, 'you gunner stand there all day with your one true love, or are you gunner do some work, Zan? Just because you just did a smash-hit gig doesn't mean you can start bludging. What did you think Sarah?'

'Great. You were all great.'

'We've got to move though, Zan, The Dugites need to set up. What are you doing, Sarah?'

'I'll wait. I'll be in the way I reckon.'

Zan still had that shine about her face. 'You could coil some leads if you want, no, actually, leave it, it'll probably be quicker if we just get on with it. Is that okay?'

139

'Stop being a mother. I'll wait here.' A tide of annoyance drifted in and out of Sarah's head.

Sarah sat on the floor, her back against the stage. A tall man in an orange shirt stood right next to her, leaning on the edge of the stage until Zan came near again. He tapped at Zan's foot. 'I just wanted you to know I thought that was absolutely fantastic. You are a wonderful performer. Where are you playing next?'

'Umm, not sure.' Zan reached down and ruffled Sarah's hair. 'We haven't been booked yet. Look out for us though.'

'Right. Definitely. Okay. I'll see you then.' He backed away, keeping his eyes on Zan until he was at the bar.

Zan jumped down to the floor beside Sarah, laughing. 'I guess that's the closest I get to an obsessed fan. The Dugites have been so supportive. Treated us like pros.'

'Have you finished packing up?'

'Yair, we can have a drink now. The Dugites start in about ten minutes, I think. I can't believe we've actually done it.'

The guitarist from The Dugites came out with two roadies and started setting up. He dropped a lead in front of Zan. 'Is this yours? That was great by the way. I really like your stuff.' He didn't look at Sarah.

Sarah's mouth was hot and dry. 'I'm gunner get a drink.' She stood up.

'I'll come with you.' Zan stuffed the lead in her pocket.

Sarah remembered the torn jeans, but said nothing.

There was a crush at the bar, Sarah felt her mouth, her head, heating up, burning up. No-one seemed to be getting served. Sarah bit at her lip. Bit harder. The burning grew bright behind her eyes. She was dizzy with fury.

'I'm going.' She walked towards the door.

Zan tugged at her hand. 'Where?'

'I said, I'm going.' Sarah yanked her hand away. She pushed at the door. Cool air danced on her skin. Zan's breath was on her hair.

'Don't go, Sarah.' She was half whispering it, bird-like. Whimpering. 'What about The Dugites?'

'I don't give a shit about The Dugites.' The fury was growing bigger now, and harder. Something to hold on to. And Zan, Zan was clinging and clawing and pleading and trying to please instead of saying Go then, go you bastard, see if I give a fuck, see if I do and her hands were at Sarah's back and trying to turn her around and Sarah didn't want to, it just happened that she turned around and Zan's face looked so weak and small. 'Please, Sarah.'

The wind outside, his feet at her face, the prisoner in the corner. *Why didn't she just say no? Why didn't she just leave?* Sarah could feel her hands, from a distance, could feel them smashing onto Zan's face. Noticed from a far-off place that Zan was on the ground, and that feet were kicking at her, Sarah's feet. Kicking at her. And kicking again. Zan was a curled-up shape on the ground with blood coming from her face all mixed with tears and Sarah kept kicking. Zan's hands were at her own throat, her mouth was open and she was yelling. The sound suddenly cut through to Sarah. Zan crying and saying 'I can't breathe, I can't breathe, I need my puffer.'

A bouncer took hold of Sarah's shoulders. She tried to shake him off, yelling in his face, 'get her puffer, she's in the band.'

When he let her go, she ran down Darlinghurst Road and kept running.

141

Twenty-Four

Sarah and Zan skirted around each other. Their words moved in circles. I-love-you-I-love-you-not. There was an uneasy settling, a desperate kind of quiet. Their fingertips didn't touch, though they slept alongside each other.

It had taken two weeks for Zan's bruising to settle and Sarah kept herself busy, dishing out apologies and pleadings. She didn't like to be alone with herself and cleaned her teeth facing the wall, avoiding the mirror. Zan was calm, she seemed to float about the place. Her back was straight and her eyes somehow glazed, blank, like the piano player with the empty tips jar. The thing was, the thing Sarah tried to say, was this: everyone has one blow-up sometime, don't they? No matter how hard you try, how sorry you are, it happens, doesn't it?

When the bruising went, a numbness came down on them. They went back to eating meals together; Zan occasionally picked Sarah up from the nursery, honking the taxi horn, if not joyfully, then at least without rage. Zan rehearsed and rehearsed, as if she had not already had a gig and been the darling of the Kardomah. Little Eric had a new girlfriend who thought the Intimate Strangers were great, just great, and she was phoning pubs, trying to get them bookings. She sat on the floor of the squat during their rehearsals, making lists and little notes to herself, as if she was a big-time manager. Most days, Sarah stuck her head inside the door of the squat and said Hi, smiling all round. The music usually paused when she did that, everyone said 'Hi Sarah', and stood waiting for her to leave, smiling politely but with hands obviously itching at the microphones and guitars, and eyes looking anywhere but at her. She hated them all, and that was a surprise, to know that as a simple and uncluttered thing. At night, Zan curled herself into a ball, her back pointing at Sarah's face and that was not fair because everyone makes mistakes.

There was a long gap between leaving the nursery and falling into bed at night. A space to be filled with simpering and politeness and carefulness and avoidance. Sarah tried to catch the late trains home and dawdled about in the nursery until Ailsa Craig told her to just get a move on. Feeding pigeons was out, they made her sick these days, with their scabbed-up beaks and lice-covered feathers and the way they tore at each others necks, horrible. She bought a piece of roast chicken from the chip-van one afternoon. It was a round fat thigh, all covered in brown skin and dripping with fat. She sat in the sun, on the Harbour wall, stretching her legs out in front of her. She rubbed the grease and juice across her face as she ate, tearing at the thigh with her teeth and hands. When she stood up, she left the bones, still with bits of flesh and skin hanging off them, on the wall. As soon as she took three steps away, a whole *swarm* of pigeons dived on the chicken bones. *Chicken.* They were fellow birds, it was disgusting, it was like cannibalism. Sarah wanted to kick at their heads, they were so revolting.

She found small pubs in The Rocks to go to and drink in. Overcrowded places, full of Pommie accents and smoke and loud voices. Sarah found herself squashed against the walls or bars, babble surrounding her. She was unseen then. She could stare right at the faces of people in front of her and they wouldn't even notice, they'd be so busy yelling into someone else's ear: 'Yes, super bloody deal, absolutely fucking *marvellous*, and what about that Bondey chap, isn't he brill? Yes another vodka, cheers.' Sarah could let beer dribble right down her chin, if she wanted to, no-one would say 'Are you all right?' or, 'Haven't you had enough?' She wanted to fall into the ease of drunkenness, the ease of becoming a regular drunk. She wanted to be able to slur at the barman, 'people jush blow-up shumtimez dohne they? Carn help it can they? They jush blow-up,' but the alcohol bored her by the time she got to the second drink.

143

It was way after happy hour, the day she wandered into a bar full of old men and green vinyl chairs. She'd scrubbed the last of the tables at the nursery, smiling hard at Ailsa Craig, then deliberately missed two trains. She walked slowly, as slow as she could, up through The Rocks. It was called The Rose, stuck on a corner and with a verandah wrapped around it. Inside, a cluster of wrinkly men sat around the end of the bar, their heads tilted back to look into the television screen above them. World Championship Wrestling. Wrong place, no invisibility here. A skinny guy – the barman – was at the end of the bar, hunched over a paper, an ashtray beside him.

One of the wrinklies called out, 'Oy,' and the barman raised his head. Goatee, long hair, grubby T-shirt. He looked past the end of the bar to Sarah, raised his eyebrows, wrapped his arms across his stomach. Too familiar, that stomach, that face. Robert. 'Oy, come on, ya friggin bludger. Gissadrink.' The fist of the drinker slammed on the bar. Sarah smiled across at Robert, trying for politeness.

He pulled his mouth into a tight little circle above his goatee, he looked like he was going to spit at her, right there in front of those pissed blokes. He didn't though, he looked around for a moment, maybe hoping she'd disappear, then back at her. 'Sarah Sweet. The one and only.' He pointed at the old guy sprawling across the bar, still banging his fist on the counter, but as if he'd forgotten what for. 'It's comin, mate.' Robert slipped a schooner glass under the Tooheys tap. 'What will ya have, Miss Sweet? Or are ya just here to make trouble?' The beer spilt from the edge of the glass as he put it down and the old bloke growled at him.

'Nothing. I don't want anything. I was looking for someone, it's the wrong place. How are ya, good?' She smiled hard, hoping he'd say yes, very good, fine thanks, no problem, nice seeing you, goodbye stranger.

He wiped at the beer spill on the bar. 'Yair, I'm okay Sarah. Happier than I was with you. Is that what you wanted to hear? Or would you like me to say I'm miserable? As if I could be more miserable than you made me. Why are you here?'

She had no words to add, her mouth was dry, tongue heavy. She wanted to be light, full of polite greetings; but somehow, instead, she was creeping out of the bar like an under-age school-girl. She walked fast down the road, back to the Quay and caught a ferry to Manly, trying not to see the picture in her head of a tear dripping down Robert's nose. Nothing to do with her. She stopped going to The Rocks after that.

The nursery grew large in her days. Children's voices managed to crowd out her own voice and fill her head. She learned this: that if she worked fast and moved quickly, there could be no time for thinking. During nap time, she coloured and cut, mounted finger paintings on the wall, tidied the kitchen, swept the floors, organised the first-aid kit. She ordered sheets of Laminex and rolls of gaffer tape and re-laminated the small work tables in bright new colours. Ailsa Craig said Sarah would turn into a star worker if she wasn't careful.

The telephone for the nursery rang often in the afternoons. Parents running late, telemarketing people with special offers, prospective clients, wrong numbers. The ringing was a dull sound in the background, rarely breaking through the comfortable noise of afternoon play. The phone never rang for staff. When Ailsa Craig tapped Sarah on the shoulder and said, 'there appears to be a telephone call for you,' Sarah expected a joke. She looked around for the laughing faces. Ailsa Craig pushed her forward, 'In the office, Sarah, off you go.'

'Yes?' Sarah's voice was wobbly, she felt cold.

'Is that Sarah?' A far away voice, small and familiar.

'Yes, who's there?' Like a game of blind-man's buff – who is it? What have you got? Can you see me?

The sound of breathing, little shudders running down the line. Something like a little creak, perhaps a sob.

'Who's there, please?'

A whisper. 'I'm sorry to call you, love. It's Kari.'

'Mum?' Hot and cold patches played on Sarah's cheeks. She couldn't think where she was.

'Oh, darl, I was so pleased to get yer letter, so pleased for ya, really I am.'

'I'm at work, Mum.'

'I know love, I'm sorry.'

Sarah tapped at the desk. *Stop apologising.*

Ruth's voice kept coming. 'I got the number from Directory, I had to. Yer father doesn't know, but he'd love to see ya.'

Just bloody well get on with it. Tell me.

'We're going to stop.' There was silence except for the jagged breathing.

'Tell me.'

'She doesn't know we're there and we've let it be for so long, poor mite, but she's had pneumonia, coughing up terrible things, they keep treating her but it's just, it has to. The doctors have advised us to take her off the drip and stop treating her.'

'Starve her? Is that what they mean?' Sarah could hear laughter through the door, the squeals of a game of Hokey Kokey. She wanted to be out there, playing.

'No. Stop treating her, stop keeping her alive. But she doesn't know anything. She doesn't. Ya need to see her Sarah. Before she goes. Please.'

Sarah tried to draw the wall around her, tried not to have the tear slipping down her face and into her mouth, wiped at it madly, and at the others that followed, making her whole bloody face wet. This was not her problem, that sister, that life. She tried, tried to yell down the phone, 'I don't care,' but she didn't.

She said, 'I'll come home.'

Part Three

Twenty-Five

The train seemed empty by the time it got to the Hawkesbury River. Sarah looked out at the neatly spaced cement pylons left from an old bridge. Pelicans squatted on two of them. She pushed her nose flat against the glass, tried to see herself out there, on top of the pylons. Or falling into the river. She could feel, if she thought about it hard enough, the cool wash of the green. She could stay there, in the river. There were houseboats on the Hawkesbury. She remembered that from somewhere. She could live on a houseboat. Live there and not talk to anyone. Except maybe once a week when she had to park the boat and go to the local shops. It would be great. No-one could ever find her there. There was a Hawkesbury River stop, but the train zoomed past it. Sarah tried to sleep instead. Tried to read the sports pages of *The Herald*, left on the seat beside her. Tried to do anything but think of the house in Boolaroo or the hospital in Teralba.

That house. Before she'd left it, there had been a blanket quietness. They had crept around each other, that mother and that father. And Sarah too, creeping around, asking nothing, asking for nothing. Now and then at night, the dull thumps through the wall. Ruth had stopped screaming by then. All eyes looking at the ground. Once, Sarah had found Ruth crying. It was late at night, after a hospital visit day. Sarah woke up to the moon in her window and the sound of little sobs from outside her room. She opened the door and walked to the lounge, placing her feet carefully on the lino floor. Ruth was huddled on the ground, her head on the couch. Even in the dark, with just a sliver of moonlight, Sarah could see her back shaking from the crying. Sarah stayed, watching, silent, until the moon passed behind a cloud.

149

Then she went back to her bed. She didn't visit Kari after that. Persistent Vegetative State they said. Terrible shame, terrible accident. The day Sarah left, Ruth stood at the back door waving and saying 'be careful, be careful' and wiping tears from her face. As if anywhere could be more dangerous than that house.

No, that's enough. Fassifern already. Sarah counted through the stops, tried arranging them in alphabetical order and calculating the time between stations. Booragul. Sarah could see the glimmer of the lake in the distance. Tried to slow the train down with thoughts of Zan, standing small on the platform of Central station, her big medusa hair waving about. She could see the sludge of Cockle Creek before the train passed Teralba. Breath was coming tight in her throat. *Think harder.* Trying to remember other, newer things. But didn't want to remember Zan either. Not Zan, not the way she'd looked away when Sarah pushed the piece of paper into her hand, saying here's their number, ring me. Zan hadn't even said, sure, sure I will. Just looked away at the station clock.

The sign for Awabakaal flashed past outside the window. When Sarah saw the light shining off the cars piled up in the yard of Ted the Wrecker's, she pushed her fingers into her eyelids, hard. The smoke from the Sulphide. Everything looked grey.

The ticket office at Cockle Creek station was empty. Sarah watched the train curling away up the hill. Her shadow was long on the cement platform. A line of ants trailed from the closed door of the women's toilets, right across to the stairs. She stretched herself out on the warm concrete and watched. One ant had a crumb of something, twice as big as its own body. Sarah watched its long journey, the crumb held over its head. When she put her hand in front of it, the ant detoured. Just veered off and set itself off on the right course again. She put her hand in front of it again. Nothing, no change. She held her finger over the insect, moving so that she kept a shadow cast over the ant-trail. No response from the ant. Even when she brought her hand down close, right near the ant's head, nothing changed. They didn't seem to panic, ants. She pushed her finger flat against it, squashing it into the cement. The ant-trail continued. Ants crawled over the small corpse. Sarah's fingers smelt of something like aniseed. Ants guts. She put her forehead against the cement and lay like that until she heard footsteps on the gravel path outside the ticket office.

Across the road from the station, the sulphide works pumped grey-white clouds into the hills. The sulphide worker's club was right next to the station, a red brick building which looked more like a suburban house than a club. The gravel car-park was full.

She stood outside the glass doors, peering in at the shadowy shapes passing behind. A man in a green safari jacket came out through the door and held it open for Sarah. 'Going in?' He was all smiles.

'Is there a phone in there? I need to ring a taxi.'

'Where are you going? I'll give you a ride, sweetheart.'

'No thanks. Really. I'm fine.' But for some reason, she wanted to fall on the ground with laughter.

'Your loss. Phone's first on yer right.'

The carpet inside was a bright orange and brown check. The giggles in Sarah's chest were beginning to swim up her throat. A woman in red stilettos teetered over.

'Member?' She had lipstick on her teeth.

'Am I a member? No.'

'I'm sorry, members only, unless you can be signed in by a member. The book's over there.' The woman looked ready to teeter off again.

'I just want to use the phone. To ring a taxi.'

'Oh. Well then. Through here.'

The lipsticked woman followed her into the small square room with two red payphones lined against the wall. Like a guard-dog, she stood at the door, baring her teeth at Sarah. A large man-shape pushed past her. 'Just comin in to use the phone Dot. Gunna ring the old lady, teller to gedder bloody arse downere. Just won twenty bucks on the pokies.'

'Well done, Macka.' The woman touched him on the arm, as if there was any skill in sticking twenty cents in a slot and pulling handle.

'Hey,' Macka was looking over at Sarah, 'it can't be, can it?' He came closer, breathed right into her face. Lager. 'It is. It bloody-well is. Isn't it? I'll be buggered with a barge pole if this isn't Mal Sweet's kid.'

The lager and cigarette smell shot into Sarah's nose. The laughing had gone and the sickness was back. She pulled the rucksack back onto her shoulders and pushed past Macka, with him yelling behind her 'Hey, isn't it?'

She mumbled at the lipstick-woman 'I think I'll walk,' and shoved past her too, and out past the orange carpet and the glass doors, and out; into the hot grey air of Boolaroo.

Twenty-Six

A haze of heat floated above the road. Sarah could smell the tar, heating, heating, ready to bubble beneath the hard-pressed surface. On the other side of the road she could see the grey vats of the Sulphide, half masked by smooth billows of smoke. There was a stretch of green behind the vats and buildings, rolling hills, like a little England. The big grey buildings of the sulphide works sat in a squat line, casting shadows across the tar. A blue van beeped at Sarah as she crossed the road, staring at the smoke curling up and meeting with the clouds. She jumped, stuck her fingers up in the air, thought about yelling 'Piss-Off-Yobbo,' but didn't. Kept crossing the road instead, keeping her eyes on the cars. A green bus passed her.

The pack was heavy and bits on it dug into her back. She laid it down on the grass while she stood and looked up at the sulphide vat. If you fell into it, that vat, you would shrivel up in an instant. Like a slug with salt poured on you. Someone had once. Someone had fallen in, some bloke back sometime. Or maybe some kid had made up the story and she'd believed it. But imagine falling in there, shrivelling and burning up just like you'd never been anything, never taken any space. She wanted to try it, wanted to see.

There was a wire fence across the grass, in front of the big buildings that were like hangars, and way in front of the tubs of streaming acid. Barbed wire across the top. Sarah pressed her face into the wire mesh, so that bits of skin stuck through and she could feel the cold of the wire making marks on her cheeks. She pressed harder, wondering if the acid would work from the inside first. Up in the works, a siren sounded for smoke-o. They didn't have weekends in there, inside that tin factory. Sarah pulled away from the fence, running her fingers over her face, feeling for marks from the fence. There were none, you wouldn't see a thing.

And there was the grass, green as anything, and soft there under her feet while all the acid smoke puffed and puffed like something beautiful and safe. You could be tricked by these things, if you weren't careful.

Sarah looked back at the Cockle Creek station sign, polished and new, glinting in the sun. Cockle Creek was like the space between things, it wasn't even properly Boolaroo and Boolaroo was nowhere. She could see the ambulance station up ahead and walked towards it, trying to breathe nice and slow and easy. Her chest was tight, though, like someone had wrapped a bar around her. The fence of the sulphide works went on for ages, right past the ambulance station and up to the sign that said WELCOME TO BOOLAROO. Sarah had seen a thumb-sized book in a newsagency in the Cross once. It had a blue cover. *Aboriginal Place Names of Australia*. She'd looked up Boolaroo, hiding behind the magazine rack, her cheeks burning. *Boolaroo: Place of Many Flies*. She'd stolen the book and thrown it away, stuffed it into an over-full bin on Darlinghurst Road. Sarah leaned against the sign, and held her hand over her eyes like Steve McQueen, squinting into the sun.

Trees had grown up in front of the primary school, and a long red-brick building jutted out, masking the view. The sun was bouncing off the monkey bars. Sarah grabbed hard onto the straps of Zan's pack and kept walking. How had she never noticed the smoke, the warm sulphur smell all around the place? And those hills, she'd never noticed them, not really. There was a road leading up, away from the primary school, away from the monkey bars and new red brick. The hills were smooth and green at the top of the street. Houses – brightly coloured weatherboard – lined both sides of the steep road. Sarah breathed in, breathed out, and leaned forward, trying to ease the weight of the pack. The sulphur smell, mixed with, what? – other smells, strong and musky – got fiercer further up. There was a big house to the left of where the road ended and the hill started. Weatherboard, but new, newer than the others anyway.

Sarah slipped the pack off her back and rubbed her shoulders. There was a low fence separating the hill from the road, low enough to step over, even if you were a kid. Sarah stepped over it, just looking, just because. Behind the big new house, about half-way up the hill, were three vats – taller and wider than the houses – in a neat line. Smoke was only coming out of one, but the smoke was dark purple. No guards, no barbed wire, nothing. Sarah wanted Zan to be there, for Zan to laugh or be angry, or anything. She'd write and tell her – about smoke pouring across the green hill and into the bright shiny houses – be better than telling her about Mal Sweet and his two girls. Nothing to tell about that anyway. Nothing Zan should know, nothing that would help. She climbed back over the fence, trying to hold her breath in. As if crap didn't get into her lungs every day. She lived in Sydney, for flip's sake.

There was a big board in front of the new house, like in front of a church: SUNNYSIDE HOSTEL. It was two houses joined together really, Sarah could see that when she looked properly. Bloody hell, a hostel in the sunny grounds of the Sulphide Works Incorporated. Underneath the big letters, in smaller writing: HOME FOR THOSE IN NEED. Sarah wondered if she would count as one in need; one needing not to be in the house she was called to, one needing to be somewhere – anywhere – else. A wide verandah travelled round one side of the house; Sarah could see rocking chairs and even a hammock near the back. Long windows at the front, wide open, letting all that fresh smoke in. Even a little garden. Yellow flowers – marigolds or something – and waratah bushes. Sarah edged closer, right up to the flowers and leaned down, putting her nose deep into the yellow petals.

A door banged at the back of the house and she could hear footsteps shuffling along the verandah. The crumpled shape of a small man folded himself into a large cane rocking-chair. Sarah stepped back, grabbed the pack lying on the grass and heaved it onto her shoulders. The chair on the verandah rocked and a slurry song drifted up from it: 'Amaaazing Grace, saved a wretch like meee.' Sarah felt her stomach go tight and water begin to fill her mouth. A woman's voice called through the window, 'Orright Jack?' and Jack creaked and wheezed and said Orright back. The woman's voice sad, 'Areya goin out visitin today, Jack?' and Jack made a sound that could have been yes. The chair was in the shadows, but Sarah could see him now. Creased up like a pack of cigarettes and dropping bits of bread onto the ground. He coughed and started on 'How Great Thou Art'.

She didn't know why, but she was running. Feet tripping over rocks and themselves, the weight of the pack on her back making her run faster, almost falling down the street, down and back down to the main road, to the primary school with its yellow rooms and strange new brick. The whole of her face was tingling, and her throat was being squeezed tight.

The fence to the school was made of hard metal, with easy footholds on it. The school motto on a red shield was painted on a long banner flapping at the corner of what used to be the kindergarten. BOOLAROO PRIMARY SCHOOL: VERA VIRTUA VINCI NESQUIT – OUR TRUE WORTH SHALL NEVER DIE. Sarah's head swirled with her stomach, everything mingling into one. The school had the over-quietness of Sundays, the absence of squeals and shouts and screams making the buildings echo. Sarah's feet sounded loud on the cement path and louder on the wooden steps leading up to the headmaster's office. She peered in through the small glass square on his door – a new name, unfamiliar; why did she think it would be the same? – and saw only another door.

Sarah felt too big for the buildings; everything was built for small bodies. She looked into the junior girls' toilets, at the doll-sized bowls and washbasins. Couldn't imagine she'd ever been so small, so easily broken.

Water bubblers shone against the brick walls, Sarah had to kneel down to drink. The water didn't ease the tight band around her throat. Speakers were stuck on high poles in the middle of the playground – black and megaphone-shaped. Sirens for going-home time instead of bells? There was a slight click in Sarah's head, memory of roughness against her hands. She kept her hands in fists and pressed her teeth together as she walked around to the other side of the buildings. Still there, the wooden platform, the flagpole flying no flag, the bell. Painted blue, and rust showing through. No rope to ring it with. Sarah stared down at her hands, remembering. The sun burned behind her eyes and made her hands look red and bubbling. She could see blood rising up to the surface of her palms, could feel again, the rough, the scratching, the fierce red numbness of the rope on her hands, her hands on the rope. And rising, rising up, a tide from her stomach. The bunching up, the rush of saliva, the winding down of her head and the rush of vomit hurling up and through her mouth, shooting out and across the rostrum and landing in a splattered pile at the foot of the flagpole. Advance Australia Fair.

She rinsed her mouth at the junior girls' bubblers and hung her head between her knees for a while. Closed her eyes. The air was getting cold on her arms and there were no more shadows on the ground when she lifted her head up and walked the rest of the main road to the police station and that house.

Twenty-Seven

The brown wooden gate, streaked with dark Estapol. The wooden slats of a fence. The tin letter box in the shape of a house – where the hell had that come from? – stuck on a white post at the end of the driveway. The crunch of gravel, and the crescent-shaped flower bed in the middle of the green lawn. The shock of it, that moon-shaped bed edged by bright blue stones.

Sarah's chest heaved up, almost without her, and something stung her behind her eyes, like a pre-sneeze tingle. In the slat of sunlight cutting across the lawn, she could almost see – if she let herself remember – the crooked callipered figure digging away at her own 'special garden'. Kari who wanted the moon for her flowers. Kari who dragged stones from the back paddock, hobbling and pausing and clinking out songs. Bright blue. Bright bloody blue. Sarah felt her whole body swell and melt with a fierce tenderness. They had to be blue, she'd had to paint them blue like the sky; the sky cuddling the moon. Like the time she wanted her room painted purple with pink polka dots like Clown off *Adventure Island*. And Mal, ready with a paintbrush, ready to give it to her, to the special cripple – to give the blue stones, the polka dots, the moon. Sarah's melting stopped and she clenched her teeth together. There was no flower bed on the lawn which bore the shape of Sarah's hands or dreams.

The cement on the driveway was cracking near the gate, and the garage at the end of it, sitting like the plain sister next to the house, had been painted brown. Fenced by wooden rails, still black and white, the main paddock was horse-less. Dry, dry mouth. Hands clenching and unclenching. Sarah felt dizzy, wanted to run into the paddock, batter herself against the wooden

158

fence. Holding her breath in, placing each foot carefully, she walked up the cement steps: avoiding the scrape of her shoes, the sound of her steps, even the sound of her breath. She leaned her head against the red brick wall, pressing against its coolness. They'd put a new doorbell in. Very posh. One with a light shining in it for night-time visitors. Her hand was right next to the button, fingers spread out, wrist poking up all bony. All she had to do was move one finger, just one, and press. Not even hard, just the smallest bit of pressure would do it. They're very sensitive, those doorbells. One press, that was all. A slight shift of the wrist. Her hand seemed stuck though, planted too firmly on the wall.

It was like moving under water, trying to get somewhere with water pushing back against your body. So easy, it looks so easy, or you think it should be, but it takes so long, the resistance is so soft it tricks you.

When she finally slipped her finger on to the bell she'd almost forgotten where she was or what she was doing there. There was a brief chime – a low, plain note – a pause of not even a breath's length, and the door swung back.

'Yer here. I'm so glad ya came, love. I'm so glad.' The voice was small, a slight tremble in its corners. Ruth was on pause for a moment, frozen in the doorway.

The jumble of light behind her made a glow around her. Small. She was small, smaller than Sarah, standing there watching this woman, her mother, with her words all catching in her throat and then, as if the switch had been flicked, falling out falling out fast too fast and hanging for a moment on her lips and anything to close the space, cover the gaping hole, the huge distance and the what ifs and whys.

'I'm here, ha, finally, terrible journey, thought they'd have coffee on the train but they didn't of course oh well it's not a very long ride really and here I am anyway and I missed the earlier train and had a wander and well. Here I am then.'

The space closed between them with a squish of breath released. Ruth smelt of Estée Lauder White Linen. She left lipstick on Sarah's cheek, then stepped back, almost cautiously. 'Look at you, hey? Tea? Cup of tea? You must be exhausted, I bet.' Her nylon frock – red, carefully fitted with a blue Peter Pan collar – shone. Sarah noticed the blue pumps on her feet, carefully coordinated with the dress. 'Put your things in your room and I'll make some tea. Oh, Sarah.'

Sarah felt herself shrink. Suddenly knew she was not to speak of her life, not to remind this tiny stranger of her long absence. She smiled, squeezed Ruth's hand and said yes, tea would be lovely and she'd just be a moment. She could find her way to the room with her eyes closed.

Nothing was different in there. The two beds, metal-framed bunks, covered in pink chenille. The white teddy propped against one of the pillows. The shining windows. Oh, god, the shining windows. Sarah laid the pack against the bed closest to the door. Kari's bed.

She wanted to be lulled by sleep, to lay her head on the white teddy and just – accidentally – doze off. She pressed her hands against her temples, hard. Tea. Must have tea and be, what? Suitably polite? Suitably silent? She slipped her shoes off, stuffed her socks in them and trod softly, softly down the dark stairs to the too-familiar kitchen.

Ruth was all bustle. Clicking the tea pot down (knitted cosy in the shape of an owl) on the Laminex. Laying out two saucers, two cups (new and white) and even a milk jug and sugar bowl. Sarah smiled, felt skin stretching across her face. 'Lovely.'

'Nothing like it is there?' Ruth's chair scraped uncomfortably as she pulled it out. 'A warm cup of tea can do wonders.'

'Yes.' Sarah smiled again. Reminded herself not to tap her fingers on the table.

'Yer Dad's over at Teralba. He'll be back later. Mad pleased that he'll be seein ya. Oh,' Ruth clapped her hand over her mouth like a girl and pushed her chair back again, 'brownies.' She reached for the blue tin on the bench and put two chocolate slices on a plate. 'They're from the shop.'

'The Coffee Pot? Are you still working there? Really?'

'Assistant Manager. Full-time.' Ruth brushed her dress down,

160

the nylon whistling like a solitary cicada. She dabbed at the corners of her mouth carefully. 'I help with the ordering. Give lists to Mrs Saint Clare. Oversee.' She pronounced oversee as if it was a word which had got stuck somehow in her mouth, a too-large chunk of cake.

'You're joking.' Sarah swallowed too fast, the tea burnt at her throat. 'Are you serious? Oh,' she swallowed hard, trying for some cool saliva to ease the burning, 'that's wonderful. That's fantastic.'

'Chocolate Fudge Brownies, these are. American. Mrs Saint Clare saw them in the Marmong bakers – you know the Marmong bakers – and decided to give them a try. They sell like hot cakes. Have one. I brought them home specially.'

Sarah bit off a corner. 'Mmm. They're good.' She ate the rest quickly, tasting only the scalding of the tea.

Ruth reached for the blue tin, placed two more on the plate. 'They sell very well.'

Sarah smiled the tight-faced smile again, across the red Laminex table which sometimes haunted her dreams. Passed a quick smile like a pay-off to this painfully familiar woman making quick little dabs at her reddened mouth. Ruth had the brittle look of someone too made up, too eager to please.

Watching her, Sarah felt something like shame wimper its way around her skin. She reached for another brownie and brushed her hand across Ruth's, letting the contact last for a moment. Ruth bit her lip and rubbed at her eyes, then smiled at Sarah.

'You should see all the changes we've had. Lots of changes. Didja see the lock-up's been done over? Metal door. Sky-blue they painted it. Honestly, you'd think it was the Taj Mahal in India the way your father fussed about.'

'I went up near the hills, up Fourth Street. There were loads of places up there painted red and yellow and blue. Has there been some kind of award for weirdest colour schemes?' Sarah rubbed her hands on her knees, began to breathe easy.

'The Sulphide bought them up, all those places. Dunno why they painted them like that, they just did. They rent them out.

161

Sam White sold his place up there and now he rents it from the Sulphide for practically nothing. His own place.'

'Is that so they can't sue when they get poisoned from the bloody fumes?'

Ruth bunched her forehead up and flicked her fingernails in and out against her thumb. That smile stretched across her face again. 'It's very low rent.'

Sarah breathed in, very very deep. 'So, the lock-up's sky-blue. What a laugh.'

The two women looked at each other in silence. Sarah stretched her hand out again, this time letting her fingers entwine with Ruth's. Both hands were cold.

'Ya sister. We'll go tomorrow. First thing. Thanks for coming, love.' Ruth wiped at her nose with the back of her hand. 'Here, darl, have some more tea.'

Sarah's voice came out in an almost whisper. A croaky late-night voice. 'No, I'm sorry, I'm really bushed. I just need, do you mind if I crash? If I go to sleep? I'm sorry, I'm so. So. It's lovely, lovely to see you. The brownies are lovely, Mum.' It felt strange in her mouth, that word, Mum. Like oversee.

Twenty-Eight

A slice of sunlight cut across Sarah's face, right over her eyes. She turned on her stomach, burying her face in the pillow. Fresh and clean and unfamiliar. The sunstream warmed the back of her head, a burning patch at the nape of her neck. Her mouth felt salty and some wafty thing was tanging at her nostrils. She slid her hand across the bed, searching for the warm patch of Zan. There was only the end of the bed, too soon, a sharp drop into air. Her eyes felt sticky, but she squeezed them open, looking across to the matching bed next to hers, with the rucksack laid out like a body on top. Her throat felt sticky too, her mouth, everything felt suddenly sticky and breath didn't know how to force its way through. Sarah sucked and sucked at thin air, opening her mouth right up, but her chest was closed, her throat was too tight. Her body went hotcoldhot; her chest was small, too small for breath and sharp needles stabbed at her eyes. Her mouth was open, sucking like a baby at the air, but nothing was coming out. She wanted Zan's puffer, or a straw to breathe through, anything to let her breathe again. And speak. She couldn't think how to scream, though she bashed on the wall with her hand. *Breathe. Breathe. Breathe.* But the breath wouldn't come.

Bacon. That's what the smell was, sizzling at her nostrils. The thought cut through, clear as breath, and suddenly her chest was open again, her throat welcoming gulps of air. She lay for a moment, watching her chest rise and fall. *In, out, in, out. Nice and easy, nice and slow.* She could hear pans clattering below her, sounds drifting up through the floorboards, and Ruth's voice coming through as a soft murmur. It had been there all along probably, that sound, but sometimes you just don't notice things. Not if you're trying too hard to breathe. There was a deeper murmur, a kind of grunt, coming through the floor. Mal. Zan's absence was a hard solid gap in between the voices. Sarah looked for the crack in the ceiling, the snake-shaped one with the dog shape at the end of its mouth. Still there. Of course. Where else would it be? Remembered the rule: if the snake didn't swallow the dog it would be all right, everything would be all right.

The sharp ring of the telephone cut over the murmuring and clattering, and Sarah's breath stopped again, just for a moment. *Zan, Zan, Zan.* It was Mal's voice she could hear, making hello noises, with little pauses between grunts. *Zan. Zan. Zan.* Sarah swung herself up, letting her feet touch the floor, and waited for the summons. She would tell her it was mad, this place, and tell her about the Sulphide clogging up the land, and tell her she'd be back in just a couple of days and tell her not to go wild or do anything stupid.

'Sarah.' A gentle tap on the door.

'I'm coming, Mum. Is it Zan?'

'Sorry darl? Can I come in?' The door opened anyway – tough luck if she'd said no. Ruth stood in the doorway, the mission brown of the corridor framing her, holding out a blue bundle. 'I found yer old dressing gown. Dooya want it? I thought it might be useful, you know, when you're here. I'll just put it here, anyway, on the other, on Kari's bed. It's there if ya want it. Now. There's bacon, eggs, toast, beans. Whaddaya want?'

'Was the phone for me?'

'No, love, areya expecting someone to ring?' Ruth's eyes had opened wide. Surprise, presumably.

'Maybe. Doesn't matter.'

'Bacon, beans and eggs?' Ruth's voice was almost crisp.

'Just coffee, Mum. Thanks. I'll be out in a minute.'

When Sarah padded down to the kitchen a few minutes later, wrapped in her blue dressing gown, a plate of bacon, eggs and toast sat steaming on the table next to a white tea cup full of coffee. 'I thought just in case you changed your mind. Breakfast is the most important meal of the day, you know that, don't you? Just have a bit.'

'Thanks, Mum. It smells lovely. Great. Thanks.' Trying not to look at the hands wrapped around the edges of the upright newspaper at the end of the table.

The hands made a flicking motion, folding the paper in and down. 'Gidday, Mate. Arya Orright?' Mal's face, when it emerged from behind the paper, looked flabby and worn. How had he got old so quickly?

'Gidday, Dad.'

'More toast, love? Coffee?' Ruth fluttered to Mal's side, snatching away his plate and cup. Moving as though her whole self was being held in, shrunk into one of those Firm 'n' Hold garters she used to push herself into.

'Sarah? Toast?'

'I'm fine, Mum. I haven't started on this yet.'

'Leaver alone, ay? Ledder bloody arrive first.' Mal flicked nothing upwards except his eyes, and Ruth scuttled away, heading for the bench. 'Got a new chestnut stallion over in Teralba you'll wanna see, Mate. Bloody bewdy he is. Never been schooled properly. Bucks and pig-roots around like nobody's business. Not for long, though. He'll be a gelding before too long, serves him bloody well right as well. So. Betta getta ride while ya can, before he turns into a lamb.'

Ruth slipped a full plate of toast in front of him. The china didn't even make a sound, didn't even clink, when she put it down. Sarah tried to smile at her. 'Nothing wrong with lambs.' That's all, that's all Sarah said; but her ears were ringing as if she'd just torn down the bloody Berlin Wall.

When he stood up, tipping his chair back on one leg and swinging it into the table like in a dance, Mal looked even looser in his skin. Smaller than she remembered, smaller than he should have been. It wasn't right for him to be shrunk like that. Sarah tried to rub at her memories, easing or erasing or making things fit. His eyes looked past Sarah, past Ruth, past everything. Like an old man. A twisting little fear bit and chewed and gnawed way inside Sarah's bones. She squeezed at her temples for a moment. *The snake did not get the dog. It did not. It did not.* Mal ruffled her hair and said he was off to Teralba because if he didn't keep an eye on this saucy bloody stallion, who would, and not to get herself into trouble. Then he said seeya and banged the screen door shut behind him.

Not to get into trouble. What the hell did he think she was doing here? But that was the thing, she was supposed to have never been away, there was nothing going on, that was the rule. That had always been the rule. The taste of vomit filled her mouth. She wanted to yell hard at Ruth, wisping away in the shadow, washing and wiping dishes: but it came out soft as soft. Soft as a lamb. 'I'll get dressed and then we can get a move on to the hospital. To see Kari.' Wanted to add, *that's what I'm here for, remember? That's why we're here*, but instead said: 'Is there a bus that goes straight there?'

Ruth folded the Snugglepot and Cuddlepie tea-towel (with a green crocheted edge) and hung it over a bar on the oven. Straightened it up, adjusting and adjusting. 'There is one, I think, but I'll drive. It's quicker.'

Sarah's head twirled madly. Her tongue felt as if it had been weighed down and when she spoke, it felt like her words came from a hollow space way behind her mouth. 'Drive? Drive a car?'

Ruth gave a final flick to the tea-towel and began polishing the stove-top. Beaming. 'Mrs Saint Clare taught me. Spent ages learnin, must have been, uhh, easily a year that I spent learnin. Terrified, ruddy terrified. Didn't believe I could do it and I didn't tell yer father, of course. Mrs Saint Clare – kept saying, go on, just have a little drive, nothing needs to come of it, just to have a go, you know? Then one day, I went for a little drive with her, laughing me head off all the way about some customer who'd been in and spent all day eating scone after scone – I think he'd had twelve scones or something, would you believe that? Anyway, I'm driving along and Mrs Saint Clare says, just pop up to Charlestown, I need to pick some things up, so I do and then before I know it, she's directed me into the ruddy licensing office, doya believe that? Well, I didn't even have a chance to be nervous. Did the test, still giggling about the scones mind you, and got it first go. I nearly died. Doreen White from the doctor's sold me her Austin for a hundred and fifty dollars. She was going to scrap it, honestly, and it's fine, it's really fine. So,' Ruth suddenly looked around the kitchen and a hand fluttered to her chest, 'we don't need a bus anyway.'

Sarah stared hard at Ruth, rubbing at her ears, at her eyes. She was talking, Ruth was talking, and you could see her shape, the whole of it. She took up a whole corner of that kitchen.

There was silence for a moment, while Ruth pulled herself in. She looked at Sarah, eyes down then quickly up. 'I had to. I had to drive. To get to the hospital. I don't drive if I'm going anywhere with yer father, of course.'

Sarah looked again at the corner of the kitchen where Ruth had been shining. The sun was behind a cloud and only shadow was slipping in the kitchen window. Ruth looked like another small patch in the darkness.

The Austin was small and the engine sounded like a series of explosions, but Ruth indicated, swerved, changed gears, pulled the handbrake on and off, braked in time to avoid a bus pulling out in front of her and overtook a green wagon on the Bay Road. Sarah kept turning her face to look at Ruth, at Ruth driving. Ruth's small wrists against the wheel, her feet in blue slippers – driving shoes – braking and clutching and accelerating. She was even more of a stranger than the lipsticked-up, desperate-to-please Ruth who had opened the door the night before. Sarah tried to fit it together: the shadow-silent Ruth and the shining, driving Ruth. She couldn't make it fit, so she stared ahead thinking of the smells of hospital. *I am not like my sister, I am not like my sister.*

'Gawd she loved you. Doted. Ruddy doted.' Ruth's voice came from far away, far outside of Sarah.

'What?' Trying not to jump, not to look caught out.

'Yer sister. Didn't she? Remember those songs she used to sing. All those bloody songs.'

Sarah was quiet. Her voice so quiet. 'I sang songs too. I sang lots of songs.' Sounding pathetic, really pathetic. She could kick herself.

'I know ya did, love. Look up on the hill, see the extension they've built to the hospital. Very new, oh it's lovely, it really is. Two new wings they built. Moved everyone around, moved yer sister from that horrible gloomy ward – what was it called? I can't remember can you? – anyway, they've put her in the other new wing, ya can't see it from ere. Princess Wing it's called, isn't that lovely? Princess Wing.'

The Austin swung across the road and into a long driveway. Ruth's unpolished nails tapped at the steering wheel as she drove. She pulled into a space labelled DISABLED PARKING ONLY and looked straight at Sarah. Mascara was running down her cheeks with her tears. Two thin black rivers on either side of her nose.

Twenty-Nine

The nurse on the desk at the entrance to the Diana Ward in the Princess Wing smiled and waved at Ruth. There was a shiny photograph on the wall with HRH THE PRINCESS OF WALES written on it in curly writing. Sarah watched the reflections her feet made on the gleaming tiles. Long fluorescent tubes hung from the ceiling, making white stretches of light on the floor which Sarah tried to walk in. It was like step-on-cracks-break-ya-mother's-back. Careful, careful, careful. Even the white of the nurses' uniforms reflected on the floor in smooth white squares. The uniforms had been blue before, and the floor a dull brown. The smell hadn't changed though. Sharp, piercing in through the nostrils.

The Baden-Powell Ward, that was it, the ward she'd been in before. The be bloody prepared ward, for it might happen to you ward. A dim shape danced behind Sarah's eyes: a shape from that other ward, with the brown floors and blue-uniformed nurses. Kari strapped in and strapped around, with pins and needles poking in her everywhere and Ruth sobbing and sobbing and Sarah in her school uniform glaring at Ruth and glaring at a nurse who didn't know where the drinks machine was and yelling at her that she was a stupid slut of a nurse. She hadn't looked at Kari after that, just stayed near the window, kicking her feet on the floor and waiting to go. Most of the other visits she'd practised number patterns in her head, just sat staring at the wall, going *three-five-seven-ten-twelve-fourteen-sixteen-nineteen*. Or sometimes just counting in twos or threes. She usually got up to at least fifteen hundred before she was ready to fall asleep right on the visitor's chair beside the bed.

It was there again, the far-away feeling, like she was floating away, like nothing could touch her. The no-feeling feeling. She watched her feet stomp along the Diana Ward, but as if her head and all the inside of her was somewhere else, away from her body.

Ruth pushed at a pair of wooden swing doors. There were three beds in a row, each surrounded by a small nestle of brown chairs and a crowd of pipes and tubes. The walls were a pale green, and fresh air was blowing through the room through a large open window. A tree was just outside, the leaves rubbing at the window, and Sarah could hear a faint chirping. Other sounds in the room. Not chirping, gurgling. Coming from the bed at the end of the room, a throaty watery gurgling. Breathing through snot. Sarah didn't want to look. It wasn't Kari, that was for sure, not that one up there, gurgling.

'Hello, darl. Look who's here to see you.' Ruth's voice was over-loud and bright, yelling towards the centre bed and bending towards it, all cheerful. She turned to Sarah. 'See, it's very bright isn't it? It's a lovely room, really. That's David over there.' She pointed to the end bed, mouthed the words 'car crash' and sat down on one of the vinyl chairs.

Sarah nodded and sat, thinking instead of Zan's curls, Zan's laugh. Then, no, that didn't work, that led to places she didn't want to be, so she remembered instead the shape of her old high-school uniform: the square box pleats and thin belt. The precise shade of bottle green, and how her white collars had always been dirty inside the neck and how she'd hitched her skirt up over her belt so that she could have room to swing her legs.

There was a coughing sound next to her, creaking and cackling. She tried harder to remember, but the coughing was right there. Coming from the small shape on the bed, the small shape with the clear tubes leading from its nose and mouth and arm and joining into one long container propped up on a metal stand. Her hair had been cut short, cropped close to her head and her eyes were still open, staring like before. The coughing made her body shake and her eyes roll back, like a shaken doll.

170

'They say it's muscular, all the coughing, but it's been worse lately. The infection's set in. She's had loads, loads of infections, it was only that this one was so much worse that they said not to use the antibiotics. I dunno if she knows ya here, but say hello just in case, love. Garn.'

'Hi Kari.' Sarah couldn't make her voice loud and bright like Ruth's. She'd never been able to do that, not in all the visits to that other ward, the Baden-Powell ward, with all the nurses saying how sad, so sweet, so easy for them to fall and hurt themselves when they're like that. And Sarah sitting, back then, with her mouth closed and her eyes fixed on a point far away. If she'd learnt one thing from Ruth, it was that, how to do that.

There was another coughing sound from the figure on the bed, the un-Kari Kari. Some dribble fell from her mouth and slid down onto the sheet. It was thick and dark, not clear at all, like normal spit, but almost black. Ruth pulled a hankie from her sleeve and leaned over to wipe the cheek of un-Kari. 'That's the girl, it's okay, love, no need to worry, ay? Nothing to worry about. Hold this would ya, Sarah?'

A sharp taste filled Sarah's mouth. The black spit covering the hankie (ladies', lace-edged). She remembered then, the other chant. *This is not my sister, this is not my sister.*

Ruth was fluffing pillows up and smoothing the sheet under the shape's chin. 'They're usually very good in here. Neat. Clean windows.' She gave a final flick to the sheets.

'Good.' Sarah smiled across the bed at Ruth. Made sure she didn't look at the face attached to the shape lying on the bed. Too thin, the face and the shape.

Ruth smoothed at her skirt. 'Sometimes I read to her. Every third or fourth day after work I come. I stopped coming every day after you left. She doesn't know. They tell us she doesn't know anything. It's not like turning off a life-support machine. It's not like that. They just stop treating her, that's all. We should have let it happen at first, but we wanted, I did, I wanted it to be okay, I thought something might happen.'

'Something already had happened.' She didn't want to talk

171

about it, didn't want to remember, but the numbness wouldn't come back. She clenched her teeth together, let the fury be there instead.

Ruth was silent, smoothing the sheets again.

'Oh for fuck's sake, the sheets are fine. Just leave it, Mum. This place stinks anyway.'

Ruth scrabbled for her purse, keeping her eyes down. 'I'll go and get some coffee. Would you like a cake from the canteen? Biscuits?'

'No. Nothing. Just leave it.' *Just shut up.*

'Okay darl. Fine.' The wooden doors swung heavily behind Ruth tottering on red heels.

That coughing again and more black gunge dribbling down. Sarah didn't want to touch it, just left it there on the pillow and on the chin of the shape. On the chin of Kari. Once, early on in the Baden-Powell ward, just after it happened, Sarah had been left alone with Kari. She'd tried to look into Kari's eyes, tried to send signals with her own, was sure – just for a moment – that they'd been received. She'd been trying to say something important, wanting to send an important message to Kari, one that would make her get better. So she'd sat and stared into the mixed-up brown and green of her sister's eyes and thought *come on, Kari* really hard. Then she'd thought that maybe Kari wouldn't want to get better, because she'd have to tell what happened. So then Sarah tried to send to her: *You'll never have to tell. I won't tell. Just wake up.* She was sure the message had gone through. But it was just the flicking about of the eyes really fast, that did it, made you think there was something going on in there inside the head. That was the biggest mistake, to think that, because nothing was. Nothing was going on. It was just muscular, like the coughing, and Sarah had been really, really stupid to think that it might get through. This time, alone with Kari, Sarah said nothing and thought nothing. She didn't even have to concentrate on it, she could just make her mind blank blank blank.

'Hot chocolate and chocolate shortcake, just in case. Do ya know, I think they're building another wing over across the

172

courtyard. There's some building or somethin goin on there. Cement mixers and stuff. Hereya go, love, take it.' Ruth handed a flimsy paper plate to Sarah, with a squashed looking slice on it.

'I don't want a cake. I said I didn't.'

'No love, I know, it's just in case.'

Just in case what? In case the hospital got besieged by Martians and they had no food and Sarah would survive because of her wonderful chocolate shortcake? Just in case she starved?

'When do they stop feeding her?' Sarah sounded sharp-edged and hard, that was good.

The steaming coffee in Ruth's hand spilt. 'Dunno love. It's not feeding anyway. They'll talk to us about it tomorrow.'

Sarah ran her nail across the top of the shortcake. *How can you not know about your own daughter. You learnt to drive, for god's sake, you're not stupid.*

Ruth took a sip from the coffee. 'I made the decision to have them stop. I want your father to be here when they name the time.' When she looked across the bed at Sarah, her eyes looked bright and clear. 'I'm doing the best I can, that's all.'

Thirty

Mal was almost cheery behind the wheel of the Holden, talking about the chestnut-stallion-soon-to-be-a-gelding, and singing 'Five Hundred Miles'. Sarah sat silent in the back seat, while Ruth – tucked small and helpless into the passenger seat – made soft little sounds: oh yes, and uh-huh, and joined in on the chorus of the song, but softly softly. Ruth, scrunched up so tiny in the front seat – the seat with the ladies' vanity mirror attached to the inside of the sun visor – that you would never have known that she could drive and overtake and oversee. Sarah pushed her back into the sticky vinyl of the back seat and watched Ruth be silent and fluttery and wanted to hit her for being so stupid.

Mal drove at twenty miles an hour, or sometimes twenty-five, and all along the winding road cars were banked up behind them. He drove even slower when people beeped their horns or flashed their lights at them, pumping the brakes to let them know he was slowing down and not to mess with him. Just before they reached the hospital, he looked in the rear-view mirror at Sarah and said, hey mate remember how we drove to Gundegai, to where the dog sat on the tucker box? Sarah let her breath out in a long slow stream, a big *haaa* of breath, and said yeah, Dad, that's right, yeah I remember. Even though she knew that they'd never driven to Gundebloodygai, they'd just sung that stupid song, endlessly, everywhere they drove together. She wasn't sure whether he really believed it, really thought for some weird reason that they had driven to Gundegai, or whether it was meant to be a joke. She did a half smiley sort of thing with her mouth, just in case, because it was better to be safe than sorry.

There was no-one on the reception desk at the hospital and

Mal wanted to get some lemon barley drops from the box-sized kiosk in the Elizabeth II Wing, so Sarah and Ruth waited on a long bench while he wandered off, whistling. Sarah kicked her feet against the floor and Ruth flicked through a *New Idea* she'd found on the low table beside the bench, licking her fingers before she turned the pages. In the quiet, Sarah looked sideways at her, ready to yell, scream out, *why are you so silent?* She didn't though, she kept it to herself, same as always.

'Here we are, I got em. No worries.' Mal strode along the corridor like the guest of honour at a royal wedding. Prince Mal. Prince Mal of Boolaroo. 'Come on then, ya lazy buggers, on ya feet.' He was all bluff and bravado, loud and happy-faced. Pretending he was at a frigging party. He didn't look at Kari though, when they finally got into the ward. He kept his eyes way above the bed, still blustery cool, looking at the ceiling and the windows and saying, hey Blossom, really loud. As if she could hear. As if she would answer him even if she could. Sarah and Zan had watched a live courtroom drama on the little black and white portable once – it was a real court-case and they'd just stuck a camera in there and filmed the whole thing – some case about a date rape. American. The bloke had been this whiter-than-white-big-teeth-square-jawed college king who kept smiling all the way through and making little jokes and saying how the girl just loved him so much. She had curly ribbons in her hair, the girl, and wouldn't stop crying, which was annoying because you couldn't understand what she was saying half the time through the snivels. The guy called the girl Petal, he kept saying, hey Petal really loud, just like Mal. The girl was chucked out of college for making false accusations.

Two doctors came in – white coated men saying, hello Mrs Sweet how-are-you, and not waiting for an answer. Sarah looked straight past them, making her face say she didn't want to be introduced, didn't care who they were, which didn't really matter because all they said was, 'is this your daughter then? Good.' As if there wasn't a daughter already lying on the bed. They didn't look at Sarah again.

The black stuff was coming out of Kari's mouth again, and Sarah looked right at her face this time. She looked like paper, her skin all crinkly and grey-tinged. Her eyes were open, they were always open, but hardly even flicking about any more. Still coughing, the shuddering running through her small body and making the crisp sheets tremble. The doctors were talking, Sarah could hear them but as if from far away: *checked blood plasma, gasses, components, quicker if, less painful, yes, absolutely.* Blah blah bloody blah. Their voices sounded dim and muffled, distant drones going on and on and bloody on. The sheets on the bed shook again, shook with the coughing. She could go far away, Sarah, far away from the thin paper skin. Someone touched her arm.

'Orright, love?' Ruth was squeezing her hand, hard.

'Yair, okay Mum.'

The doctors had stopped droning on. One of them had left and the other one – dark-haired and round – was muttering with Mal and scribbling on a clip folder. He gave the folder and pen to Mal – a signature – then left, his white coat making a billowy cloud behind him.

'Right. Lessgo.' Mal was gatherer, wrapping them up, pushing them out with all his bluster. 'Over and done with anyway, that's the way. That's the best. Best for everyone.'

Ruth scuttled ahead of him, dabbing at her eyes and mouth and making soft agreeing noises. Her back was stiff though, Sarah could tell, even paces away from her she could see that. Mal looked bigger with Ruth in front, scuttling away, all hunched over like that. He would shrink in an instant if she stood up. It was only when Mal opened the back door of the Holden for her and half shoved her inside – meant to be a friendly pat on the back maybe but really it was almost a shove, making sure she got in the car – that she realised she'd done it too. Just scuttled along behind him, asking no questions, making no sounds. She didn't even know what was going on, what had happened, what anyone had agreed. No-one asked her anything.

Mal slid into the driver's seat and slammed the front door. The skin sagged around his ears; the back of his head was sunburnt and sandpapery. Except just near the neck, below the end of his thinned-out hair, there was a patch of skin, smooth and pink and loose. Soft looking, like it would tear. It wasn't fair, it wasn't fair for him to make her hate him so much and then to let her see that one weak bit of flesh.

All the way back to Boolaroo she watched that patch of skin and tried not to feel the ache in her belly and tried not to hear Ruth saying that was it: that was it, no more treating Kari, dignity this, peace that – as if dignity or peace had ever been important in Boolafuckingroo. Sarah tried to make herself, no she *did* make herself, go away far away and only hear the blah, blah, blah of Ruth's bloody endless voice. That was good then, because she hated that, the endless rattling on, the never shutting up of the stupid voice, and then she could think about that, feel about that, the hating and the fury instead. Instead of the soft skin and the shape on the bed and the black gunk and herself saying, *I won't tell, you'll never have to tell.*

Mal parked the Holden on the front verge; he never used to do that, said that's what hooligans did, but now he drove right up over the gutter and parked there like he didn't even care. He slammed the screen door when he went into the house. Ruth stayed behind him, stayed on the front porch spitting on her hankie and rubbing at the doorbell even though it was only plastic. Shrinking right inside herself. When Sarah went into the kitchen, Ruth followed like a pet and started pulling bleach and surface cleaner and Windex and rags and window chamois cloths out of the cleaning cupboard. Sarah sat silent at the table while Ruth scrubbed around her, making puffing noises with her mouth and nose.

'Yer gunna have to move, love, I'll need to do that floor. It's flamin filthy, look at it.' Ruth piled chairs upside down on the table.

Sarah looked. 'It's clean, Mum. There's nothin wrong with the bloody floor. Siddown, for god's sake.'

'Oh I couldn't, darl. The whole house is in a real state. I've let it go. Ya can hardly see through the windows, they're that filthy.'

'When are they gunna stop feeding her?'

'Whaddaya mean?'

'When will they stop feeding Kari?'

Ruth paused in her scrubbing and looked at Sarah. 'You were there, darl. They've stopped treating her, if that's what ya mean. They stopped today. We'll be out there first thing. Move yer feet.'

Sarah felt the silence fill her mouth with dryness. Her whole body swelled with all, all the silence. All the time of saying nothing, of never telling. And they'd just left, just got up and gone like that was it, no point hanging around waiting. She put her feet down hard on the floor, hoping to buggery that they left big filthy black marks. 'You didn't even tell me. You didn't, so, what? That's it, is it? Not that there's any frigging point in saying good-bloody-bye.'

'Please Sarah. We'll be out first thing. She won't, she doesn't, we don't know how long it will take. They've treated her so many times, she's got so many bugs goin' on inside her it's just not true.' She looked at Sarah, looked right at her. 'We're not starvin her, stop sayin it like that. We're not treating her. That's all. And it's better, just not to use the antibiotics. They said it would be better. This way.' Ruth squeezed at the cloth in her hand. She pushed her lips together, but a little sound, a whimper, came out of them.

Sarah turned away. 'You didn't tell me. You didn't tell me anything.'

The cloth flew hard out of Ruth's hand, right across the kitchen. It landed smack on the wall and stuck there. Her voice came out loud, loud as Mal's, and sharp-edged. 'For God's sake, Sarah, you were there, you were listening. *It's not my fault.*'

Her yelling hung in the air for a moment, bouncing around in the silence. Sarah stared at her, her heart going bang, bang, bang, in her ears.

Ruth put her hand against her chest, took a deep breath in, then picked up the window chamois cloth from the bench, not looking at Sarah's face. The scrape of Sarah's chair as she pushed it back sounded loud in her own ears.

Outside, the sky-blue of the lock-up melted into the sky. Sarah stood on the bottom step, her hand resting on the rail, remembering King Jack and a finger tracing through the lock-up bars. The police station had had a new extension built to it. New white brick. Two new sergeants in there Mal had said, and three constables – a big operation. She kept her eyes on the new wing and walked, one foot in front of the other, across the grass. Her whole body felt like paper and she could see her hands shaking. But Kari was dying today or tomorrow or next week and it had to be someone's fault. Manslaughter it would be, wouldn't it? And Kari wasn't even a man. Vomit at the back of her throat. They wouldn't believe her, would they, they wouldn't listen, surely? But she kept walking, closer and closer to the door of the station, being careful not to think too hard. Just walk. The grass crisp under her feet, rustling against her shoes.

The sign above the station was one of the new blue and white electric ones: POLICE in nice big safe letters. She'd seen a poster, way back, way back in the Boolaroo Primary School. It was a picture – a photo – of a big friendly policeman bending down and listening to a little boy. Underneath, in black letters: POLICE: WHEN YOU'RE IN TROUBLE, WE'RE HERE TO HELP. But what if the police were the problem, if they started the trouble, what then? The door was open and she poked her head in first, then her body. There was only one sergeant inside the new office. It smelt of furniture polish and the sergeant looked too young and shiny, like the doctors. He looked up when she came in.

'Gidday. You lookin for ya dad? I saw ya leavin this mornin. He's out the back in the paddock, or he was a minute ago. Givin Macka's new Arab a fair bloody thrashin. Two years old and the poor bastard's not been broken yet. Bloody criminal. Still, if anyone can do 'im, Mal can, ay? Ya can go out the side door, if ya want.'

Sarah smiled and said, no thanks, it was okay, she'd go out the way she came in, and backed herself out the door.

He was in the back paddock. He'd been there all along. She stood near the shed, well back in the shadows, and watched him. He'd taken his shirt off and thrown it on the ground, right in the dirt, and he still had the trousers on from the hospital visit. Stupid bastard hadn't even got changed. He was bent forward, right up close to the horse's ears and his body looked wet. He didn't have a whip, he was just belting at the horse with his hand, yanking on the reins with the other hand, so that the horse kept turning around on itself and bucking all over the place and every time it bucked he'd belt it harder. She could see the blood at the corners of the horse's mouth, it was running down its chin and Mal was yelling in its ears, 'carn, ya bastard, you can give me more than that.' She leant against the wood of the shed, very very quiet, watching his rage. Her head felt light and her lips moved, but no sound came out: poor bastard. Poor bastard. She almost ran forward, almost yelled over the fence: 'yer not angry, ya stupid bloody bastard, ya know yer not.' Standing in the shadow of the shed, she could see that the fury, the wet on his back, all the sweat running down him like water, it was the closest he could get to tears.

Thirty-One

It felt endless, the driving back and forth to the hospital. Like the back-and-forthing of the ferries across the Harbour, the endless trips Sarah had used to fill herself: but without the soothing wash of water, or the comfort of invisibility. There was a bubbling happening beneath Sarah's skin. Something rash-like, ready to break out and spread across her flesh. At the hospital, she stared ahead, making herself absent while pale-skinned nurses wiped at Kari's mouth, measured her pulse, waited. Sarah was like Kari – saying nothing, keeping her mouth shut. Driving back to the house each day, she stared at the back of Mal's head, listened to him sucking his teeth. Wanted to ride like him, ride hard enough and rough enough to have sweat like tears all running down her body, to at least feel something, to at least get near it. Sometimes she could find a solid edge of hate inside her belly – she had to look hard, probing for it, coaxing up memories or wishes: but mostly, even the anger had gone. She was limp, feeling nothing, nothing at all.

After four days, it felt like for ever. Waiting and staring over Kari's head and drinking sickly coffee and driving to and from and to and from. Sleeping-waking-eating-driving-hospital-eating-hospital-driving-eating-sleeping-waking. It was stupid, all very stupid and Zan hadn't phoned, not even once.

After four days of waiting for something to happen and four days of nurses saying, no it could take weeks and four days of waiting for Zan to phone and thinking maybe she'd phoned while they were all at the hospital, how about that for an idea, Sarah woke up on the floor next to her bed. She had no memory of having fallen from the skinny single bed onto the floor, and no aches or bruises. Her body still felt sleepy though, desiring softness, and there was a chiming sound in her ears. Loud and high, bell-like. She sat up, rubbing her legs. The dinging sound didn't stop. Ringing. Doorbell. She counted eight dings of the bell before she wrapped the fluffy blue dressing gown about herself and scuffled downstairs, holding tight to the stair-rail.

The back door banged shut. 'Was that the door, darl? I've been tidying up the garden since dawn. Absolute state. At least yer up now anyway.' Ruth was all rush, gloves and gardening fork in her hand.

Sarah leaned against the wall, her arms folded cross herself. The doorbell rang again.

'Hold these willya, love? Ta.' Ruth shoved the dirt-covered gloves and fork into Sarah's hands and pushed past her to the door. Even as she put her hand to the handle, the bell rang again. 'Oh ruddy hell, talk about impatient.'

Light swooped into the hall as she pulled the door open. Sarah squinted out into the sun, trying to look through the brightness, but it made her eyes swim and all she could see were bright shapes dancing in front of her eyes.

'Jack Fir, ya lovely old bugger, fancy meetin you here, ay?' Ruth's voice was loud and warm, bouncing about like the sun.

There was a raspy mumbling from the doorway. Sarah shifted closer to the door, trying to peer out. He was a hunched-up shadow on the porch. His voice was loud, but the words all slurred together. 'Fffprot some flouhs for her.' Even with the sun in her eyes and the shape of Ruth in front of him and the distance of half the hallway between them, Sarah could see the spit flying from his mouth.

'Ah Jack, yer the biggest sweetheart this side of the black stump.' Ruth's voice was still warm, but something like surprise was in it. She took a handful of flowers from Jack's hand. 'Bless ya, darl.'

The door clicked shut behind her and Ruth leant against the wall. Her shoulders moving up and down and a gentle sobbing

182

falling from her mouth. Her face crumpled in on itself, became small and creased up like Jack's face, and the sobbing for a moment grew loud. Sarah looked at her feet, then at the wall, then went into the kitchen. Opened the fridge door, pulled out orange juice and drank from the bottle. Grinding her feet into the cool lino. The sobbing in the hall settled and Ruth followed her into the kitchen. She had three marigolds in her hand.

'He brought her flowers from her own bloody garden. He's a bloody character and a half I swear. Still the flamin same too.' Ruth filled a Vegemite glass with water and put the marigolds in it. 'They built a residential hostel up the road, but he still wanders about all over the ruddy shop – drops in here, the school, visits the nuns, gawd knows who else. They just let him get on with it. No-one minds really.' Her face still looked slightly crumpled. 'Well then. Anyway,' she smoothed her skin down and smiled at Sarah, 'are you gunna get yerself dressed so we can getta move on out there? We'll take the marigolds, I reckon. Why not? Brighten that ward up.'

'I'm still really tired, Mum. I didn't sleep very well at all. I might go back to bed for a bit. Get a bus out a bit later. Yer gunna be there all day anyway, aren't ya?' Thinking: ring, telephone, ring.

'Oh. Well. Fine. Yes, well, whatever you want to do darl. Of course. Areya all right? Yer not sick?'

'I'm fine. Just tired, I need a bit more sleep.'

'It's not good to go back to sleep when you've woken up, ya know that doncha?'

'Oh, bloody hell, Mum, I'm tired.' There was no need, no need at all, to speak like that, so sharp, she didn't know why she did, it just came out, it always came out like that. She made her voice softer, warm like Ruth's: 'I'm waiting for a phone call, okay? I'll be out by lunchtime.'

Ruth slipped her hand into Sarah's. Smiled. 'You could take my car. Save ya gettin the bus.'

Sarah pulled her hand back to herself. Wondering how people did it, how they managed to drive cars and not be terrified of killing someone. Wrapped her arms about her waist. 'I'd rather get the bus.'

She shuffled back up the stairs and into the cold bed. Left her dressing gown on and listened to the sound of the doors slamming and the Holden starting and the engine revving then fading into silence. She lay on her back looking at the snake-getting-the-dog crack in the ceiling. *Ring, Zan, ring.* The silence stretched. The sun was warm on her eyes and her arms. The heat through the glass of the window making a burning spot on the back of her hand and making a whitehotyellow stripe across her pack lying on the other bed with clothes tumbling out of it like guts. She let her breathing come soft and slow and easy. The sun warmed her face, melted her skin, made everything slow and soft. Her eyes closed, her mouth went loose, she could feel her jaw dropping open, her tongue slipping heavy behind her teeth.

Then, the swirling of colours and voices. In the dream, Kari was a child again, but walking free, jumping free. She had a baby, a very small one – small as a hand and without a name – which she gave to Sarah to hold and protect and name. And Sarah named it Zan. In the moment before the phone rang, pulling awakeness from her, dream-Sarah realised she'd lost the baby: just put it down somewhere with her coat and a bottle of Coke. The funny thing was, dream-Sarah wasn't worried for the baby, or even that Kari would be angry – only scared that Kari would cry and all her make-up would run. The phone cut in quickly, and Sarah was jarred awake in a sudden rush. She tripped over herself running downstairs, trying to remember where the phone was. Her mouth was sticky and her body still heavy, but even in the tumble of dozey waking, finding the phone in the hall and getting her hand to it, she managed to think *Zan Zan Zan.*

'Hi.' She was breathless and loud, her voice in the over-brightness of no-I-have-not-been-sleeping. Blood thumped up-down, all around her body: sounding loud, sounding like it echoed in the hallway. There was no sound for a moment from the phone. She waited for the silver of Zan's voice to float through.

A jagged breath. A small croak. A shudder of half a word. 'Darl.'

Then silence again, shaking breaths slicing out from the phone. 'Oh, Sarah. I'm sorry, darl.'

'Mum? Where are you?' Although she knew of course, exactly where she was and who she was and what she was doing and why she was calling.

'She went just a few moments ago, oh God, Sarah, just after we arrived.'

The hall seemed huge suddenly, the ceiling stretching way above Sarah's head, even the phone soared up, grew large in her hand. 'She can't, how could she? They said days more, even weeks. How could she?' Her voice tiny and thin, but her body still and safe, wrapped up with everything seeming far far away.

'I know, love, it just, she just went very quickly, no-one expected, oh, Sarah,' there was a creak of tears, 'it was very peaceful, very quick. She just stopped breathing. She'd been coughing up all through the night.'

Sarah floated above herself, watching, feeling nothing. 'I'll get dressed.'

'The keys to the Austin are in the third drawer in the kitchen. Ya won't have time to get a bus.'

'I can't drive, Mum, I thought you knew that.'

A quiet little 'oh' from Ruth, then: 'Fine. Get a taxi. The number's in the book. They said they wouldn't touch her until you get here.'

'How nice of her to wait.' But the words were so quiet that they didn't even come out of Sarah's mouth.

She sat in the back of the taxi, watching the meter, slipping from side to side as the car screeched around the bends. She hadn't ever paid for a taxi, not since Zan. Bloody expensive, the meter ticking over like mad. Watching and counting and the bald-headed taxi-driver being careful with her feelings, saying nothing but trying to get her there fast. All she'd said was 'it's an emergency, ya have to get me to the Stuart Hospital, quickly.' Poor bloke drove like he could save someone's life. No point in telling him it was too late, had been too late years ago. Had always been too

185

frigging late. She shoved ten dollars into his hand and said keep the change even though she could see the meter came to thirteen dollars and fifteen cents, but he said, thanks love, good luck as if she'd given him a massive great bloody tip and then she was out of the car and running across the car-park, puffing hard.

She was still puffing when she crashed through the doors in the Diana Ward. Ruth was standing in front of the window, looking out. She didn't turn around. 'Yer father's out on the lawn. They're gunna take her soon. I wanted you to be here.'

'Thanks.' It seemed to be expected, so she said it, not looking at the bed, looking only at the window.

'I'm gunna go outside for a bit, let ya say good-bye. I've already said it.' Ruth turned, reached for Sarah's hands and squeezed them, almost roughly, then pushed through the doors.

The gurgling was still coming from the bed at the end of the ward and the pipe was still lined up next to Kari's bed. Her hands were folded on her chest, like in all the pictures of dead people, and the fingers were a pale blue. Sarah touched the cheek. Cool and thin. They'd closed her eyes and taken the tubes from her nose. *Say good-bye.* Nothing. It was like starting the conversation at some poxy party, not knowing what to say or how to say it. She had nothing to say. *Feel something. You must feel something.* She stroked her hand down Kari's arm, feeling the coldness, feeling the bone beneath the skin. Wanting to feel, at least something. At least anger, at least hate. But it was gone and there was nothing in its place, except maybe a mild nagging, a picking at her intestines. *I won't tell.*

The doors thumped behind her and she felt Ruth's hand around her waist. 'It was peaceful, love. Dignified.'

'Closest she got to dignity in her fucking life then.'

'I don't think so, Sarah. I don't think that's true.' Ruth still had her arm about Sarah's waist and her thumb was making small circles, pressing into Sarah's back. 'Yer father's gone to the car. He's had enough.'

The circles were pressing harder in Sarah's skin, annoying. 'Enough of what for god's sake?'

'He's cut up, darlin, he always has been. Ya know he adored her.'

'At least he adored one of us, then.'

The circling thumb stopped. 'He adored you both.'

'Oh fer god's sake. For fuck's bloody sake.'

'Anyway. He's in the car. Doyer want to wait for them to cover her and take her through? Have ya said yer farewells?'

'She's dead, she can't hear me. What's gunna happen then?'

'When?'

'Now. Next. About Dad. Ya have to do something, Mum.'

'I don't know what you mean, darlin.'

'Bullshit, Mum, don't give me that.'

'No.' Ruth looked down at her hands, took a deep sigh inside herself, then looked back to Sarah. 'You know he doesn't, not any more, I mean, he doesn't hit me, is that what you mean?' She said *hit* in a whisper.

For fuck's sake. 'I mean she's dead. He killed her. What are ya gunna do?' There. It was out, and it hung suspended and heavy as a gong.

'No darl. No.' Almost a whisper. 'That's not right. Ya know it's not. She fell.'

'Oh, Mum, please. He threw her. I heard, I heard everything, remember, I was there.'

'No, darlin. *I* was there. She fell down those stairs. She ran at him and – you know this, I know you know this, I can't believe you don't – he moved. God knows why, but she flew so fast, it happened fast, and she fell. Right down the stairs and so fast. She just fell. You know that.'

'I don't. It's not true.'

Ruth turned Sarah around, so that they were face to face, their breath almost touching. 'Sarah, it should never have happened, I'm not sayin it should have, I'm not sayin it's okay. But he didn't throw her. Believe me. I can't believe ya thought I was lyin all this time.'

A breeze slipped in through the open window and a branch of the tree creaked. The light through the leaves made the room look green and sickly. Everything, everything, everything. Everything seemed to be shifting about, Sarah held on to the wall, but it all kept moving.

Thirty-Two

Ruth was brittle and caked-on, cutting crusts off white bread sandwiches, marking the lino with her heels. Her wrists looked bony poking out from the ends of her navy twin-set, her marquasite watch glittering above her square-trimmed nails. She'd spent the morning heating electric rollers and turning the ends of her hair under. The bathroom smelled of Estée Lauder Youth Dew and Blue Grass talcum powder. The buzz of Mal's electric shaver zizzed through the house. Ruth found his bottle of Brut 33 – an old Christmas present from Mick Newton, the third-class sergeant in the Boolaroo station. It was still half wrapped in Christmas paper with a Santa card and a note inside about Mal trying to do something about his terrible bloody pong (ha ha). Made a worse bloody pong than there'd been in the first place and stung his skin like salt. Ruth was all clean lines and bright lips, dressed and ready to go with hours to spare: but Mal's blue ironed shirt was laid out on the bed with his uniform, all gleaming buttons, and his officer's cap next to it. He spent almost an hour polishing his presentation cufflinks with Brasso and by the time he'd finished you could see your whole face in them, you really could. Sarah held her stomach in, tried to be thin and invisible, kept her eyes, her face, her whole self away from Mal. Not knowing anything, what to think, what to feel. She sliced sandwiches into quarters and put lemon icing on cup-cakes and put a carton of beer in the fridge, following Ruth's instructions carefully and silently. She peered out from inside her skin like a stranger, not sure what it was she was supposed to feel, but sure that there was something – there must be something.

The phone was loud in amongst the quiet busyness and

desperately bright getting-on-with-it, the shrill ringing a welcome distraction. Ruth wiped her hands on a blue tea-towel and handed Sarah a fish-shaped glass plate covered with small tomato sandwiches. 'Glad-Wrap these, would ya love?' Her voice was light and neat and bright, tossed back over her shoulder as she headed for the phone. 'That'll be the funeral directors.'

Sarah pulled a long slice of plastic from the Glad-Wrap box and stretched it across the plate. It was nice, satisfying, tucking the ends under the plate, squashing the sandwiches down almost flat. Ruth had put sprigs of parsley in amongst the sandwiches. Garnish, she said. Apparently they swore by garnishes at the Coffee Pot.

'Sarah.' Ruth's voice was almost as sharp as the phone. She stood in the hallway, holding the mouthpiece up, not covering the receiver or anything, and yelling as if Sarah was miles away. 'It's for you. Sam. Quickly, it's long distance.' She spoke into the phone again. 'She's coming, Sam. Won't be a tick love, she's just Glad-Wrapping the sandwiches.'

Sarah took the phone, slid the door into the kitchen shut behind Ruth and stretched the cord as far as it would go, edging towards the lounge. 'Zan?'

'Was that your mum? She didn't seem to be able to cope with me being called Zan at all. I said it three times, but she couldn't deal with it. She's got a nice voice.'

'Where are you?'

'I'm in Sydney, where do you think I'd be?'

'I mean whereabouts?' It was important somehow to be able to imagine her.

'Martin Place. I got two bags of twenty-cent pieces from the Telecom office and I'm sitting on the little ledge next to the phone. Where are you?'

'Hallway.'

'Great.'

Silence for a moment. 'Why have ya called today? It's not a good time. Not at all.'

'Sorry. I'll hang up then, shall I?'

'Don't be, you know, don't. It's just today. Everything's a bit weird. I've been waiting for you to call. Why haven't ya called yet?'

'I've been busy. I needed time to think too, and I thought, you know, with your family and everything, it would be better if I just left it. Are you all right?'

'Yair. Fine. You?' Sarah was twisted up inside, why wasn't it easy? She waited for a tinkle of light from Zan.

'Fine. Very fine.'

Big breath, tight throat. 'Missed me?'

'Um. A lot's been happening. In some ways I have. I've been sleeping downstairs in the squat cause the flat felt too big.'

A knife sliced through Sarah's chest. 'Who with?'

'Oh Sarah, don't be silly. With myself.'

The sliding door opened and Ruth's face appeared. 'The car'll be here in a tick, love. Just letting you know.' Ruth's whisper was a loud screech.

Sarah nodded, mouthed 'okay' and pushed the door shut again. 'So, the squat's okay then?' She felt like she was calling down from the moon she was so far away.

'Well, yair, it's not bad. Sarah, listen.'

'I'm listening.'

'I've chucked me job in.'

'Yer joking. What, completely?'

'Mmm. We've been offered a tour with The Dugites. National support. I can't believe it. Five months. Do ya believe it?' Zan slipped a giggle down the phone, like a pay-off.

Lead filled Sarah's mouth, her hands, feet – everything. She was heavy, but numb. 'Great. Excellent.' She sounded like Eric, cool and quick. 'Are ya gunna take it then?'

'Oh, bloody hell, Sarah, what do you think? How could I not?'

'So I don't matter at all then.'

'You nearly killed me.'

'Do you have to do this now? On the phone? It's my sister's funeral today for fuck's sake.' Although it meant nothing to her, touched her nowhere.

'I'm sorry. Oh I'm sorry Sarah. Are you all right?'

'Yep. I'm fine. Wow. National tour. Congratulations.'

'I wanted to wait until I'd decided. It's only five months. Maybe if you get your shit together, maybe we'll see. I don't know.'

A tap on the door and Ruth's voice calling through: 'they're here Sarah. We have to go.'

'I can't talk about this now. Call me again. Please.'

'I might still be downstairs, when you get back. But I'm not changing my mind. You hurt me a lot, Sarah. You wanted this to happen, you know, it's better now than later. I'm sorry about the funeral. I hope it's okay.'

Ruth tapped again at the door.

'Bye.' After all the *Zan Zan Zan* wailing through her head all that time, it was like Zan was someone she'd never met. She put her mouth to the phone after she'd clicked the button down. 'I don't fucking care.' That was that. She didn't, it was true. Sarah Sweet: you couldn't hurt her, no way.

Outside, two long black cars and a white police car – Highway Patrol – were lined up behind each other. A small coffin in the back of the hearse with a wreath of white carnations on top of it. A woman in a blue suit stood at the door of the hearse, smiling with her lips closed. Mal was square-shouldered in his uniform, shaking hands with the driver, everybody's mate. Ruth slid without a sound into the back of the second car and pulled at Sarah's hand. Sarah sat beside her, smelling the deep smell of the vinyl, not looking at the car in front, at the long window with the small coffin. The locks clicked on when Mal squished himself in. The driver had a crew-cut, spiky black hairs at the nape of his neck, and no-one spoke at all. Behind them, the police car – full up with two of the bright-eyed sergeants and a pimply constable – flashed the blue light in silence. Sarah could see the blue reflected in the mirror, but she would not look ahead at that long black car.

The heat pushed in through the open windows and Ruth mopped at her face with a pink tissue. They kept the silence in the car right until the crunch of the wheels on the gravel of the crematorium driveway. Mal got out first, marching forward, hup two hup two, arms and legs almost straight, eyes up and forward – to the back of the hearse. The grey-suited funeral director waited until the police car was emptied of its load before opening the back of the hearse. The four blue uniforms reached in and began pulling at the wooden box. Ruth opened her mouth and a deep-down sound came out. She put her hands over her lips. Nothing would fall out. The woman in the suit took Ruth's hand and said come inside.

It was cold and grey inside the chapel: stone walls and floor so that feet and voices echoed. Three long pews on either side of the room and a small opening, like a stage with an open purple curtain. A grey-haired, frocked-up minister stood in front of the curtain. 'Mrs Sweet, welcome. Such a sad occasion.' He spoke like he was reading the words from a book, all sing-song, and he looked over their shoulders at some other place, a spot behind them, over their heads.

Sarah turned around, looking to see what he could see, and Ruth tapped her on the arm. 'This is my daughter, Sarah.'

'Reverend Anderson.' He held his hand out, like a dog waiting for his paw to be shaken. Sarah looked behind his head, at the organ, and he dropped his hand. 'Such a sad occasion, Sarah. We'll keep it very simple, as we agreed, Mrs Sweet. Short, simple, and sweet.' He smiled hopefully and Sarah looked at his feet. Shiny shoes. Fascinating.

The suit-woman pointed to the front pew and Ruth held tight again to Sarah's hand. Sarah wanted to shake her off but stared at the curtain instead. Velvet. Suit-woman sat down at a wooden organ tucked to the side of the stage and pressed at the pedals. Ruth's breathing sounded too heavy until the organ sound swelled and swam over the top of it. Even looking straight ahead, Sarah could see the shadow blotting the doorway, could feel the absence of heat and light. She turned her head, twisting on the pew. Beside her, Ruth was as still as stone.

The four blue uniforms blended into each other. Mal walked at the front, rubbing his shoulder against Mick Newton, giver of

Brut 33. There was no room between them, their shoulders all pressed together. It didn't need four people carrying it, that coffin; it was a joke to have it hoisted up on all their shoulders. Mal probably could have carried it on his own – it was as small as a child. They pushed it carefully onto the small stage, making a bump when they set it down. The crew-cut driver put the wreath on top of the coffin, and then lay the metal callipers on top of that. Ruth's body shook.

'The Lord be with you.' The sing-song voice of the very reverend, the more reverend than anyone else. A silence for a moment – he seemed to be waiting for something, so Sarah said thank you. The very reverend smiled above her head. 'A selection of readings from scripture as this young woman, Karen Frances Sweet, goes to her home, the home where she will at last be free to walk, run and roam.'

Sarah closed her eyes and let the voice wash and slap about the stone walls. Sun reflected from the callipers inside her eyes, shining too bright. She could feel the skin of Ruth's hand, could recall the hard coolness of a calliper bridge, the sound of callipers on cement. There was no Karen Frances Sweet in her memory. Something hard was swimming up her throat, something too big for all the inside of her, trying to break out from her body, pour down over her skin. Her face felt like china, ready to break, to be cracked open. She could hear the very reverend voice still rattling on and on, could feel the bursting things swimming and swelling up. For a moment, wanted it to burst out, and then: what if it did? who would gather her pieces up? She pressed her hands hard against herself, to keep her intestines neatly inside. Think, think, think. Stare ahead, look away, think hard about being somewhere else. Think about hating Zan, about how-dare-she-who-the-hell-does-she-think-she-is. She couldn't find it though – the hard little wedge of hate – so she breathed in, breathed out and let herself be empty. She was gathered up in a burst of music, a scattered stamping of feet as everyone stood. The curtains closed with a mechanical click-whirl-click and the small wooden box was whisked away from view, away from memory.

Thirty-Three

All the way back to the Boolaroo house, sitting in the back of the long black funeral car, Sarah floated outside herself. Ruth had stopped shaking and sat in the car humming one of the funeral tunes. Mick Newton's wife turned up at the house with a plate of Lamingtons and too much blue eyeshadow. Kissed Ruth on the cheek, said, 'ohh such a shame, love, such a bloody shame, what can I do?' and shook Mal's hand. Ruth said no, really, just sit down, and started laying things on the cloth-covered table. By the time the grey minister, the two sergeants, the constable and the blue-suited woman arrived, the table was covered with plates of small sandwiches and little cakes. Mal handed all the blokes beer and asked the two ladies and the minister if they wanted sherry.

Sarah sat in a tight ball in the living room, watching them swell and talk and crack open cans and drop crumbs on the floor. The swelling thing was back inside her, snaking around and up – she could feel it if she let herself, if she could find how to, how to let it snake its way up and out and too bad if no-one could pick up the pieces. Mal slapped his uniformed mates on the back and they slapped him and Sarah watched: waiting for Mal to burst out into anger. He didn't though – Mal kept himself numb like Sarah.

The backslapping chat and tinkle of glass stopped for a moment when the doorbell rang. Everyone looked around with a trace of almost-guilt. Mal nodded his head at Ruth and she scuttled to the door, handing her sherry glass to Sarah.

'Oh, gawd, flip-a-dip Jack, how do ya do it? Whenever there's a spread on, you manage to find yer way there, ya old bugger.'

195

Ruth's voice zoomed into the living room, cutting right through the cakes. 'Come on in love, that's the way.'

Jack followed her in, a slightly battered waratah flower in his hand.

'Is that for me love? Yer an angel.'

Mick Newton wiped the beer from his moustache and grinned at Mal. 'Bloody Jack Fir ay? Sniffs out food from a mile off I reckon – he turned up at Noreen's bloody PTA meeting a coupla weeks ago – didn't he love? Great White Scrounger of the North.' His teeth showed – slightly pointed and brown – when he tipped his head back and let a roar of a laugh fall out.

'Come on in, Jack, I'll get ya some sangas lovey.' Smiles and soothing sounds from Ruth, as she pushed Jack into the corner near the table. He sat quietly, almost invisible.

Sarah, curled up in the big chair in the corner of the living room, could see through to the kitchen. Invisible herself, she could see the hunched solitary shape, pushing sandwiches into his mouth. In all the talk, drifting and dabbling about her, no-one mentioned Kari. The voices talked about: weather, saddles, fencing, land prices, golf, the new commissioner of police ('total friggin bludger, bumsucked his way up'), the day Sam Wright got nabbed speeding out of hours in his police car, the difficulties of baking a perfect sponge, the difficulties of funerals-weddings-christenings, the difficulties of yearlings – until Sarah wanted to stand up, become visible, and scream in all their bloody faces – but no-one mentioned Kari.

The shiny young constable was turning pink around the edges and his voice was becoming louder. He put his arm around Mal's shoulders and waved his beer glass about the room. 'This bloke – here – Mal bloody Sweet, this is the best bloke, the best bloody bloke ya could ever, *ever*, meet. This bloke has given his bloody all and ya can't ask for more than that. He is a bloody good bloke and I'd like you all to change yer glasses – to *charge* yer glasses – for a toast. C'mon ya bastards, on yer feet. To a bloody good bloke.'

Sarah stayed tucked small and neat in the chair while the glasses

196

clinked and the voices repeated 'bloody good bloke', like a bit of magic.

'Hey, whass this, c'mon – on yer feet, this is a toast. That means everyone.' He was staring right at her, right at Sarah; somehow he had seen through her invisibleness. She felt too stiff to shrug or smile politely as he grabbed at her hands. Even the *no* stuck in her throat. She could still see Jack in the kitchen – cramming cakes into himself – and as she stood, his mouth and eyes opened wide. A hacking sound fell out of him and his body shuddered, his arms waving about like wings. The hacking, coughing, scherr-acking sound again, and his face tightening up. Sarah's own mouth opened and the words were a dry croak: 'Jack. Get Jack.'

Everything got very noisy then – Ruth running into the kitchen, yelling, 'carn, Jack, spit it up mate,' and slapping him on the back, while Mick Newton called encouragement and the constable muttered, 'bloody good bloke', into his glass. Sarah felt slow as mud, wading through the wide opening into the kitchen. She felt hands shoving at her back, heard Mal in her ear: 'Move it mate, he's chokin.'

It was Mal who picked Jack up and laid him over his knee, thwacking and thwacking Jack's frail back.

'Don't hurt him, Mal, he's only tiny.' Ruth rubbed at the place where Mal hit. 'Stand him up, it's not workin.'

Mal didn't argue, didn't even sneer, he just turned Jack up, and stood him on his feet. There were words coming out with the cracking chest; breaking sounds: *Hriim sho-hing*. Sarah stood big and useless and lifeless, watching while Ruth shusshed and rubbed soothed and said, 'it'll be all right, love,' and Mal stuck his hand right down into Jack's throat.

'Flamin bastard bit me.' Mal pulled his hand out, speckled with blood. There was a circle of bodies now, standing, watching like a footie game: 'carn Mal, you can do it, get in there.' Again, Mal's hand in, then out with teeth marks and red flecks.

Jack's face was deep purple and his breath in little jagged gasps. Ruth rubbed his back, whispering, 'c'mon love, c'mon,' and Mick Newton ran to the phone to call the ambulance and Sarah stayed frozen, her hands heavy lumps by her side. When Mick came back from the phone, Jack's back wasn't shaking any more and his eyes were still. Ruth shook him again and nothing fell from him: no breath, no piece of cake. Mal yelled in his face, told him not to be such a stubborn bloody bastard and swung his hand way up high and whacked Jack on the back so bloody hard it could have knocked his teeth to Timbuktu. Nothing changed, so Mal rubbed his back instead saying, 'Poor bastard, poor bloody bastard', really soft. Mal's face went all soft, too, and he rubbed and rubbed, as if Jack were a prize mare.

Sarah could feel her mouth opening and closing, like she was trying to get something out, some words or a sound. Even her throat was moving, but nothing falling out. The ambulance siren blared up, blaring louder and louder, getting closer and closer, and then another sound, a shcerrack hack ha sound, the sound of Jack Fir's cough, the sound of his voice breaking free, his throat waking up, his mouth opening up and letting the great ball of spit and bread and cake fall out, out across the room, out across the floor, flying in a perfect arc and landing on Mick Newton's shoe. Jack coughed again, wiped his throat, looked at the table and reached for another cake. The siren screeched closer.

And then, the siren coming closer and closer, right outside the door, and Jack looking pleased with himself and Ruth saying, ya lousy bugger, Jack, but kissing him on the cheek like she never ever did before, and then, and then, and then:

and then another siren sound, loud and wailing, round and high, falling, falling out from Sarah's mouth, out across the floor, and spilling onto everyone's shoes. She could see herself, just for a moment, mouth open and face wet, tears falling and falling. Her face turning into sponge with all the wetness of it, melting and flooding over them all. She could see her arms wrapping about herself, holding herself in. Then her arms unwrapping, letting go of herself, letting herself fall out.

In the loud high cries falling out from way deep in herself, Sarah could see patterns, odd pictures swirling about with the sobs and sounds. Kari and Ruth and Zan and Mal all twisting in a dark mix and Sarah, sitting on the edge, feeling nothing except the fierce lovehate for them all, wanting them to notice her, love her, see her. Protect her.

And then she couldn't see anymore, because she was inside her skin and the scream was hers and the tears were hers and the inside falling out was hers, all the pieces bursting out fresh and wet and clean like new fruit. All hers, she could feel it. And if no-one ever picked all the pieces up, she was there, alive, inside her skin. Touching home.